# DOUGLAS DAY

# *Journey of the Wolf*

PENGUIN BOOKS

PENGUIN BOOKS

Published by the Penguin Group
27 Wrights Lane, London W8 5TZ, England
Viking Penguin Inc., 40 West 23rd Street, New York, New York 10010, USA
Penguin Books Australia Ltd, Ringwood, Victoria, Australia
Penguin Books Canada Ltd, 2801 John Street, Markham, Ontario, Canada L3R 1B4
Penguin Books (NZ) Ltd, 182–190 Wairau Road, Auckland 10, New Zealand

Penguin Books Ltd, Registered Offices: Harmondsworth, Middlesex, England

First published in Great Britain by Max Reinhardt 1977
Published in Penguin Books 1988

Printed and bound in Great Britain by
Cox & Wyman Ltd, Reading

ONCE AGAIN
FOR
ELIZABETH
WITH LOVE

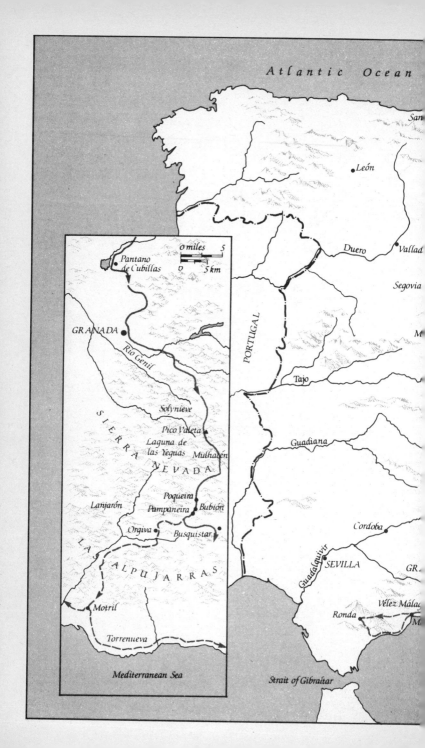

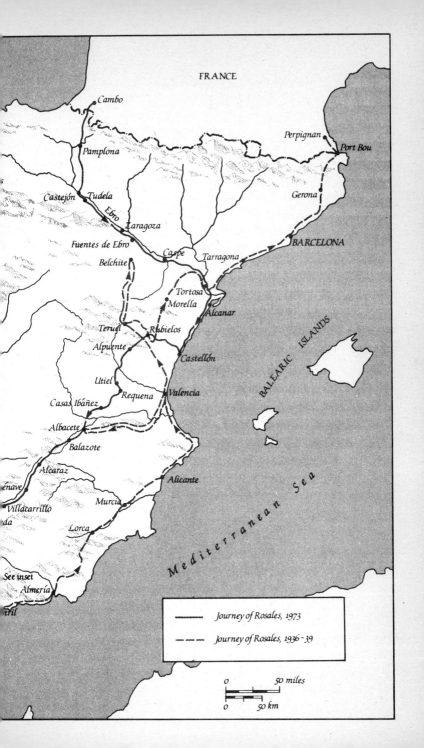

FRANCE

Cambo
Perpignan
Port Bou
Pamplona
Gerona
Castejón  Tudela
Ebro
Zaragoza
BARCELONA
Fuentes de Ebro  Caspe  Tarragona
Belchite
Tortosa
Morella
Alcanar
Teruel  Rubielos
Alpuente
Castellón
Utiel
Casas Ibáñez  Requena
Valencia
Albacete
Balazote
BALEARIC ISLANDS
Alcaraz
énave
Alicante
Villacarrillo
da
Murcia
Lorca
Mediterranean Sea
See inset
Almería
ifil

——————  Journey of Rosales, 1973

– – – – – –  Journey of Rosales, 1936~39

0        50 miles

0      50 km

*Era España tirante y seca, diurno*
*tambor de són opaco,*
*llanura y nido de águilas, silencio*
*de azotada intemperie.*

Spain was taut and dry, daily
drum of opaque sound,
plain and eyrie of eagles, silence
of scourged rough weather:

PABLO NERUDA, *Como Era España*

# Prologue

Sebastián Rosales, known in other times as "El Lobo," wanted badly to smoke, but was afraid that the harsh smell of one of his black-tobacco Gitanes would reach whatever passersby there might be on the road below him. So he sucked instead on one of the frail blades of grass that grew up through the green moss on the floor of the beech forest in which he was hiding. Shivering slightly, leaning his long back against the smooth gray trunk of the tall tree he hoped would shelter him from the chill rain that was beginning to fall, he crouched and nursed the blade of grass as if it were in fact the cigarette he craved.

Rosales was annoyed with himself for feeling tired so soon along the way, and for being so ill-equipped for crossing the western Pyrenees in December. His black city-man's shoes, sunk deep in the moss where he squatted, already showed signs of wear. And his vinyl jacket, torn and unlined, hardly stopped the cold from reaching through his blue workshirt to the flesh beneath. He had taken the blanket from his wife's bed that morning, and rolled it in the old fashion so that he could sling it crosswise across his shoulder and chest. But the blanket, like the black beret he had pulled down almost to his ears, was sodden, and only added to his chill. Thirty-four years in their fucking country, he thought, and all I can carry out of France is less than I took into it.

Cambó, the village that since 1944 had been his home, his and his wife's and his two daughters', was only twenty kilometers behind him. An hour before he had passed through the Basque town of Aïnhoa. Now, from the forest, he could look southward down into Spain, his land which had expelled him long ago and which was going to have to take him back tonight, like it or not.

Last night he had been sitting at the table in their small and crowded kitchen with Inés, his wife for twenty-nine years. Their daughters, married to a pair of the Frenchmen whom he had always despised, had just left, their little Citroëns packed with fat and loud children. There had been the usual boring fight: Why did Rosales refuse to learn even the most rudimentary sort of French, why was he so openly contemptuous of his sons-in-law (whose very names he often affected not to remember), why would he show no fondness for his five grandchildren? Why wouldn't he see, and see with satisfaction if not pride, that his family was becoming French, that it

4

was getting ahead? The Gaullists had decorated him after the Big War for his exploits in the *Maquis*, he had a pension as a wounded hero from the French government: Why therefore must he insist on regarding himself as an alien in a bad country?

Rosales had sat through this routine assault with his usual cold silence, his face impassive behind all its years and scars. At the end of their tirade he had smiled his wolf's smile, his thin lips stretched tight over teeth that were still white and even, and barked at the women who surrounded him: "Because I am *andaluz*, and so are you. And because I hate this woman's country of people who speak and act like *maricones*," like faggots.

"Then go away, peasant," Inés had said, her great melonbreasts pushing against the cloth of the black dress she wore, had always worn during the years of their time together. "There's been an amnesty for four years: Go back to your filthy *pueblo* and be an old man with the other old men. You embarrass us here. Go back and sit with the other senile ones at the café and smell like wine all day and like piss all night. You Spaniard." Then, tired from such a long and angry speech, she had pulled herself to her feet and gone stumping about their house, cleaning up the mess the grandchildren had made. Over her shoulder she called to him once: "And how long has it been since you shaved, *sucio*—a week? Do you ever look at yourself in a mirror?" Rosales felt the gray stubble on his chin and cheeks. *¿Y qué?* he thought: *So what?*

Ah, *Jesú*, Rosales murmured to himself, running the gnarled fingers of one hand through the gray hair that, still thick and stiff, grew low over his forehead. So this is how it is to go into one's age, with a sow for a wife, daughters married to French pimps, and grandchildren of bad milk.

It had not always been this bad, not at least in the early years of their marriage. Inés, when he found her living with other exiles in a Bordeaux tenement, had been almost pretty, and full of admiration for him, the decorated hero. Since she was without a *novio*, and Spanish— it would never have occurred to him to marry a *francesa*, no matter how beautiful—he had married her, and taken her to live with him in Cambó. Because he could not return to his own *pueblo* in Andalucía to take up again with Ana María, the thin and lovely *novia* he had only just begun to court in the months before the war began, there was really no alternative, unless he wished to remain single. So they made their lives in Cambó, with Inés dutifully producing children and growing sourer by the day, while Rosales never ceased to think of the faun-eyed Ana María and his home in the south, and of all the things he had lost.

He sat alone in the kitchen now, his flat black eyes roving from the liter bottle that had held their evening's wine, to the plate before him with its few scraps of *tortilla española*, and across the room to the stained old gas stove with the tiny window above it. Through the window he could just make out, in the glow of a single street light, a row of ragged small houses, all very nearly identical to his own. Here was where they all lived: all the Spanish exiles in Cambó, most of them like Inés resigned to lives as laborers for French landowners and shopkeepers, trying at one moment to hang on to their Spanishness, and at the next to melt smoothly into the life of the country that had begrudgingly taken them in once it had become clear that the Franco régime would never allow them to return home—never, that is, until the surprising declaration by Franco in 1969 of a general amnesty for all who had fought for the Republic.

With some of the men Rosales had discussed this amnesty. It was 1973, now, but very few had dared to take advantage of it. Everyone in his *tertulia,* his bunch of old veterans who gathered at a café almost nightly to say the same old things to one another, agreed that it meant precisely nothing—at least not for those exiles who were not men of *categoría,* of status. For thirty-four years men like Rosales had dreamed of returning to their villages, of living out their lives where they belonged, in their own terrain. But letters had come from Spain which warned them against accepting the amnesty, and which told them what to expect if they did try to return. Old Valentín, a crippled apothecary who had been raised in Lavapíes, a workers' district in Madrid, had the year before got a letter from his brother who had stayed behind, waiting out all the years of political executions, of near starvation, of the routine humiliation and harassment that the régime offered the old Republicans in Spain.

"Come home if you wish," the brother had written, "but here there is more shit to eat than a man can stand. There is now no real hunger nor daily fear. But there is no freedom, and no honor for a man. And they will hate you, and will make sure you wish you had not returned. Stay where you are. Wait until the Little Frog dies, and then we'll see. But for now, don't come. Do not think you can come quietly and live in peace. They will have your names still written down."

But the Little Frog, or whatever his enemies chose to call Francisco Franco, had not died, nor showed any signs of doing so. And for Sebastián Rosales there was no more time. In Cambó he saw before him only the daily ten hours in the bakery where he worked, and the nightly return to his fat Inés and her heavy sullenness. And the *tertulia:* glasses of oversweet French wine, old men's coughs, cheap tobacco, and, always, the same bleak hopelessness.

Then, this last night, Rosales had made up his mind. After the bad evening with Inés and the daughters and the grandchildren, who noticed him only long enough to mock the old language he continued to speak, he had gone to the *tertulia*, taken the same straight-backed chair at the same plastic-covered table as always, and sat silently through the same ritual complaints. His mind was full of Poqueira, his *pueblo* high in the steep green-brown hills of the region called the Alpujarras, ringed about by the snowy peaks of the Sierra Nevada, only sixty-five kilometers north of the Mediterranean. He saw the white stone walls of the houses of Poqueira, the narrow dirt-and-cobblestone paths that ran through the town, the dirty central plaza scattered about with chickens, dogs, children, and tight knots of old women, seated on rush stools mending their black dresses in the warmth of the morning sun. He saw himself as he should have been: going out at dawn into the fields that he owned to spend the day cutting the *trigo alonzo*, the bearded wheat that he and his fellow farmers grew almost up to the snowline in the mountains. He pictured his wife (definitely *not* this old Inés, but someone thin-

8

ner, happier, younger—someone, in fact, like the Ana María he kept so strongly in his memory), coming out to join him at noon with a liter of tart local wine, some goat cheese, and a large slab of the flat, unleavened village bread. Perhaps she would bring a few olives, or an orange. After lunch they would rest for an hour in the shade of a poplar, and maybe there would even be something in the way of lovemaking, languorous and drowsy. Then he would return to work until time for a *copita* of something—a *montilla*, probably—with his friends in one of Poqueira's three cafés; and finally he would be at home for the evening with his *andaluz* family, all speaking quietly and happily in the fluid and decorous accent of the Alpujarras. He had not seen Poqueira since he was seventeen, thirty-seven years before, but Sebastián Rosales knew that this was where and how he should have lived: This was what They had stolen from him. This fight tonight with Inés was the last one, the one too many.

Just after eleven, without having spoken a word to the old men of the *tertulia*, he had arisen, left some coins on the table, smiled faintly at his fellow exiles, and said quite calmly, "*Bueno, voy a buscarme la vida*": Okay, I'm going to find myself some life. And they, thinking that Rosales was merely speaking the first part of the old *andaluz refrán*, had given the prescribed response: "*Claro, porque la muerte siempre viene sola*": Right, because death always comes alone. But Rosales had known that he was speaking no *refrán*: He was going to find his life in the only place it could exist for him. He was going home.

*　*　*

So now Rosales crouched, less than a day later, only a few hundred yards from Spain. He had said no good-byes, nor had it occurred to him to do so. His mind was fixed now on the Alpujarras, eleven hundred kilometers to the south, and what did any of those in France have to do with that? As for the celebrated amnesty: Let it, with Generalísimo Franco, go shit in the sea. Rosales had with him no passport, no workman's papers, no identity card. He would cross the border south of Aïnhoa because there was no *aduana* there, no Customs Office where *flics* and *Guardias Civiles* would question him and then certainly stop him. Taking to the hills after Aïnhoa, he had followed the smugglers'. trails that crisscrossed the Pyrenees; and now here he was at dusk, waiting for darkness to hide him from whatever travelers, tourists, or police might be on the road below him. Shortly after nine, in the same soft, cold rain that had fallen all day, he rose, paced about for a few minutes to loosen up his aching legs, then commenced the steep descent to the silent gulley below. By ten o'clock he had crossed the gravel road and was standing once again in his own country. He was as cold as ever. The ground beneath his feet was still soft and mossy. The tall beech trees around him, so far as he could make them out in the moonless night, looked no different from those that had sheltered him all afternoon. But it *was* all different, just the same: That other had been France, and this was Spain.

The first crossing of the border, that of the last retreat in 1939, was something else altogether. Sergeant Sebastián Rosales, age twenty, veteran of three years, called El Lobo, the Wolf, by all who knew him in Colonel Juan Modesto's Army of the Ebro, was in a situation that he knew to be very dangerous. Shrapnel from an Italian bomb had torn much of the flesh away from his left forearm, and he was lying in an emergency hospital in Barcelona. Next to him was a young *alférez*, a second lieutenant from his battalion, dying from a chest wound. The enemy—regular troops from the Nationalist army, Italians, and Moors from Franco's old Foreign Legion— were only a day's march from the city, and El Lobo knew that as a member of a Communist regiment he would certainly be shot if captured.

As he lay on his side, silently watching a large blood-stain spread across the bandage of the dying officer, El Lobo heard voices from the end of the crowded ward.

"*Hombre*," someone was saying in tense exasperation, "they are almost on us. For the love of Christ, let's at least get the officers up and moving. They'd be killed first, anyway. And it's a danger for the rest of us to have them around. Let's get them dressed and out of here. Find them a truck, get them to their damn battalions if they still exist."

With almost imperceptible slowness, El Lobo drew back the single blanket that covered him and slid over to the bedside of his unconscious neighbor. From the brass headstead of the bed hung the peaked cap of the *alférez*, with its single gold bar surmounted by a woolen red star. "Good luck to thee, my officer," whispered El Lobo, "and may their Christ be kinder to thee than their *moros*." He returned silently to his own bed, with the man's cap clutched under his wounded arm.

An hour later El Lobo, wearing the officer's cap,

stood in the back of a mottled and rusty old *camión*, headed for what remained of the Catalán front north of Barcelona. He and the other wounded men with him, whom it pleased him now to think of as his brother officers, knew only that they were to try to locate their various units, and function however well they could in the exodus of the last 250,000 men of the Republican army from Cataluña into France. El Lobo's arm ached only slightly, but he felt thirst and dizziness from time to time. Fever, he thought. It will pass when it is time for it to pass.

The *camión* moved slowly, not only because of its age and debility, but also because the road north was clotted with those who were fleeing before the Nationalist advance. El Lobo was sure there must be hundreds of thousands of them, straggling on toward Gerona and Figueras: wounded soldiers with their blankets wrapped around them like ponchos; civilian men pulling large two-wheeled carts piled high with mattresses, chairs, old clocks, family photographs in ornate frames, and crates containing nearly frozen rabbits and chickens; women and children of all ages—all caught up in the panic of flight that El Lobo had seen more than once in this war. Somewhere ahead, presumably, lay the remnants of the Army of the Ebro, holding on in the late January snows. El Lobo hoped that their discipline, created and enforced by Modesto, the furious little ex-woodcutter who had grown into one of the Republic's best leaders, would hold against the constant bombing raids of the Italian Air Force and the German Condor Legion. We finally make ourselves into a real army, thought El Lobo sourly, and then all we can do with it is run up into

France. There was no longer any hope for victory, he knew: The best they could hope for was enough bad weather to keep the bombers away so that there could be an orderly escape, with perhaps a little dignity. He hoped that they would at least be able to march across the border as an army, and not as a confused mass of *sinvergüenzas*, shameless ones.

At Gerona they found their companies, dug in at many points in and around the city, protecting themselves as best they could from the waves of enemy planes that came over both day and night now that there were no more Republican squadrons to oppose them. El Lobo tossed aside his officer's cap and became Sergeant Rosales once again. His men, when he found them gathered about a heated brazier in the basement of an office building, nodded to him with deference and perhaps a little fear.

"Welcome, our old sergeant," said one of the privates. "How goes your arm?"

"It hangs onto my shoulder, as always," El Lobo answered.

He glanced casually around the brazier at his men, and saw on them all the signs of fatigue and tension that he had expected. They had been steadily retreating ever since the disastrous Battle of the Ebro the preceding July, and they had very nearly exhausted all their resources for combat. Their rifles, old 7 mm. Mausers dating from 1916, were, he noted with some satisfaction, still being kept clean and oiled. Their uniforms—most of them wore heavy brown corduroy jackets and trousers, black berets, and shapeless gray Russian overcoats—were filthy and tattered, but nonetheless still recognizable as uniforms. They had not abandoned the hated leggings which Modesto insisted they wear, but which always seemed to come unwrapped at the most inopportune moments of combat; and they had not ceased to keep clean their large leather cartridge cases, clipped to the web belts with which they held their buttonless overcoats closed over their bodies. El Lobo did not need to ask how many rounds those cartridge cases held: At this stage of the war none of his men could have fired more than five shots before their rifles fell permanently silent.

Most of them were bearded, since luxuries like razors had ceased to exist, as had the water they might have used to wash themselves. Their eyes were sunk deep in the gray, taut flesh that showed above the beards, and they stank with the sourness of fatigue and fear. It was a soldiers' smell: They might not be able to fight much longer, but at least they should be able to march with discipline to whatever reception they would find at the border. It did not occur to Rosales to wonder very much what the French would be able to do with the sudden appearance at Port Bou of almost five hundred thousand Spanish civilian and military refugees. He knew only that the French government had been more or less sympathetic to the Republican cause all along; and he supposed vaguely that some sort of provision had been made for them all.

One month later, at noon on the tenth of March 1939, El Lobo and the Army of the Ebro began to learn what the French had planned for them. Since dawn his battalion had been stationed on a hill overlooking the international bridge, which lay in a gulley filled with smooth, rounded stones. All about the hillsides were groves of delicate almond trees already in blossom. Just to the east were the rugged cliffs of the Costa Brava, falling hundreds of feet down to the placid sea. It was a pretty scene, thought El Lobo, or would have been if it were not for what was happening on the road below them.

The soldiers were waiting to move across the bridge until the last of the civilian refugees had passed by. So far as he could tell, they were proceeding with dignity, moving slowly forward with a kind of diffident trust along the dusty road, which the French had sprinkled with chloride of lime. On the hills beyond the bridge stood hundreds of French troops of some sort—they were the *gardes mobiles*, an officer told El Lobo—who were presumably there to ensure the orderly passage of the Spaniards.

El Lobo let his eyes move across the scene below him. Beneath a flowering shrub just across the bridge lay a dying man, his face yellow, his eyes staring sightlessly up at the blossoms. Several men lay huddled together, drinking at a stream. A shaggy-haired man with a donkey, which had apparently refused to go any farther, was seated on the ground, waiting for anything at all to happen.

Next something occurred that gave El Lobo his first notion of what sort of welcome they could really expect. A large group of civilian men moved toward the bridge, holding their left arms high over their heads, fists clenched in what El Lobo took to be the Leftist salute. Some of them were singing in Catalán; what it was he could not tell. Like most of the *andaluces* in the Army of the Ebro, he had not bothered to learn this language, which seemed to him like a kind of barbarous Spanish. Then there was a commotion at the center of the bridge: One of the officers of the *gardes mobiles* had stopped the men, and was angrily slapping at their raised arms. El Lobo saw handfuls of reddish dirt falling onto the stones of the bridge floor, and realized that these Cataláns had been trying to carry a last piece of their own soil with them into exile—and that the French were not going to let them do it.

"We are being greeted by the Sons of the Great Whore," he muttered to his company commander, an ascetic and authentic Communist who stood beside him, silently watching the spectacle.

"You're the killer, Lobito," the officer responded, with a smile at his sergeant that had no humor in it. "Want to start killing Frenchmen now?" El Lobo gave an answering grin to the officer, and lightly touched the bayonet that hung in its scabbard from his belt. The officer moved away a short distance, disturbed perhaps as so many had been since the beginning of the war by the cold and implacable ferocity that he saw in the face of his sergeant.

El Lobo looked down at the bridge again. He saw a young girl holding in her hands the broken head of a doll. He saw an old woman, moving slowly along with the others, clutching to her bosom a small child wrapped about with a shawl. He watched as a *garde* stopped the woman, peered at the bundle she was carrying, then took it from her with a gesture that looked to El Lobo very much like contempt. The child was dead, clearly; and the *garde* moved to the northern end of the bridge and deposited the small cadaver beside a row of others who had died that day. The old woman said nothing, but resumed her place in the procession, her face a blank. El Lobo watched it all, squatting now in his peasant's fashion, feet flat against the sandy soil of the hillside, the seat of his trousers almost touching the ground.

Some time later, with the last of the civilians, came a small band of somber men carrying a long shape on a makeshift litter of canvas stretched across pine boughs. "Another one for the pile of cadavers," observed El Lobo to the company commander, who was standing again at his side.

"You don't know who that is, do you, Lobito?" The officer was pale and agitated. He was standing very straight, his hands stiff at his sides. El Lobo looked at the sand between his feet, thinking how much these ideological officers, these political ones, were more like priests than most of the real priests he had known.

"You ought to know, Lobito, really," the officer continued. "That's the poet Machado, an *andaluz* like you. Or do you recognize the existence of poets in Andalucía?" El Lobo shrugged. This catechism bored him. "Poets die, too, my captain," he said absently, watching the litterbearers move across the bridge.

"Yes, of course, sergeant, they do die. But they leave words for men like you and me, if we choose to hear them." And he began, his voice, his earnest priest's voice, shaking slightly, to recite:

*Sabe esperar—*
*aguarda que la marea fluya*
*así en la costa un barco*
*sin que el partir te inquieta.*

Know how to hope—
Watch for the rising tide
like a boat upon the shore
and do not fear for the departure.

El Lobo looked up at his commander. "Poetry is for intellectuals, Comrade Captain: for officers and commissars. But I might say, as a poor *campesino*, a man of the fields, that that old one down there had better begin hoping with some speed, because his departure is upon him."

The officer jerked his head back as if assailed suddenly by a very bad smell. El Lobo laughed silently, thinking of how a priest might react if he found something unspeakable placed for a joke in his chalice.

Then finally it was the turn of the Army of the Ebro. The troops formed themselves in columns of three, shouldered their rifles, came to attention, and then, at the command of the perpetually angry little Colonel Modesto, began a slow march down the road toward the bridge. The red, yellow, and purple flag of the Republic moved along at the head of the column, carried by a young soldier of great seriousness.

At the precise center of the bridge, a *Prefect* of the *gardes mobiles*, very elegant in his blue uniform with flat-topped cap, stopped the advance, his hand raised before him in the universal policeman's traffic-stopping gesture. He said something to Modesto, who, understanding no French, looked away from the *Prefect* impatiently. A foreign civilian, probably, thought El Lobo, a correspondent there to record the final moments of the Republic, came forward to translate. Then they were moving again, across the bridge and into France.

The long single column was split into four smaller ones, each of which was directed to move toward sites that had been prepared for them a kilometer or so beyond the bridge. Once positioned properly they were halted, and allowed to stand at ease. Squads of *gardes* approached each unit, and indicated that the Spaniards were to surrender their weapons. El Lobo gave his twelve men the order to stack arms. In the prescribed manner, a little self-consciously proud of their soldierliness, his men attached their rifles one to the other by interlocking the stacking swivels of the old Mausers, so that their rifles stood like a row of three tent frames, their working parts elevated above the sandy roadbed. One man, another old veteran, held on to his rifle for a long moment, and for the last time ran his hand caressingly over stock, bolt, and barrel. As El Lobo watched, a *garde* strode rapidly toward the man, seized the rifle impatiently, and tossed it to the earth. The soldier said nothing, nor did the other Spaniards. Something shameful had happened, something that their pride did not permit them to acknowledge.

And then more. The *gardes* began to move down the line of troops, demanding that each man empty the contents of his haversack into the ditch that ran along the roadside. Soon the ditch was strewn with each man's poor possessions: underclothes, fragments of food, letters, photographs—all went into the layer of chloride of lime in the ditch, so that, thought El Lobo, this precious France should not be contaminated by Spanish filth. "These people are very clean," he said not very softly to the man next to him. "I wonder if they will consider allowing us to shit in their country."

As he spoke, he looked up at the *Prefect* and a small group of senior officers who stood above them, smoking idly and commenting casually on the proceedings. It occurred to El Lobo that perhaps he had made a mistake: Might it not have been better to have stayed in Spain and taken his chances with the Nationalists than to have come here to submit to this humiliation?

Then there was another foreigner, another correspondent in their midst. Russian? North American? English? The man, with tears in his eyes, had leapt into the ditch and was retrieving what he could of the men's personal belongings. He came out of the ditch toward El Lobo, handed him the tattered photograph of Poqueira that he had carried with him for three years, and said, tears lining his cheeks now, "*Lo siento*": I'm sorry. El Lobo took the photograph, looked calmly over the man's shoulder, and replied, "*No hay de qué*": It doesn't matter. He took a quick look at the picture—a blurry white knot of a town grown onto the side of a steep green mountain, with snowy peaks in the background—and then placed it in his jacket pocket.

They had not eaten that day. A *garde* who spoke

Spanish now appeared before them to say that they would be taken to "rest areas" nearby where they would be fed and sheltered. After a five-hour march in the direction of the town of Argelès, up the coast toward Perpignan, El Lobo learned the worst. The "rest areas" were vast stretches of sand surrounded by barbed wire. For shelter there were hundreds of shallow trenches. Not so much as a hospital tent or a latrine. The "rest area" was in fact a concentration camp, and El Lobo, like every other refugee, was a prisoner.

A Red Cross truck stood by the entrance to the camp, and a handful of foreigners who called themselves "Quakers" went about among the men offering them cups of black coffee and slabs of chocolate. But El Lobo touched none of this. He stood alone, his long face full of contempt. A cold wind had come up from the mountains behind them, blowing sand back into the trenches that the Frenchmen had dug, but El Lobo scarcely noticed. He thought only of the end of his honor and the commencement of his disgrace.

# Chapter 1

By midnight the cold rain began to turn to snow, and Sebastián Rosales knew that he could not remain where he was. The Pyrenees south of Aïnhoa were neither particularly steep nor high, but in early December a man could still freeze there if caught by real snow. So he pulled his socks up over the cuffs of his trousers, wrapped the thin woolen blanket more tightly around his shoulders, and began his descent. The night was almost completely dark, so much so that he could find no traces of the smugglers' trails that had got him safely past the Customs offices yesterday afternoon. He found that he had to walk with his arms held out in front of him to guard against falls or sudden encounters with trees. Again he cursed his city-man's shoes, whose leather soles and heels caused him to slip often in the wet

22

snow. For much of the way down he had to walk almost crab fashion, kicking the sides of his shoes into the mountainside with each step so as to gain some purchase.

Rosales knew little about the geography of this part of Spain, but he supposed that by dawn he ought to be nearing the foothills of the Pyrenees; and he knew also that somewhere not far to the west was the main road that ran south to Pamplona. His general aim was to get clear of the French border by as many kilometers as possible, and then to find himself a ride in some sort of truck or auto heading south. Spain was not so very large, after all: If he kept his direction mainly southward, and did not delay any more than necessary along the way, he saw no reason why he should not be in Andalucía within four or five days at most. He had no road map, no papers, and almost no money (fifty new francs were all he could find in his house on the morning of his flight); but none of this seemed to him much cause for worry. He was large, he was still stronger than most men he knew—and he had been through much worse than this, many times. There were quite a few things more fearful than bad weather.

From time to time Rosales stopped to rest and to listen. There was a slight wind from the east, and now and then the sound of a truck reached him: The road could not be far away—probably not more than a kilometer or two—though, he knew, it was difficult to judge the distance a sound could travel on such a night. He had heard that there were many wolves in the Pyrenees, and it gave him some comfort to reflect that there were not liable to be any hereabouts, where there were roads, people, trucks making noise. He had heard somewhere, too, that wolves rarely attacked humans, but a childhood memory made him doubt this.

Though there had been no wolves in the Sierra Nevada when he was a boy, there still were whole packs of them in the Sierra Morena to the north, at the topmost edge of Andalucía. Once two men from Jaén had appeared in Poqueira with a full-grown wolf, which they had penned up in a wooden cage, carried on a mule-drawn cart. These men apparently made their living by capturing wolf cubs and raising them. When the cubs were fully grown they would haul them from village to village, collecting *céntimos* from the people who came running to see them. On lucky days, the trappers would find a shepherd gullible enough to believe that the wolf had just been caught nearby, probably on its way to raid the shepherd's flock. Out of gratitude, the shepherd might give them as much as twenty-five pesetas.

When the men and their wolf came to Poqueira, Rosales had crowded in as close as he dared to the bars of the cage. He was only ten, but still old enough to be struck by the indomitability of the captive wolf. It could scarcely move in its narrow cage, but when people teased it with straws it drew back its lip and snarled with frightening ferocity. If it had been captured as a cub, Rosales now reflected, where had it learned this savagery? Was it instinct, or had the men who captured it treated it cruelly, to make it so vicious?

The notion that there might be wolves around him in the Pyrenees now was something Rosales could use to tease himself: It was no real fear to him. What truly concerned him was men: *They* were the genuine enemy, and had been since he was seventeen years old. And though there was no certainty about the presence of wolves, Rosales had every reason to believe that there were men in these forests. He was in the Vascongadas, the ancient land of the Basques, and over the years in Cambó he had heard much of these strange people, with their impossible language and their hatred of the French, who ruled them on one side of the border, and of the Spanish, who ruled (not ruled, *dominated*) them on the other side. From what he knew of them, Rosales had much respect for these Basques. The ones who had fought for the Republic in the Civil War had done well, he had heard, until their resistance in the northern provinces had been stamped out by the Nationalists in 1937. But he himself had seen nothing of these Republican Basques. Those *he* knew were on the other side: Carlist Basques, fierce monarchists and Catholics, who fought against the Republic with an ideological fury that made them more feared even than the Moroccan troops from the Spanish Foreign Legion. Rosales still had vivid memories of these Basque battalions, or *Requetés* as they called themselves, racing at him across open fields, their red berets like poppies in the barren soil of Aragón. These were no people to fool with, Rosales thought; let me meet none of them on my way.

This was a real fear, not like the business of the wolves, for Rosales knew that the Basques in Spain had been waging a campaign of terrorism against the régime for some years. There had been murders and kidnappings by Basque separatists, men who wanted the seven Basque provinces to unite as one country. It seemed very probable to Rosales that the smugglers' trails he was trying to follow were being used at this moment by these Basque terrorists, and that it would not do for any of them to come upon him as he moved down out of the Pyrenees. Worse, though, would be for a patrol of Nationalist troops (he still thought of them as Nationalists) out in search of Basque guerrillas to come upon him, a fugitive with no papers, instead. He had better get out of these mountains very quickly: Never mind cold, snow, and wolves. So he continued his descent.

Gradually through the night the snowfall lightened, then ended altogether, and by dawn Rosales found himself in a rolling countryside, with the forest broken often by large fields, obviously used for the grazing of sheep. Soon the sun rose above the mountains to his left, and he began to feel that now he truly *was* in Spain. Dryness and heat were parts of his natural condition. He knew how to deal with them much better than with the cool and humid climate in which he had been living for so many years. When he came to a small stream at the edge of a pine forest, he stopped to rest.

Rosales wanted very badly to sleep for a couple of hours before seeking the Pamplona road, but before he could allow himself this luxury he had to see to the drying of his clothes. He twisted four small branches from a pine at the edge of the stream, and tied each corner of Inés's blanket to a branch. The gray-black soil of the field at the edge of the forest was so hard that he could not force the branches into it, and it was necessary for him to gather stones from the banks of the stream to place around them and so hold them erect. When he had done this, the blanket was elevated above the ground like a small tent roof, and he knew that it would dry as soon as the sun began to warm the day.

Next he emptied the pockets of his trousers and jacket, looking with rueful good humor at the meagerness of his possessions: a clean pair of socks, a box of matches, a pack of Gitanes, a penknife, fifty francs tied up in a handkerchief, and a piece of stale bread he had taken from the kitchen table as he left his house the day before. All were as wet as if he had not tried to keep the rain and snow away from them, but this was no great problem. He laid them in the field beside the blanket, then took off all his clothes—trousers, jacket, shirt, drawers, socks, and shoes—and placed them beside his other belongings in the sun.

Still ruefully, he looked down at himself, shivering, his skin covered with goosepimples. He could not say that this was the body of a fifty-four-year-old man—there was no paunch, no sagging muscles—but he was, he thought, no thing of great beauty. On his left forearm was the ugly red scar from the shrapnel wound in 1938 that had sent him to the hospital in Barcelona, and on his right thigh there was the puckered lump of flesh from the bullet that had struck him thirty-six years before, in the retreat from Málaga. He ran his hand across his face, and felt the deep lines left there by a barbed wire fence he had encountered when running away from a German ambush during his days with the *Maquis* in the Big War. He felt also the gray stubble that had grown out even more on his face in the past day, and briefly regretted that he had neglected to bring his razor with him. Then he shrugged, smiling to himself, and reflected that he was now after all in his own country, where he would know how to take care of himself: What he needed, he would find. And besides, it had seemed necessary when leaving his French home to carry away as little as possible in the way of belongings.

He hunted about on the floor of the forest until he had collected several handfuls of dry pine needles. With these he rubbed his body and limbs briskly until he could feel the chill retreating and the circulation returning. He went back to his small pile of belongings and bent to pick up the piece of bread. It was still soggy, and almost tasteless; but he squatted by his clothes and his makeshift tent and chewed the bread, meditatively and with apparent satisfaction. He was too tired to be hungry yet, but he knew from the earliest lessons of his life that when one had food, one should eat. There had been, there would be, many mornings without bread.

This done, Rosales made himself a bundle of pine needles to use as a blanket, and stretched himself supine upon the ground at the edge of the forest. The day was still cold, and there were patches of snow in the shadows where the sun had not yet reached, but Rosales was happier than he had been in a long time. The sky was by now clear and of a blueness that Rosales had never seen except in Spain. As the ground around him dried and warmed, it began to give off a faint scent that brought to his mind the fertile soil of the Alpujarras. He fell asleep watching a hawk wheel far above him, curvetting in the thin mountain air.

When Rosales awoke the sun was almost directly above him. The day had become warm, almost balmy for December. He climbed slowly out of the burrow of needles he had fashioned and walked stiffly over to his clothes. They were still not quite dry, but certainly dry enough to wear. The cigarettes and matches, though, were ruined. Rosales regretted this, because his belly was rumbling now with the beginnings of real hunger, and he knew that a couple of cigarettes would stave off for a brief time the feeling of emptiness. But hunger was a minor problem: He was sure that he would find some way of eating before long. His shoes, though, were something else. In drying, they had begun to curl and crack; and he knew they would not last more than a day or two more. As it was, he could barely force his feet into them, and it was impossible to lace them more than halfway up, they had warped and shrunk so. New shoes, he worried, would be harder to come by than food.

After he had dressed himself, he rolled the blanket tightly, and slung it again across his shoulder. Settling his beret squarely atop his head, he squinted eastward, where the road to the south lay. Limping slightly because of the shoes, he moved off, still quietly happy, not doubting at all that with a little luck and shrewdness he would soon be in his own mountains before many days had passed.

In an hour he found the road: a two-lane asphalt highway heading directly south. It would not do for him, he knew, simply to stand on the shoulder and wait to hail whoever came along: This might be his own country, but it was after all a land still occupied by the enemy. And he had no papers: A man with no papers was no one. So he walked along until he found a cluster of boulders at the end of a long stretch of straight road. Here he could hide, and watch for a possible ride.

This was a fortunate precaution, because he had not been squatting by his boulders for more than ten minutes before a gray Land Rover appeared at the far end of the road, heading swiftly southward. He threw himself down, and watched as the truck passed by him. In it were two men wearing the green uniforms and the patent-leather tricorn hats of the *Guardia Civil*, the national police force, which had always symbolized for such as Rosales all that Spain could provide in the way of brutality and oppression of the people. "*Cabrones*," he hissed, full of sudden hatred. Instinctively he raised the forefinger and little finger of one hand to the top of his head, to ward off the evil eye, and chanted: "*Lagarto, lagarto, lagarto*": Lizard, lizard, lizard. These were bad men, these were the worst: One needed the strongest spell possible to dispel the miasma the very sight of them produced. Rosales did not even want to begin to think of how many Spanish peasants and workers had been maimed and murdered by the *Guardia Civil*, who were ostensibly only keepers of the peace, but who were actually (especially in his Andalucía) at the service of the large landholders, who used the *Guardia* ruthlessly to quell any hint of unrest on the part of the people who lived and worked in poverty and hunger on the huge estates that took up almost all of the usable land in his province. Rosales was shaken that the first Spaniards he should see on his return should be this pair. "*La pareja*," he murmured, only beginning to relax minutes after the Land Rover had passed by. "They still travel only in twos, afraid to go out alone." He did not move from behind the sheltering boulders for at least fifteen minutes, lest one of the men in the gray truck

30

should chance to look behind him and see the fugitive by the side of the road.

*Come on, man; did you return to Spain in order to hide behind a rock, like a quail?* Rosales came out, and resumed his wait. The traffic was slight in either direction: Within the space of perhaps an hour there were three or four cars heading north—Frenchmen going home, he thought, noticing as they passed the license plates and the badges with F printed on them, and large trucks carrying—what? oil? petrol?—south to Pamplona or Zaragoza, hurtling along much too rapidly to stop for such as he. Finally Rosales saw a likely prospect coming over the rise to the north: a black civilian car of no newness, dusty and slow. He stepped to the roadside and held his arm before him, his thumb turned to the south. The car, an old Opel Rekord with German license plates, slowed as it passed him, then stopped some fifty meters down the road. An arm beckoned him from the right front window. *Dignity is all,* he reminded himself, and sauntered casually up to the car, holding himself in a manner appropriate to Sebastián Rosales, El Lobo, a man of a certain age and stature, an authentic son of the *pueblo* of Poqueira.

He did not relish the notion of becoming beholden to a carful of Germans, for whom he had no great respect. They did seem to have more of a sense of manhood than the French, but as soldiers (to judge from the occupation troops he had fought against in France) they were not much when compared with most of the Spanish troops on either side in the Civil War. It had been, after all, no great feat for the Condor Legion to obliterate in one day's bombing much of the undefended Basque town of Guernica; and in most of the rest of the Civil War the Germans had never opposed (never *dared* to oppose, he thought) Republican troops on the ground, but contented themselves with artillery shellings, aerial bombardments, and the advisement of Nationalist generals. And in the Big War, at least in the small corner of it he had seen, the Germans had been a bumbling if brutal lot: His Spanish company of *Maquis* had never been really hindered by the *Wehrmacht's* occupation of France from coming and going almost as they wished. Indeed, he reflected as he neared the Opel that was idling roughly on the road ahead of him, we had more to fear from French informers than German soldiers. Perhaps, though, as he had heard, the Germans were good at running factories and making money. If one gave much value to such things.

As he reached the old car, trying to remember how one said "Good afternoon" to Germans, Rosales was startled to hear a voice say to him in Spanish: "Come on, old man, get in. If you make us stand here much longer, this sick cow of a car will die on the road, and we'll never get to Zaragoza." On guard, but expressionless as always, he bent to look through the windows at the Opel's passengers. Inside were four young men, all dressed in cheap suits of dark serge. Only the two in front were awake, gazing impatiently out at him. The two men in the back were sprawled across one another, asleep in the manner of those who have been drinking for some time.

"Get in, old one," said the driver in the harsh, staccato

accent that Rosales remembered as typically Aragonese. "If, that is, we pass your excellency's inspection. Push those *borrachones* in the back to one side, and climb in beside them. If we can stand the smell of their puke, so can your lordship."

"I give you thanks for your kindness," Rosales said stiffly and formally, touching the edge of his beret with his hand as a sign of respect—a respect that he was far from feeling, however. What manner of Spaniards were these, to display rudeness to a stranger, and—in the case of the two with whom he was to share the rear seat, at least—to be so visibly and totally drunk in public, in daylight? Pushing the drunks' arms and legs to one side, and breathing shallowly against the smell of vomit, Rosales seated himself behind the driver. He had to bend his long legs almost double to make himself fit into the little space there was for him; and even so his head scraped the ceiling of the car, so that it was necessary for him to bend forward and cast his head sideways. "A ride is a ride," he told himself. "I will worry later about the cramps that this one will give me." He had learned long ago to ignore physical discomfort when there were no alternatives; and now he made his mind as blank as possible, turning his gaze to the closed window beside him, wishing only that one of the men in front would invite him to let in a little air. The Opel jerked forward, an empty bottle on the rear seat banged against his hip, and no one invited him to do anything.

After perhaps a quarter of an hour the young man in the front passenger's seat half-turned to Rosales and asked, without much interest, where he was going.

"South," he answered, thinking that there was no need

to tell strangers—especially such *antipáticos* strangers as these—more than was absolutely necessary.

"South," the young man echoed. "Clearly, we can see that. Would you care to use a little more specificity? Is there a *pueblo* you wish to reach, or are we to deliver you to your suite in the Castellana Hilton in Madrid?"

"No, *hombre*," the driver said. "Look at him: This one is without doubt a holy pilgrim, in search of the Camino de Santiago. We are fortunate. We can drop him in Pamplona, so that he can go along to Compostela with the other pious ones to pray for sinners like you and me and the two poor unfortunates who are sleeping like lambs beside him."

Rosales wanted fervently to be able to inform this pair of *cabrones* that it was his one desire to go wherever he might be able to shit on the graves of all their ancestors, but all he said was: "I am *andaluz;* I would wish to go as far in that direction as you might want to carry me."

"*¡O, señó, tú eres andalú!*" exclaimed the driver, glancing quickly at the companion beside him, drawing out the last vowel over the space of two seconds. "We would never have guessed such from your accent." Still mimicking the *andaluz* manner of speech with its elisions, its long vowels, and its broad rhythms, the driver continued: "Perhaps you are the owner of an enormous *ganadería* near Ronda, and are roaming through Navarra and Aragón in search of truly brave bulls to breed with your cows." His companion smiled, putting his left arm across the back of the driver's seat. On his wrist was a gold-plated watch that looked very expensive to Rosales.

"No, *señores*," Rosales answered, carefully keeping his voice as smooth as possible. "I am only a poor man, as

34

you surely can see; and I have in mind to go to my *pueblo* and live out my life with simplicity and peace." To himself, he continued: "Or do you understand such terms, you pimply sons of whores?" Ten more minutes of this *tontería*, this stupidity, he knew, and he would attack these two mannequins, and leave them, their drunken friends, and their filthiness of a German car in the ditch for the crows to find.

"This is a truly noble man we have with us, Rafi," said the driver to the man beside him. "We should leave him in peace, and envy him his simplicity." Turning his head toward Rosales, he continued: "Do you take back to your *pueblo* enough foreign wealth to be a big man, a *cacique?*"

"As you see, I take nothing."

"What a pity," said Rafi. "Then you haven't been working in the right places. If you had been with us in the factories of Frankfurt you would have made enough to go back to your town as *don Tal y Cual*, Master Whoever. You could have *bought* the damn town, probably, and lived in something better than simplicity and peace. Do you see the watch that I wear?" Rosales nodded. "It's a Zentra, the best there is; and I didn't even have to work for it—not in the factory, anyway."

"But you *did* work for it, *hombre*," the driver laughed. "You sweated for hours over the fat German pig who gave it to you."

"It's true," Rafi sighed. "But, Jesus, how those big blondes love us up there."

"And down there, too," said the driver, making a quick grab for Rafi's crotch.

"That's true, too," laughed Rafi, his voice full of

pride. "All you have to do is be a Spaniard, and in Germany you're don Juan Tenorio. My God, *they* pay *you*."

"It's the life, all right," said the driver. "One works his hours in the factory, then goes with his friends to the bar at the train station for a *copita* or two—and then one reaches out his hand and grabs the biggest blonde he can find walking by. And the night shift begins. Show him a little money, Rafi."

Rafi dug his hand into a trouser pocket, and came up with a roll of thousand-peseta notes, which he held up for Rosales's admiration. "How much do you think is here, *don Tal y Cual?* For six months' work, how much? One hundred thousand? No, man, there's a lot more. Easy money. Are you still sure you want to go home? Want us to drop you off so you can turn around and go to Germany?"

Rosales, who had never seen more than four thousand pesetas together at one time, and who could scarcely believe in the reality of what he was being shown, could only shake his head. Could it really be possible that such louts as these could become so rich? "You will surely live like princes in such a grand city as Zaragoza, *señores,*" he said. "Undoubtedly you will be honored for life, there." He thought of the fifty francs in his own pocket, and unaccountably was struck by how hungry he was becoming.

"Sure, we'll live like princes there—but only until after the holidays," said the driver. "Then we'll go back. Who wants to live in Spain now, anyway?"

"Forgive me, *señores:* but *I* do," answered Rosales. "And I wouldn't know what to do with such money. I would wish only enough for some food and a little wine. There will be sufficient for me in my *pueblo*, where I can grow enough food to eat, and enough more to trade for the little necessities."

"How long have you been away, old one?" asked Rafi. "A long time, I suspect. Don't you know there's nothing for anyone in the *pueblos*, now? If yours is like the others, when you reach it you'll find no one there but the priest and a flock of old women. Every man with balls is like us: up in the real world, getting rich, and living like *hidalgos*."

*Your balls are in your mouth, so far as I can see.* In Poqueira, he told himself, things will be as they have always been: The men will be there, behaving like men, working and keeping their mouths shut and their balls where they belong.

Beside him, one of the two drunks stirred, groaned, and half sat up. "For the love of Christ," he muttered, "what is all this noise? Where are we now? Stop this filthy auto so the noise will cease and I can piss. I am dying, without doubt."

"Welcome to Spain, you great cistern of wine," said Rafi. "We're almost to Pamplona. We can stop there to buy you something more to drink to last you until Zaragoza, and perhaps to allow you to empty that cow's bladder of yours."

"Your mother," the drunk beside Rosales answered; and slumped back, apparently unconscious again. The Opel drove on, down through the rolling and wooded countryside of Navarra, with the afternoon sun warming the interior of the car so that Rosales was on the point of asking to be let out. His thirst and hunger were great enough now to make him quite faint, but he had little hope that his companions would think to include him in whatever meal they were to have in Pamplona.

By four o'clock they crossed the Río Arga and entered the city, and the driver of the Opel slowed as the highway narrowed into a street that pointed toward the Plaza de Toros. The sidewalks were nearly empty of people (siesta time, thought Rosales), and many of the shops and restaurants had already lowered curtains of wooden slats across their fronts, where they would remain until the life of the city resumed at six. When he found a bar restaurant that was still open, the driver stopped, opened his door, stepped out of the Opel, and began banging his fist on the roof of the car. "Out, sons of whores!" he cried. "Out! Time to eat the first Spanish meal in months and taste real wine again!" Then he and Rafi pulled the two drunks from the rear seat and shook them until they were awake enough to follow them into the restaurant. Rosales had not moved.

"What's the matter, *andaluz?*" asked Rafi. "Don't they eat where you come from?" Rosales shrugged, thinking of his handkerchief with its little cluster of fifty francs. "They eat, of course," he answered. "But I have little money, and far to travel. You go in, and I will guard the car for you."

Rafi snorted. "Come on, old one: your belly has been growling so much for the past two hours that it's kept my friends here upset. Eat a little; we won't watch if you're timid."

"I have not changed my money into pesetas, yet. I will wait here and perhaps you might bring me some bread if there is something extra on the table."

"Ah, the famous Spanish pride," laughed Rafí. "You

38

embarrass us. Come on, let us allow ourselves to be exploited a bit, as the bloated capitalists we are. *Mahlzeit,* man."

"*Mahlzeit?*"

"It's what we say in Germany, *andaluz.* It's like *qué aproveche:* Eat, enjoy yourself. Do you want to offend us?"

Rosales shrugged again. "I would not wish to offend. Perhaps then I will take a little something." And he followed the four inside. It was not much of a restaurant: the sawdust-covered floor was littered with scraps of paper, toothpicks, and various débris from shellfish that earlier customers had left behind; and the odor of stale olive oil was strong. None of this bothered Rosales, however: In fact, the disorder of the place pleased him, as a kind of antidote to the comparative sterility of French restaurants.

An hour later, full of chicken roasted in garlic and four glasses of wine, Rosales was back in the Opel, cramped again into the back seat, and drowsy enough not to mind either the discomfort or the company. As they headed south toward Tudela and the broad valley of the Río Ebro, he began to doze, worried now only about the problem of his shoes. The ride would end in Zaragoza, and he had to assume that he would be on foot again by nightfall. He had to think of something: The shoes in which he had crossed the Pyrenees would not get him five kilometers down the road before they fell apart.

By eight o'clock, as the Opel drove southeast along the Ebro toward Zaragoza, the solution presented itself. Of the four with him, only the driver remained awake.

39

Rafi was asleep with his head inclined against the window, and the two drunks were once again sprawled across the rear seat. The legs of one of them—he who had stirred briefly before Pamplona—were across Rosales's lap; and at the ends of those legs were a pair of feet encased in good, sturdy German workman's shoes, double soled and heeled. Over the space of an hour, with infinite patience, Rosales untied the man's shoes, then pried them carefully from his feet. The man never moved. Rosales silently unzipped his jacket, slipped the shoes inside, and then zipped himself up. "Let this drunk sleep until we reach the outskirts of Zaragoza," he prayed, "and then I'll be off. If these people are so rich, they can buy their friend a pair of patent-leather cavalryman's boots in the morning, and have a good laugh while doing it." His only worry now was that the shoes might not fit him. They had looked perhaps somewhat too large, but that would not be so bad: He could always wear both pair of socks, and stuff the toes with paper if need be.

As the Opel turned to cross into Zaragoza by the old Roman bridge over the Ebro, Rosales lightly tapped the driver on the shoulder and whispered, "Here is where I leave you, *señor*, and a thousand thanks for your great courtesy to me. I would wish there were some way to repay you."

The driver, surprised, began pulling the car to the side of the road. Whispering also, he asked Rosales whether he would not prefer at least to be left off nearer the road south out of the city. When Rosales shook his head, the driver stopped the car at the curb. In front of them was an enormous cathedral of great ugliness. Rosales carefully slid out from under the legs of his unconscious benefactor, touched his beret respectfully, and—holding his blanket roll across his swollen midsection—climbed from the car. Gesturing toward the hideous cathedral, he said good-bye to the driver: "May the blessed Virgin of the Pillar, who I am told resides within that holy place, bless you and your friends, for your generosity." Still wearing his surprised look, the driver of the Opel nodded and drove slowly off, leaving the solemn Rosales standing behind on the sidewalk.

In two minutes Rosales had found a narrow alley leading away from the broad plaza in front of the cathedral, and was sitting on a bench as far as possible from a streetlamp. Seeing no one coming his way, he pulled off his old shoes and hid them beneath the bench. As he had suspected, the drunk's shoes were too large, but not irremediably so. He pulled on his extra pair of socks, and tiptoed over to a garbage can at the entrance to the alley. "My luck continues," he said to himself. "This Zaragoza is clearly a city of great dirtiness, a place where the people throw trash away with considerable abandon. I can choose the exact sort of paper I require." Selecting a large wad of soft wrapping paper, he went back to his bench, stuffed the paper into the toes of his new shoes, and laced them up. Now he had all that he required: His belly was full, his feet were well-shod, and he had regained most of the pride he had lost during his long ride with those Germanicized Spaniards. Perhaps he was right: Perhaps all it took was a little shrewdness and luck. Now all he had to do was to get away from this ugly Zaragoza and into the countryside again, and his way would be clear. With some complacency, he looked about him. "We tried for eighteen months to take this *maldita* city," he mused. "I wonder what the hell we wanted with it."

By the time he had walked through the gray and grimy streets of Zaragoza for two hours, he was even more cynical about the Aragonese capital. It seemed composed of an intricate series of mazes, each calculated to keep him, Sebastián Rosales, from finding a way out. Every time he came upon something that looked like a *gran vía*, main thoroughfare, it would constrict itself within a few blocks into a dark tunnel of a lane leading, so far as he could tell, nowhere at all. It hurt him, as a man, to ask directions of strangers, but from time to time he would try to stop one Zaragozano or another to ask how one might find a road out of this city that might take one southward. None of this came to any good, however: Either he found his accent or his ignorance mocked, or he was given intricate and insoluble directions in the rapid Aragonese that made no concessions to those of slower Spanish. Finally, well after midnight, by pure luck he found himself at a place called the Plaza San Miguel, looking at a road sign that said: N232. CASTELLÓN DE LA PLANA, 277 KM. This meant nothing to him, but at least it indicated that there was some way out of Zaragoza; so off he set, hoping that this N232 would head at least generally southward.

By dawn, he had covered twenty kilometers, walking steadily along the flat highway, which, as it turned out, lay along the south bank of the Ebro. Just ahead of him was a large truck stop, brightly lit and obviously open for business at this hour. He stepped into the café beside

42

the filling station there, hoping for he knew not what—perhaps only for a little warmth against the chilly dawn, or for a place to sit quietly for a few moments. He sat down at the bar, and looked across it at the reflection of himself in the large mirror, framed by two placards advertising San Miguel beer and something called "Agua San Narciso." The face that peered back at him was certainly not that of the warrior he thought of as El Lobo: It was an aging man he saw, with matted gray hair, a nine-day growth of beard, and a face that was scarred and tired and weathered. This will not do, he thought. I must repair myself.

He saw a door marked CABALLEROS, and went through it to find another mirror, a dirty sink, and a dirtier toilet bowl. There was a small remnant of soap on the sink, and it occurred to him that he might at least try to shave. He took his penknife from his pocket, opened it, and placed it on the sink and then attempted with indifferent success to lather his beard with the sliver of soap and the cold water that trickled from the single tap. The blade of the knife was as sharp as he had been able to make it before leaving Cambó, but Rosales had little luck with the thick stubble that now was almost a quarter of a centimeter long. After he had nicked himself several times, and covered his jaw with blood, he gave it up, splashed his face with water, grinned at himself, and returned to the bar.

When the bartender, a young man who looked tired and bored, came over to Rosales, who was the only customer there, Rosales hesitated a moment, then said, "I would like a *café con leche* and perhaps a *bollo*, a roll of bread; but I have only French francs. I suppose you

43

would not accept them."

"What would I do with francs, old one?," the waiter asked. He looked at Rosales for a long moment, then said, thoughtfully, "Still, it's a cold morning, and *café* and a *bollo* don't present a major problem. How many francs do you have? I don't even know what they're worth in pesetas."

Nor did Rosales know, but he offered the waiter five francs. "Done," said the waiter, and turned to the coffee machine behind him. Hurriedly, Rosales took out the knotted handkerchief from his trousers pocket, untied it, and separated five francs, which he placed on the zinc surface of the bar. When the waiter returned with the coffee and the roll, he scooped up the coins without counting them, and laid them next to the cash register. "Perhaps a French tourist will come along and want his change in francs," he said, not very convincingly.

"That is very probable," said Rosales. "In any case, I thank you for your kindness." He ate and drank very slowly, thinking that this might be the only meal he would find that day. When he had finished, he called to the bartender, who was standing by, watching the occasional truck pass. "As a favor," he asked, "can you tell me where this road leads?"

The bartender yawned. "One can do many things with this road. In twenty kilometers, one can turn south to Belchite and Teruel, if those names mean anything to you." *Do they not: These are names I will never forget.* "Or one can continue southeast, through Caspe and down to Tortosa, in the Ebro Delta." *Those names mean something to me too.*

Before the bartender could turn away again, Rosales

said, "I do not wish to bother you unduly, but if one were hoping to travel very far south, as quickly as possible, which would be the better way to go?"

"More coffee?" Before Rosales could raise his hand, palm outward, to signal no, the bartender took his cup to refill, gesturing as he did so that this was free. Then, leaning his elbows on the bar, the waiter thought for a moment. "Well, through Teruel is faster; but there's not much traffic that way. You'd probably do better to head for the coast, and then down. The roads there are so full of tourists, here for the winter sun, that you'll never be stuck. I'd go to Tortosa and hit the coast road if I were you. But if I might offer a suggestion, I'd get that blood off my face, and spruce myself up a bit before I began to hope for more than a ride in a cattle truck. At least get some sleep, first: You look like death, old man. No offense."

Rosales looked again at his face in the mirror. In truth, he was no man to give a ride to. "No offense," he said. "Is there perhaps a small corner here where I might rest for a few hours before setting off?"

"I do not own this place, *viejo*, and the owner would not enjoy my turning it into a hostel during his absence. But I work here until noon, and I would not mind it if you were to stretch out in the storeroom for a few hours."

Rosales stood, noticing as he did so how unsteady he was becoming. Indeed, this was real fatigue. "You are very generous," he said formally, "and I accept your kind invitation."

The waiter led him back to a small, unheated room behind the bar, and indicated a flat space on two cardboard boxes where Rosales might lie. "It's not much, *viejo;* but rest well." They shook hands, and the waiter returned to his position at the bar.

This was more like it, thought Rosales, rolling his blanket about him and lying down on the cartons. The man asked me no questions, and treated me with courtesy. This is more like the old Spain. In five minutes he was in deep sleep.

Shortly before noon the waiter woke him, gave him more coffee, shook his hand again, and escorted him to the door. He and Rosales were still alone in the café, but the waiter seemed nervous, now—anxious, thought Rosales, lest the owner return early and be annoyed by the presence of such a one as he. But as Rosales was about to turn toward the road, the young man stopped him. "Here, *viejo*. Something against the cold. You'll need it, and the boss won't miss it." He held out to Rosales a small paper bag, and a bottle of Fundador with almost five fingers of the brown *coñac* left in it. Rosales opened the bag: Inside it were a pair of hard-boiled eggs, a box of matches, and a packet of biscuits. The bartender waved away Rosales's thanks, and hurried back into the warmth of his café. In truth, Rosales thought, I did right to return. There are still Spaniards.

Still undecided as to which route he should take, Rosales set off down the road toward Fuentes del Ebro, where the route lay south to Teruel. The day was bright but cold, colder even than the Pyrenees had been. A sharp wind was blowing from the west. He remembered that wind: It was called "El Moncayo" and it came from the mountains west of Zaragoza. In winter it could blow a man off his feet, bring on frostbite with great suddenness, lock the action of his rifle—ruin a battle, cause a town to be lost.

This Aragón was no place for a man to live, let alone fight. Only the banks of the Ebro ever showed much greenness. The rest was all steep and barren hills, barely able to support a flock of sheep. No wonder the Aragonese had such a reputation for toughness: The winters were colder than anywhere else in Spain, and the summers were so hot and dry that a man could die of thirst in twelve hours' time. Rosales looked around him. He saw no trees, few shrubs, an occasional clump of thyme or esparto grass: Aragón was rock, sand, and wind. No one stopped to pick him up, and he could not blame them: Who would want to stop his car in Aragón, especially for such a frightening-looking *campesino?*

Hungry again by four o'clock, he stopped just before the *pueblo* of Fuentes del Ebro, where the road forked south. If he were to pass the night here, he knew, it could not be in the village: There would be no place to sleep, and the ever-present *Guardia Civil* would learn of his presence almost immediately. They would stop him very politely, ask to see his papers—and then, without doubt, arrest him. He drew from beneath the blanket in which he had kept himself wrapped his paper bag and his bottle of *coñac*. Seating himself on a large stone below the slope of the roadbed, he began to eat and drink, slowly and methodically as always, until the food and liquor were gone. He felt quite well, almost lightheaded. If he could not enter the town, so what? He would find shelter in the earth—dig a cave in this awful soil, if he had to. Without much on his mind, Rosales

47

turned his head from west to east. He felt small, almost dwarfed in this blasted terrain: Except for the occasional car or truck, the only sign of life he could detect from horizon to horizon was himself. His shoes, his handsome new shoes, had raised blisters on the balls of both feet. When he stood, he found that his trousers were noticeably looser than they had been when he left Cambó. I have got to take care of myself, he thought, still a little giddy from the *coñac*. It would not do to appear in Poqueira as a skeleton, something to frighten children.

The ceaseless, sharp wind shifted to the south for a moment, and Rosales heard a faint *tunk, tunk, tunk* sound that filled him with immediate nostalgia. It was a sheep bell, of the kind used all over Spain to attach to the bellwether of a flock. Before long he was able to make out a smallish mass of moving bundles approaching him over the hills to the south. A few minutes more and he could pick out the shepherd, and even the shepherd's little dog, who was racing merrily about the perimeter of the flock. Here was a good sign, thought Rosales: Where there are shepherds, there are shepherds' caves—places where they could shelter themselves against midday heat and sudden storms. All he had to do was walk south, climb around on the lee slopes of a hill or two, and there would be his home for the night—a cozy, windproof cave where he would be free from molestation.

Rosales did not want the shepherd to see him—shepherds were famously silent people, but this one might go home tonight to a garrulous wife and mention the sight of a stranger on the road—so he ducked down, and looked for a *barranco*, a ravine, that would carry him south, but downwind from the sheep-dog's good nose.

An hour later, at dusk, he was reclining contentedly in a small cave halfway up the slope of a hill that was mostly reddish stone and shale. Beside him was a *bota*, a small leather winebag, which the shepherd had left behind for himself. It was more than half full, Rosales was happy to discover. He told himself that he would sleep early, and rise at dawn to make his decision about which route southward to take.

At dawn he awoke, totally alert in an instant: There was something in the cave with him, something moving. Rosales held himself absolutely still, completely aware of where he lay in relation to the entrance to the shallow cave. Very slowly, without turning his head, he opened his eyes. By his left shoulder, no more than a meter away, a large brown rabbit sat on its haunches, its round liquid eyes fixed on his.

"*Psst, psst, conejo, conejito,*" Rosales said quietly to the rabbit, who would, he knew, flee instantly if startled. Distracting the animal with his caressing murmur, he reached with his right hand for a stone on the cave floor. The rabbit did not move as Rosales's hand closed around a hard clump of shale almost as big as his fist. "Little rabbit, little rabbit," he continued to whisper, as he tensed his whole body. Then he moved, swifter than he had moved in years, and slammed his right fist over his chest into the face of the rabbit. Still alive but stunned, the rabbit made a lurching bound for the cave door. Rosales leapt to his feet and dove for the rabbit, catching it by one of its long hind legs. He stood at the entrance to the cave, cradling the rabbit gently in the crook of his arm, reflecting that he now had his breakfast. Did he

49

dare to risk a fire, or should he try to eat this rabbit raw? The idea repelled him. He would kill the rabbit, clean it as best he could with his penknife, and cook it over a small fire made from whatever poor scrub this awful landscape would yield.

Gently he grasped the stunned rabbit by the hind legs and let the body hang down. As he continued to croon to it, Rosales began swinging the animal back and forth in an arc, holding both hind legs with his right hand. Suddenly, as the rabbit swung up, he slashed his left hand down sharply, striking the creature at the top of the spine. Its head snapped back, the neck broken.

Rosales built a small fire, then moved away from the entrance to the cave, and began to operate on his prey. First came the skinning. Quickly he bit a piece out of the loose neck skin and inserted his fingers under the flap. He had not done this since he was a boy in the hills above Poqueira, but all the necessary memories returned. Methodically and expertly he began to peel the whole skin back from the carcass. This done, he knew that it was essential to see whether the rabbit was diseased: He had to check its liver. With his penknife he probed and pulled out the soft pulpy meat from the rest. It was bright red, with no spots. Good, a healthy rabbit. It took him only a moment to clean the rest of the animal, scooping the guts out of the stomach cavity. He was careful to pull the intestines out without breaking them, remembering that this could be done—that there were no ligaments holding the organs to the carcass. Within two minutes after striking the startled rabbit with his fist, Rosales stood, with its entire guts in one hand and its carcass in another. Breakfast, he announced proudly to himself.

With a flat stone he dug a shallow grave for the rabbit's intestines—no point in bringing the vultures over his position unnecessarily—and then settled back to strip what flesh he wanted from the carcass. The meat was red, and so tough and sinewy that he was hardly able to tear away more than a few bites to lay across the fire he had started from handfuls of thyme using all the matches the waiter had given him. He buried the remains of the body beside its entrails, and scoured his hands with the rough earth of the hillside. There was no wind yet, and Rosales could feel the early morning sun beginning to warm him. He was content enough, and decided to rest before his cave for an hour before setting off again. He pulled his blanket from the cave, draped it over his shoulders, and settled himself into a sunny spot on the south slope of the hill, where he would be least liable to be seen from the road or from the nearby town.

Wishing he could smoke, Rosales stared off to the south. Thirty kilometers away, over ground that he remembered still with utter clarity, lay the *pueblo* of Belchite. Mother of God, he said to himself: That I should ever see that place again! Belchite had been one of the worst times, one of the few times of his life that he had felt shame for his own actions.

---

Throughout August and September of 1937, the Republican Army of the East (later to become the Army of the Ebro) had launched a series of offensives against the Nationalist forces, which lay along a front that extended from north of Jaca, in the Pyrenees, straight down through Aragón to Teruel, the southernmost city of the region. Presumably, the goal of these offensives was the city of Zaragoza, from the beginning of the war a Nationalist redoubt of considerable strength and strategic importance.

On August 24 the Republican attack began at eight points along the front, as usual without aerial or artillery preparation. For several days the Nationalist divisions fell back slowly, and by August 26 only the town of Belchite, surrounded and fifteen kilometers behind the new front lines, was holding out against the Republican advance. For reasons known only to the general staffs of both sides, Belchite was important: General Franco radioed to the commander of the town's garrison that he must hold out to the last man; and the Republican attackers, consisting mostly of the Fifth Army Corps of Juan Modesto, were ordered to seize the town at all costs.

To Sebastián Rosales, El Lobo, a *cabo*, a corporal, in the Eleventh Division of Enrique Lister (a former quarryman from the Asturias, and as tough and dedicated a Communist as Modesto), Belchite looked like no great prize. His company lay entrenched for days at the eastern edge of the town, sniping away at the Nationalist troops and civilians, who were fitfully firing back at them from behind barricades of bedding, cement slabs, and timber they had torn from the walls of the town's houses. The heat was ferocious; and, since Lister's encircling troops had cut off the water supply to Belchite two days before, El Lobo reasoned that thirst if not bullets would conquer the town soon. He knew little of strategy, and cared less, but it seemed to him that Modesto and Lister might just as easily ignore this dirty little Aragonese town and bypass it to march on Zaragoza.

Belchite, though, was evidently something of a symbol: Therefore it had to fall.

And finally, on September 6, it did. El Lobo and his men ran through the streets of the town, firing at anyone who offered them resistance. Then they followed the usual mopping-up procedure. The mayor of Belchite had died days before at the walls of his *pueblo*, a rifle in his hands. But the Assault Guards attached to Lister's division soon rounded up all of Belchite's other prominent bourgeoisie, lined them against a stone parapet near the central plaza, and shot them. So much for Belchite, thought El Lobo with no great satisfaction. Now perhaps we can rest for a day, then begin the drive on Zaragoza.

But, as was so often the case in this war, the Republicans did not press ahead when they had the advantage. As El Lobo sat in Belchite, looking about at ruined buildings and swollen corpses bloating in the September sun, the attack along the Aragonese front stalled; and by the end of the month the Army of the East was on the defensive. Lister did venture forth once to the north, using a group of Russian cruiser tanks as his spearhead; but his attack was beaten back, and the conquerors of Belchite now became its defenders.

El Lobo's company was positioned on the forward slope of a hill west of the town, looking out across the road from Cariñena, along which Nationalist troops were shortly to appear, with tanks, artillery, and aerial attacks to support them. At dawn on October 16, El Lobo heard the approach, far overhead, of the inevitable Italian bombers. Two hours later he saw a column of German tanks on the Cariñena road, dust billowing around

them as they moved slowly toward him. At two kilometers' distance from El Lobo's position, the tanks
moved into a line abreast, and opened fire with their
howitzers as they continued to advance. The Republicans had had it again, El Lobo knew: Once the large
field guns that had doubtless been set up behind the distant hills in the west opened fire, the Republicans would
be blasted off their hill and back into what the Italian
bombers had left of Belchite. He felt a great thirst. His
mouth was full of the brassy taste that he knew came
from simple fear. He waited throughout the tank and
artillery barrage for the order to retreat down his hill
and back into Belchite. But no order came: Once again,
it seemed, this insignificant Aragonese town was to be
defended at all costs. "*At all costs*," he said aloud, his
voice full of contempt: This was an expression that had
clearly been devised by men who sat far behind the lines,
making marks on maps. When the staff officers said "*At
all costs*," men did not simply die: They were slaughtered. So he sat in his trench, firing 7 mm. bullets at
German tanks, and watching his hillside burst apart
around him. Smoke and dust were everywhere. Men
screamed, men were blown apart, men ran to the rear,
tossing their rifles aside as they leapt back over the crest
of the hill.

But—yet another inexplicable event in this strangest
of wars—the attack ended by forenoon. No Nationalist
troops had advanced toward them through their covering tanks. The bombardment ceased, the smoke cleared.
El Lobo raised his head above his trench, and saw most
of his company still there, where they were supposed to
have been. Finally, at dusk, his company commander

passed along the order to fall back to Belchite for the night. Their positions were taken over by a company of Assault Guards that had been standing in reserve on the reverse slope of the hill. By nightfall, El Lobo and the remnants of his company were camped behind the walls of the old Augustinian seminary, the largest building left standing in Belchite. Not even bothering to eat, El Lobo fell asleep.

He was awakened at first light by a foot kicking at his boot. He opened his eyes to see standing above him his company commander and his regimental commissar, a Russian who spoke rather little Spanish, but whose function it was to preside over the ideological discipline of the Spanish troops under his authority.

El Lobo jumped to his feet and stood at attention, noticing as he did so that behind the two officers were standing a cluster of four men: two Assault Guards who appeared to be watching over a pair of soldiers from El Lobo's company. "*A sus órdenes, mi capitán*," said El Lobo, sensing trouble but still not awake enough to think of what that trouble could be.

"You know these men, *cabo?*" asked the commander.

"*Sí, mi capitán*, they are our men, men who have been with us for months." They were, indeed, veterans of as many battles as El Lobo had seen—and, moreover, they were *andaluces*, men from near Ronda who had been fighting since the old days when they were not an army but a militia. El Lobo knew them well, these men from his *patria chica*, and he knew suddenly that they were somehow the grave trouble he had sensed on awakening.

Turning to the commissar, who stood casually somewhat aside from the group, allowing his eyes to wander around the little encampment behind the seminary, the company commander said, "This is the young *andaluz* we call El Lobo, because he has something of a reputation as a killer. He may look like a boy to you, Comrade Commissar, but he has done things in this war that would surprise you. He has the necessary discipline, which is why I have chosen him for what you wish done."

"Then tell him what to do," said the commissar, his voice bland and bored.

"Lobo, these men you see here ran yesterday in the barrage. The Assault Guards caught them fleeing like rabbits down the hill. They have been sentenced to die, and the comrade commissar and I have chosen you for the job. Do you understand?" El Lobo looked across the officers at the two *andaluz* peasants, both men perhaps ten years older than he. They gazed back at him, expressionless; men who had no doubts as to their future. He understood perfectly: This captain from the regular army and this *ruso* commissar wished to enforce a little discipline on men who had been not only *andaluz* militia, but anarchists to boot.

"They are my friends," El Lobo protested, still at attention. "Anyone might run. These are good fighters. They have between them killed more *fascistas* than this *ruso* has ever seen. Have we so many good men that we can now commence shooting our own?" The commissar looked at his fingernails; perhaps he had not understood El Lobo's speech.

"*Cabo.* We shoot cowards," said the company commander, his face reddening. "These men ran; therefore they are cowards. Discipline must be maintained. You are to take them over the hill south of town and shoot them. Do you submit to my orders?"

*Or do I wish to die, too?* Then, to the commander: "I understand, *mi capitán*. But why not let these Assault Guards, or this *ruso* here, perform the execution? These 'cowards' are men from my region: What sort of barbarity is it to require *me* to kill them?"

For the first time, the commissar spoke, his narrow blue eyes fixed on El Lobo's chest. "You kill these men, now. Enough talk."

El Lobo nodded, and bent to pick up his rifle. As he did so, the company commander stepped forward and offered El Lobo his semiautomatic pistol. "You know how to use this, *cabo?*" Again El Lobo nodded, looking with some disdain at the tiny weapon in the officer's hand.

"Good. Go now and obey. Report back to me when you have carried out your orders." El Lobo touched his beret briefly, brushed between the two officers, and walked quickly over to the four men who stood behind them.

"Go fuck your mothers, assassins," he said to the two Assault Guards. "This is an affair involving *andaluces*, real men." The Assault Guards lowered their rifles, looking at the company commander as they did so.

"*Bueno, compadres*, we have work to do, no?" El Lobo said to the two *andaluces*, who had turned to face him.

"*¿No hay remedio?*" asked one of them, his eyebrows lifting. "There's nothing to be done?"

"Nothing."

"Then let's go, Lobito," said the prisoner who had

spoken. "It's already getting hot, and we're hungry. Only treat us like men: You know us."

"I know you," replied El Lobo. "I will behave with respect, and we will do this business as quickly and cleanly as it can be done."

"Good then," said the second prisoner. "March us off."

El Lobo pointed to the hillside nearby, and followed the prisoners as they turned and walked away, their backs as straight as though they were on parade. When they had reached a spot of sandy soil one kilometer south of Belchite, El Lobo called for the men to halt. He looked back over his shoulder, and saw the two Assault Guards following them at a distance. He realized that if he did not carry out his orders, he, too, would die this hot morning.

"Kneel." The men knelt.

"Bend your heads forward." The men bent their heads forward in unison, as at the elevation of the Host. Both were trembling slightly, but El Lobo knew that these were men who would do nothing to shame themselves in death. *Mother of God: What am I about to do to these men?*

El Lobo walked quickly up to the man on the left, pointed the barrel of the pistol against the back of the man's neck, and pulled the trigger. Nothing happened.

"You must cock the mechanism, Lobito. Pull the receiver rearward. That will chamber a round." The voice of the prisoner who said this was as matter-of-fact as if he were giving instruction to a recruit.

Sweating, El Lobo did as he was told. Again he pressed the barrel of the pistol against the man's neck, and pulled the trigger. There was a sharp report, and the prisoner pitched forward, face down into the sand.

"Well done, *hombre*," said the second prisoner. "Now do as well with me." His voice shook as he said this, but the words were said with as much detachment as possible.

El Lobo moved to the right, and repeated the act of firing. The second man fell forward like the first, but rolled over on his side. In the front of the man's neck El Lobo saw a large red wound, with blood pumping out at a great rate. The man writhed about in the sand, a gurgling moan coming from his torn throat. El Lobo, furious, bent over and fired again, this time into the man's left temple. The noise and motion ceased. El Lobo looked at the hillside around him. All was silent. He turned around: The Assault Guards were not far behind, appearing to El Lobo like mildly interested spectators at some sort of village game.

"Must I bury them, too, you pair of sick whores' cunts?" El Lobo was shaking.

"No, *hombre*, go back to your men. We will finish your assignment."

El Lobo paced rapidly back to the village, strode toward the two officers, stopped, and saluted. Ignoring the commissar, who was still apparently bemused, he held the company commander's pistol out to him.

"I have accomplished your orders, *mi capitán*," he said steadily. "But may I say one thing?"

"Say it, *cabo*."

"You have caused me to perform a shameful act, *mi capitán*. I do not know whether you are to blame, or this *ruso* here; but I have been made do a bad thing. I am a soldier, not a worker in a slaughterhouse. You have shamed me, truly."

"Go away, soldier," said the commissar. El Lobo

looked for an instant at the flat blue eyes of the Russian, then turned and walked back to his resting place against the seminary wall. Perhaps he could sleep again, but he doubted it. This Belchite was a bad town: The Nationalists could have it, for all he cared.

# Chapter 2

No, Rosales would not follow the Belchite–
Teruel road, even though it led almost directly south.
He had done that once before, in the long and depressing
autumn of 1937, retreating steadily as the Aragón front
collapsed. The business with the Russian commissar
stuck in his mind as being the time when the *extranjeros*
began to dominate his war: A time when something that
had seemed simple, almost pure, in its Spanishness had
become complicated and foreign. If he had thought
about it, he would have said only that he was fighting
because it was time for Spaniards to fight. He had never
himself been a Communist, and had felt a little uneasy at
fighting in the armies of men like Modesto and Lister,
who (he had heard) were given their military education
in Russia. But these men were at least Spaniards, peasants

61

and working-class men like himself; and he had no difficulty in accepting their authority.

Yet the longer the war lasted, the more he found himself fighting alongside Englishmen, Belgians, Germans—God knows what sorts of foreigners, all in Spain for who knew what reasons. He supposed they were good enough men; certainly they were brave, and they died in great numbers and with a willingness that he, Rosales, found hard to understand. This was Spain, after all, and this had been a war among Spaniards: Why did the rest of the world have to join in, on both sides? There had been a certain amount of political instruction, to be sure; and Rosales had been told much about the Cause, and the World Struggle against Fascism, and the Need for Ideological Solidarity. But these were finally only words: What mattered was that the Republicans won small victories and lost great defeats until one day, in March 1939, he had found himself in his "rest area" in southern France, surrounded like the rest of the beaten Republican army by the barbed wire and the scorn of their French friends. And the road from Belchite to Teruel had been the scene of many of the confusions, delays, and routine defeats that for Rosales characterized this war in which so many foreigners had dabbled. To hell with all this cold, all these mountains: There was too much remembered death in them. He'd head east, toward the coast, and then roll down the shores of the Mediterranean to Andalucía.

A bitter wind had arisen from the west, and the sky was no longer sunny, but gray and heavy. He felt the kind of dampness that precedes snow, and knew that he could remain no longer perched on his hill near his shepherd's cave. It would be necessary for him to skirt the south edge of Fuentes del Ebro, and quickly, and then to return to the highway some way to the east of the *pueblo*. He stood, wrapped his blanket over his shoulders, slung the shepherd's *bota* across his chest, and set off along the bottom of a *barranco* that curved eastward, in a way that appeared roughly parallel to the road through the town he wanted to avoid. He must not be seen. *I am a man with no papers.*

After a half-hour's walk over this rocky bed of what had perhaps, a thousand years ago, been a lively stream, Rosales heard the sound of voices. Women, he thought, not more than three or four; and near. Cautiously he went on, in the direction of the road. Suddenly he was on level ground, and the road was there, not more than fifteen meters before him. And on the road were three old women, all motionless, all dressed in black, all staring at him. He glanced beyond them: There was the *pueblo* of Fuentes del Ebro, only a kilometer to the west. He had miscalculated. From where he stood he could see very clearly the clay-and-mortar houses of the town, with their red-tiled roofs. A row of stunted and leafless plane trees lined the road as it emerged from the narrow streets of the village; and at the center of Fuentes del Ebro was the inevitable belltower of the inevitable church, rising high above the other houses. A perfect place for snipers, he thought; why did we ever leave it standing?

The old women had not moved as he examined their village. They watched him with an unswerving and silent attention that made him think of the cows that moved about in tiny herds across the hills below Poqueira, his own *pueblo*, still hundreds of kilometers to the south. If he hollered, if he clapped his hands, would they turn and lumber off up the road? They would certainly not be able to lumber very fast, he saw: They were old, very old; and each was bent beneath a load of dry sticks she carried in a fat bundle across her shoulders. Well then, courtesy.

"Good morning, *señoras*," he said. "It is a cold day, no?"

No answer. The women did not move.

"Do you gather wood for your fires?" No answer.

"You must be preparing to bake the day's bread," he tried again, thinking that in Poqueira the daily baking would long since have been accomplished, and such old women would be back in the *pueblo*, nagging at their grandchildren. Truly, these Aragonese were a backward lot, hard and dull.

Finally, one of the old women spoke. Pointing with her free hand at the leather bag Rosales wore around his neck, she twisted her face around her toothless mouth and asked, in a voice that he could scarcely understand, "Whose *bota* is that?" My Jesus, thought Rosales: Is this *pueblo* so poor they know each man's *bota* by sight? To the old woman who had spoken, he answered, "It is mine, *señora*, carried by me from my home in the mountains of the Asturias." He could not think of the name of a city, let alone a town, in the region of Asturias, but this was the first place that had come to his mind.

The women looked at one another, then back at Rosales—then turned as one, and began hobbling back toward the town.

"Good day again, *señoras*, and that the Holy Virgin

64

and all the saints should bless you each," he intoned after them. And may you all be rotting in your graves by nightfall, he added to himself. They'd talk when they returned, he knew. They probably *did* recognize the damned *bota*, and were off to the shepherd's house to report the theft. He really could not blame them for being suspicious about *forasteros*, strangers. Even in the Alpujarras, almost everything that went wrong in Poqueira—missing sheep, illnesses, unwanted pregnancies, soured milk—was blamed on someone from one of the neighboring villages of Pampaneira or Bubión. Or worse: from the dangerous big cities of Granada and Málaga, the sources of evils beyond the imaginings of the Alpujarreños. So it seemed reasonable to Rosales for these crones to look on him with distrust and hatred.

Still, he had better get away from their *pueblo* before they had the *Guardia Civil* out chasing him. He began to trot down the road toward the east, hoping that someone would stop for him before those two men in their green uniforms and shiny tricorn caps began searching for him.

Rosales was lucky, once again: Within minutes a small red Seat sedan pulled up beside him and stopped. The driver, a tall man with a blond beard, leaned over to open the righthand door.

"Good morning, please get in. May I give you a ride?" Before Rosales could respond to any of this, as he stepped into the little car, the tall man continued, "It is very cold today, right? Are you going far? I am glad to have your company. Do you know why?"

Rosales, confused by such garrulity and by this man's curious accent, only shook his head. What in the name of God have I encountered this time? he wondered. The accent—or rather the monotonous delivery, the near *ab-*

*sence* of accent—made him think of the Robot Man, a machine, which, for a peseta, told fortunes on the Ramblas of Barcelona—a thing he had seen when he was recuperating there in 1938.

"Yes," he said slowly. "It is cold. I do go to the coast, if possible. I do not know why you wish my company, but I am glad that you do." He thought of the three old women of Fuentes del Ebro, doubtless now gabbling away at the *cuartel*, the barracks of the *Guardia*.

"Perhaps you notice that I am a foreigner," said the bearded man, who could not have looked less like a Spaniard. "I am a visitor to your country, and I want very much to learn your language and something of your customs. Can you understand me?"

"You speak the language very well, very correctly," answered Rosales politely. "But I am an old man, a peasant, and I doubt there is much I could tell you that would interest you." He composed himself in the right seat, and looked out his window as if to discourage conversation. But the driver did not notice.

"I am *norteamericano*," he said, "but I am a great student of things Spanish. I have real admiration for your country. Are you Aragonese?"

"No."

"Do you not find this bleakness, this desolation, dramatic beyond words?"

"Aragón to me is a frozen cow turd. I leave it to the Aragonese."

The man laughed. "So you are not from here. May I ask where you *are* from? I hope you do not mind if I ask you questions this way: It is only in the spirit of friendly curiosity, and so that I might practice my *castellano*."

66

In his largeness, his boyishness, and his naïveté, this *yanqui* reminded Rosales of some of the English and Dutch who had fought near him in the Fifteenth International Brigade along the Ebro delta. One could not dislike such people, but they *were* a little lacking in dignity, he thought. Or, simply, they talk too much. And like robot men, with the Spanish coming out correct but stiff.

"I am not from here," Rosales answered after a moment. "But I know this land very well."

"Ah. Do you work here? Or no: Let me guess: you are from Extremadura or Castilla, and are passing through on your way to the coast to grow rich on the *urbanización*." The American smiled, turning toward Rosales a row of teeth that were whiter even than his own.

"No, *señor*, I know nothing of this *urbanización*, wherever it is going on and whatever it is."

"You'll see when we reach the coast," said the American. "Spaniards like you are finding work and growing rich there, working in construction, and in the big hotels. The small villages of Spain are emptying themselves of men, who all go to the coast to become rich."

Except for those who go to Germany to become rich, thought Rosales. I have been in my country three days, now, and I have seen two Spaniards—a bartender and a shepherd. Perhaps this toothy man is right.

The American swerved to pass a tractor, waved to its driver (who raised his arm in response, palm inward, fingers extended—casual contempt), and went on: "May I ask then how you know Aragón?"

"I was here during the war," said Rosales in a tone

that another Spaniard would have recognized as final—
an end to conversation.

"Ah, you were in the army," said the American. "On
which side, may I ask?"

"The losing side," Rosales said curtly. "The Republic.
The Left. The *Rojos*. Whatever name you like."

The American seemed awed. "May I shake your
hand?" he asked. "In my country, any true liberal
honors the men who fought for the Republic."

Rosales let his hand be shaken. *What's to honor?* He
looked from the *yanqui* to himself. *What does this ami-
able fool know? This man lives and eats well: He wears
good clothes, goes to doctors when he's sick, keeps a
little healthy fat on his body. He's clean: My God, I
have never seen such cleanness. And look at me, the
honored one. I have stolen the shoes I wear, and the wine
I drink. Last night I slept in a cave and tried to eat a half-
cooked rabbit. Just now I was frightened by three old
women. I stink like a pair of goats. I have nothing except
a home in the south to go to—if I still have that. For this
I am to be honored?*

On their left the Ebro appeared, swollen now and
flowing swiftly, full of the winter water that poured
into it at its source, far to the northwest, in a lush and
green province Rosales had never seen. He wished that
this friendly man would leave him alone. He pulled his
beret down over his forehead until it almost covered his
eyes, settled himself farther into his seat, and pretended
to go to sleep. But the American wanted to talk.

"Things have not been easy for you who fought for
the Republic, have they?" Rosales grunted, briefly rotat-

ing his open left hand, palm outward, to indicate indifference. The American did not notice, or did not recognize, the gesture, and continued his questioning.

"We are going through some very historic country, now," he said, as they passed a weathered blue sign saying: A CASPE, 10 KM. "From here to the coast was where the great Battle of the Ebro took place. Were you by any chance a participant?"

"Yes." *My God, yes: For six months I was here, burning in summer and shivering in the autumn snows. This was a good battle, one of their best, and they had called it a great victory—but it had lost them the war, in the end. What was always wrong with us?*

"Look," said the American. "We'll be in Gandesa soon; shall we eat lunch there, and talk a little about your experiences? I have never spoken with a participant."

*I am invited to perform for my meal. Very well: One must eat, and one must pay however one can. Besides, it would be good to see what Gandesa looked like from inside the town. The great Army of the Ebro had almost taken Gandesa before whatever it was that made them fail had happened.* He nodded briefly to the American, then again pretended to sleep. As he had feared, a light snow was beginning to fall.

What would this polite tourist wish to hear? How he and his platoon crossed the Ebro near the town of Cherta almost every night in the early weeks of July, wading through the shallow water to the west bank, where the Nationalist armies were gathering? How they were ambushed on one of these reconnaissance missions by Moroccan troops, and he had had to watch from behind an ilex tree as one of his men was beheaded by a laughing Berber tribesman with a *gourmia*, a short, curved saber? Would this sort of talk earn him his meal in Gandesa?

But when the Seat pulled up before a clean, new restaurant on the road skirting the southern edge of the town, Rosales was in no mood for anecdotes. As they seated themselves at a small table covered with a throwaway paper tablecloth and beckoned a waiter, Rosales resolved to tell the American only formally about the Ebro as it had been for him: a time of large hopes, boredom, frustration, immobility, and then the inevitable retreat.

The waiter—smiling and deferential to the American, haughty and almost insolent to Rosales—brought them a carafe of red wine and plates of *entremeses*, cold sausages, blades of pale asparagus, bits of salted fish speared with toothpicks. The American, accustomed no doubt to better than this, ignored his plate and looked at Rosales with respect and anticipation. As he ate his own food with slow pleasure, Rosales began to speak in a matter-of-fact way about what he had seen.

"I was part of Enrique Lister's Fifth Army," he said. "We understood it was our job to break up the Nationalist positions along the Ebro so that the regions of Valencia and Cataluña, which had been separated by our loss of terrain, could be rejoined. One night—it was moonless, I remember, and near the end of July—we all crossed the Ebro, either in boats or on pontoon bridges. I went across near Miravet, which is just to the east of here. The assault was a complete success: They knew we were coming, but they did not know we were a whole army. And we fought well. You understand, I am not bragging, but we were trained men, and had the advantage of surprise."

The American nodded, smiling encouragingly, chewing away with pleasure now on the veal steak the waiter had put before them.

"For once we had artillery to prepare our way, and there were reinforcements when we needed them. With us in the platoons were machine guns, and we killed many *moros* and *Requetés*. And for once when we advanced we did not do so on foot, but were carried forward in Russian trucks, *Sturkas* they were called. In two days we were all over the Sierra de Caballs, which you can see over there, looking down on Gandesa. Then we lost it all. In four months we were back across the Ebro—what remained of us."

"What happened, *señor*—? May I know your name?"

"Sebastián Rosales."

"What happened, Sebastián? Were you overpowered in counterattacks? Were you bombed out of those mountains? Did you run out of supplies?"

Rosales was taken aback for an instant by the presumptuousness of the American.

"All of those things, *hombre*, and more. I don't know; political things, too. The International Brigades on our flanks were pulled out of the lines. The Russians took away their support. I don't know. One day we were winning; then the next day we were sitting; and then many Nationalist planes came over, and there was an artillery barrage such as we had never seen, and finally we looked up to see the whole Nationalist army climbing up the hills after us. 'Resist, resist, resist,' our officers kept telling us. But soon we had nothing with which to resist." Rosales raised both hands, palms upward. "They ran over us, *hombre*, that's all. I was a sergeant, not a general. No one explained large matters to me. And that's all."

The American seemed a little disappointed. *What does he want from me? Should I have told him how it was so hot our men fought each other over canteens of bad water? Or about the lieutenants and captains who were shot by their men for ordering retreats without authorization from above? What about the squads of* Guardias Civiles *we saw below us, shooting those of us they had taken prisoner? Or how the German planes strafed us as we waded back across the Ebro, until we could walk across the goddamned river on the corpses of our own men? Would he like to know that, not far from where he is sitting and enjoying his meal, the Ebro ran red for days with our blood?*

But to the American, Rosales said only, "I am sorry, *señor*, but I understand little of how things happened. And anyway, I was wounded soon after, in November." He pulled the left sleeve of his jacket up to his elbow, and held out his arm for the American to see the long and still livid indentation that the Italian bomb had caused. He did not wish to shock or offend his host: He simply wanted a way to say clearly that so far as he was concerned, his account was finished.

The American ordered them *flan*, coffee, and a glass of *coñac*. When the meal was over, he paid the bill and tipped the waiter (fifty pesetas! Rosales marveled, closing his eyes in disbelief), and they returned to the auto. A light coating of snow lay over it. He could barely

72

make out the Sierra de Caballs now, and their dim outline in the late afternoon gloom made Rosales feel depressed and old.

But the American had recovered his good spirits, and was eager to continue practicing his Spanish and to increase his knowledge of the war. "Those International Brigades you mentioned. Did you know any of the *norteamericanos* in the Lincoln Battalion?"

Rosales shook his head. "There were some at the Ebro, I'm sure. All the *extranjeros* were there—until they were taken out and sent home. But there were so many different sorts in the Fifteenth Brigade that no one could say who was what. I saw some black men, once, at Albacete. Would they have been your countrymen? Or are all *norteamericanos* like you, *rubio*, blond?"

"Oh, we're all kinds," the American laughed. "But there *were* blacks here from my country, and workers of all kinds, and intellectuals, too. I like to think that *I* would have been here also, if I had been old enough."

"Why?"

"This was an important war, Sebastián. To many of us, it seems now to have been the last *pure* war, where right was fighting against wrong."

Rosales thought for a moment. He was not so sure of this purity business. For him it had been *them* against *us*. The longer the war had lasted, the less he saw signs of right against wrong. There had only been the killing, the hunger and thirst, the confusion, the constant retreat. "I was never a political man, *señor*, though there were many among us who were. I joined the Republican militia when the war came only because that's what all the men of my village did. In the next village they had diff-

73

erent politics, and the men joined the Nationalist army, or the Falange. You must understand: For us Spaniards, it was a private war. You *extranjeros* supplied the ideology. Or so it seemed to *campesinos* like me, anyhow. Perhaps if we had been left alone, to fight it out as Spaniards, then the end might have been different." It wouldn't have been any less bloody, though, he thought: Once we get started, we Spaniards kill one another with great dedication.

They were approaching the Ebro delta now, as the city of Tortosa appeared in the distance. An idea came to Rosales.

"*Señor*, you are clearly a serious student of this war. Would it interest you to see the battlefield where I was given the wound on my arm? It is at Amposta, only a few kilometers south of here, on the coast road."

The American smiled. "That would be an act of real friendship, Sebastián. I am honored that you would serve as my guide." He swung the car onto the road that continued south of Tortosa, slowing now as the heavy coastal traffic began to clog the highway.

Rosales was amazed at the volume of traffic. As far as he could see in either direction, there were trucks and automobiles, all traveling at great speed, in spite of the snow that was still lightly falling. The noise was tremendous, and the reek of diesel fumes was enough to make him feel a little nauseated. "What in the name of God is all this?" he asked the American. "All of Spain is on this road."

The American grinned at Rosales. "This is the *urbanización* I was telling you about, *amigo*. The whole Spanish shoreline, from the Costa Brava around to Gibraltar, is one huge building boom. Here's where all the big money is. All of Europe is down here—Germans, Swedes, Dutch—throwing up whole new towns for the tourists. You can go for days without hearing Spanish spoken, up and down the coast. This is what you would call your capitalist exploitation with a vengeance. Look at that, over toward the shore." He pointed to a group of unfinished buildings of a height that Rosales would not have believed possible. On their tops were large cranes, moving around even in this snow, lifting wooden beams and concrete up to the construction workers who climbed about on steel girders. Around the foundations of the buildings, many hectares of sandy soil had been bulldozed away. Streets were being laid. Rosales could see teams of laborers pounding away with sledgehammers at piles of coarse gravel to make roadbeds. Trucks of every sort moved about, carrying construction material to the building sites.

Rosales was filled with wonder. "What is this all for, this 'boom' you speak of? Who lives in these places? What do they *do* here? Spain must be becoming very rich."

"With all respect, Sebastián, you are a little naïve. Where have you been all this time? Spain is the great European resort, now. *Turismo* is its biggest industry. All of Europe comes here for the cheap vacations in the sun. There's only one hitch to all of this *urbanización:* It's being done with foreign money, and the people who are growing rich off your country are not Spaniards—except for certain government ministers and industrialists—but large European consortiums, who buy the land, put up these great hotels, which may look very grand to you, Sebastián, but which are almost always shoddily made, and then sit back to pick up the tourists' money. Your government tells you that all of Spain will profit from this business, Sebastián. They say they are creating jobs for all Spaniards here, jobs that will pay them much more than they could have made in their *pueblos*. And there *are* jobs; but they will end, just as *el turismo* will end; and all the poor people who came here to work as laborers and waiters and waitresses will find one day that they are as bad off as if they had stayed at home. You are looking at false prosperity, Sebastián: Spain is being ruined by all this."

Rosales listened with some indifference to the American, who was no longer smiling. Privately, he doubted that whatever happened here on the coast could have any effect on Poqueira or the other *pueblos* of the Alpujarras. And that was *his* Spain, not this madness on the coast. Let the *extranjeros* come, as long as they stayed away from what mattered to him. He remembered this coast as he had last seen it: scrubby delta country, bad roads, the shoreline dotted with an occasional ragged fishing village, where men went out before dawn each day to net fish that they would sell for next to nothing to those who gathered on the beach at dusk. There are worse things than what the American was describing, he thought: poverty, for one. Again, though, he excepted his own terrain from this observation: There might not be wealth in the Alpujarras, but the land was rich enough to support all who chose to work. Corruption, whatever that was, would not reach the Alpujarras, in spite of the Spanish government and the crazy foreigners who built such palaces as these. In any case, this complex conversation was beginning to bore him a little. "I was going to show you Amposta, *señor*."

"This *is* Amposta, Sebastián. Perhaps your old battlefield is now occupied by a *supermercado* and a row of cafés made to resemble English pubs." The American's voice was ironic. "But you tell me where to stop, and we'll see what we can find."

In truth, there was nothing that looked familiar to Rosales. But he looked to the west, in the direction of the range of hills called the Montes Blancos; and in a few minutes he said to the American, "If you find a small road to the right, heading toward those hills, then let us take it, *señor*. Where I was wounded is not so beautiful a place that rich *extranjeros* would wish to spend their vacations there."

Within minutes they had turned inland, on a dirt road, and Rosales began to recognize certain landmarks: a dry stream bed, a small forest of stunted ilex trees, a series of rolling sandy foothills. He knew this land, all right.

"Stop here," he said suddenly to the American. They were far enough away from the coast road now for the noise of the traffic almost to have disappeared. There was only a faint breeze, blowing light flakes of snow about them. It was not nearly as cold as it had been on that day thirty-five years earlier, when the remnants of his battalion had been dug in here in the last days of the Battle of the Ebro, knowing that they had lost everything, and wondering how their leaders were going to get them away to the north, to those parts of Cataluña that were still in Republican hands.

"My platoon was posted on that hill, *señor*. Shall we walk up there, or shall I simply describe things for you?" The American was shivering, pulling the collar of his sheepskin jacket up around his ears, but he seemed to have lost none of his curiosity.

"No, show me, Sebastián. Take me to your exact position, if you can." Rosales nodded, and moved off rapidly uphill.

"Here was the battalion headquarters tent, and just over there was an emergency hospital. We must have had five hundred wounded with us, waiting for ambulances to take them away. Our troops were spread around in a large circle on the crests of these hills, waiting for the Nationalist advance. A battery of howitzers was positioned here"—he indicated a flat space at the base of one of the hills—"but since we had no ammunition for the guns, their presence did little for our morale. Chiefly, we were cold and hungry. We were allowed to make fires for warmth, but as you can see, *señor*, there is little around here that would burn." The American nodded, and appeared concerned mainly to keep up with Rosales, who was moving forward at a pace that was more like a lope than a walk.

Finally he stopped. "Here were our trenches, *señor*: You can still see where they were." A series of shallow indentations did in fact crisscross the hillside, in places still deep enough to offer shelter to a man.

"I was just here," Rosales said calmly, "just waking at dawn. I remember being happy to see that the weather was clearing, and that we would have sun that day. I sent some men down to the main encampment for bread and coffee, and was lying here on my poncho, watching my men begin to stir themselves. In war, even in defeat, there are sometimes days when one can rest and feel almost happy."

"Like camping out, I suppose," said the American. "I know the feeling: I do a lot of hiking in my country."

"Yes," said Rosales, not knowing what "hiking" was. "And then we heard the sound of many planes heading toward us from the northwest. When they came close enough, flying very low straight toward our positions, we saw they were Italian bombers, the ones with three motors. Someone later told me there had been over a hundred of them. I suppose he was right. Anyway, as each wave of bombers reached our position it let loose its bombs on us. There was nothing we could do but dig deeper into our trenches and hold our hands over our ears. You cannot imagine such noise, *señor:* It was noise past noise, the kind of thing a body cannot support. It was as if there was left of me only a knot, something hard *here*"—and Rosales prodded at the center of his chest—"and no wind, nothing else. One tried to curl up around that knot, and hold oneself together somehow. How long it lasted I do not know: I only lay there. I could not breathe or move or think. *Me habían sacado el alma:* They had taken my soul away from me."

The American looked at Rosales, worried. Very lightly, he touched the old man on the shoulder. Rosales looked at him, not seeing him. He continued: "When it was over, I lay for some time as I was, unable to move. Then I remember being lifted up, pulled by the arms. I had been buried by the bombardment, it seems. I looked around me, but I could see almost nothing, only a blur. Nor could I hear. They put me on a litter, and carried me from the hill. The battalion was gone, destroyed. I was put beside other wounded. I remember looking across at a man who lay near me. He had almost no face left, but he was conscious. I knew this because he was screaming. But you know, *señor*, the funny thing was that I could not hear him scream. But I could *see* him screaming."

Rosales shrugged. "And that was my wounding, *señor*. I do not know when it was that I learned my arm had been hit by shrapnel. It was some time later, and I gave it little importance. As things went, it was nothing. I was put in an ambulance and driven north. And that is all the story of my wounding. It is not a very dramatic or interesting story, I am afraid."

"Jesus Christ," said the American. "Jesus Christ. And that happened *here*, right in this place? A whole battalion blown to pieces, right here. How many of you were left, Sebastián?"

But Rosales was not listening. Something had caught his eye, something in one of the ruined trenches a few meters from where they stood. He walked over to the spot, bent down, and pulled the object from the sand in which it lay almost buried. In his hand was a bayonet. Its brass handle was eroded badly, and the leather grip had long since rotted away. But its steel blade, buried for three and a half decades in the sand of the hillside, was still bright and sharp. He laughed. "Here, *señor*, here is what we had to defend ourselves against the bombardment."

Rosales held the bayonet up before his face, smiling. The American looked at him, rather as the three old women outside Fuentes del Ebro had looked at him earlier that morning.

After a moment, Rosales lowered the blade, and remembered the presence of this polite *yanqui*, so gloomy now at his side. "Well, *señor*," he said. "That's the end of the show, and I'm sure you're ready to move on. If you would carry me past just a little more of this *urbanización* of yours, I'll hop out and go on my way. How far do you go, today?"

The American, who hoped to reach Valencia by nightfall, hesitated a second, then replied, "Castellón only, I'm afraid, only two hundred or so kilometers south. Will that help you any?" The prospect of carrying this now-formidable Spaniard any further than necessary was not appealing.

"Castellón would be very good. Perhaps I can find a place to spend the night there, and then be off for the south early tomorrow morning."

"Do you intend to keep that bayonet as a souvenir of this battle?"

Rosales did indeed intend to keep it, but he was not thinking of it as a souvenir. There had been a saying in the Alpjuarras: *El hombre que lleva un cuchillo, se muere por cuchillo:* The man who carries a knife will die by the knife; but he thought of himself more than ever as a man traveling through the country of his enemies, and this bayonet gave him a certain confidence. A man with such a weapon was not a helpless man.

"I shall keep it, *señor*, but only as a protection against possible attack," he explained. "I shall not always be on this very civilized road of yours, and the land between here and my home may present dangers in which a man might need such a blade." As he spoke, Rosales was worrying about how he should carry the bayonet. It would not do simply to stick it in his belt, where all could see it, and it would be useless to him if tucked away in his blanket roll where he could not reach it quickly. "Have you a piece of string, *señor*? I might secure it to my waist that way, and let it hang within my trousers."

The American opened the Seat's glove compartment, and came up with a short length of thin wire. "Might this help? It's not very long, but perhaps you could twist it about your neck, and let the bayonet hang from it down your chest, inside your shirt."

"Perfect," grinned Rosales. "You should have been one of us in the war. You would have made a formidable *guerillero*."

Rosales did as the American suggested. He ran the wire through the ring with which the bayonet was to have been attached to the barrel of its rifle, then hung it around his neck. As he entered the car, he could feel the point of the blade resting against his belly. He felt secure.

The drive to Castellón passed quickly, with the American largely silent. Rosales, beside him, noticed with growing concern that tourists and construction trucks were not the only traffic on the congested highway. At least once every ten kilometers they passed, or were passed by, police of one kind or another. There were the ubiquitous pairs of *Guardias Civiles*, some on motorcycles, wearing crash helmets and large white gauntlets; and some in gray Land Rovers such as he had seen on the road from the Pyrenees. Others, of a type Rosales had not seen before, wore gray uniforms and rode in staff cars or personnel carriers. When he asked the American about this new variety, his companion grimaced, and answered, "Those are *los grises*, Sebastián, the gray ones. They're the political police, the ones who exist to put down riots and demonstrations. Spain can thank them for its great social order. They use truncheons, mainly, I hear, long lead-weighted ones; and they have been cracking the skulls of students and dissidents for some years, now. Watch out for them: They're worse than the *Guardia*."

Sebastián did not like this plenitude of police. How could he dare stand by the side of this coast road, signaling for rides, if every tenth vehicle that passed him would be filled with those who would like nothing better than to capture him? "Why are there so many, in an area of such prosperity?" he asked.

"I don't know," the American answered. "Perhaps your government wishes to demonstrate to the tourist population that it is safe from . . ."

"From dangerous people like me, right?" Once more Rosales smiled, and the American looked disturbed, as he had done when he had watched this man fondling his bayonet back at Amposta.

At the outskirts of Castellón de la Plana, the American stopped the Seat by the side of the road. "Here is as good a place as any for you, Sebastián," he said. "From here you can continue south along the coast, or turn inland toward the mountains."

"I give you a thousand thanks, *señor:* You have been kind." Rosales held out his right hand to the American, who took it firmly in his.

"Look here, Sebastián, I would not wish to offend you. But you clearly are traveling very light. Do you have any money at all?"

Rosales held up his hand in negation. "No, no, *señor*, I have what I need to reach home. Only—"

"Only what?"

"If you have a cigarette or two, I would be grateful."

"Good Lord, man, of course. Wait a minute."

As Rosales stood by the side of the Seat, the American reached in his pockets and came up with a small packet, which he passed out to the old man. Rosales took it, touched his beret in thanks, and gave a short wave as the American smiled one more time, then put the Seat in gear, and moved off into the traffic.

When he was alone on the highway, Rosales looked at the small bundle in his hand. There was a full pack of Ducados, expensive black-tobacco cigarettes, a box of matches, and—folded around the cigarettes—a green one-thousand-peseta note. Truly I am lucky, he said to himself. A good ride with a rich *yanqui*, and a generous reward for my pleasant company.

He lit up one of the Ducados—his first cigarette since leaving Cambó—and inhaled deeply, full of a sense of well-being. When he had finished smoking, he reached inside his jacket to touch the blade of his bayonet for reassurance, then began leisurely to saunter toward the city. He was far enough south now, and close enough to the sea, for the weather to seem warmer, even at dusk. He was thinking that tonight he might buy himself a bed and a meal at some small *posada*, and perhaps even rent himself a half hour in a bathtub. He wondered whether his bayonet might be sharp enough to shave with. Perhaps.

Then, as he rounded a bend in the highway, all his sense of ease vanished, and the old visceral fear struck him. Not more than two hundred meters ahead of him were a pair of motorcycles, one parked on each side of the highway. Standing together on one gravel shoulder were two *Guardias*, smoking and chatting idly. They had seen him, and were perhaps asking one another whether it would be worth the trouble to beckon him to them. He had not been so frightened since the war.

*Mother of God, what am I to do?* Rosales couldn't run away: They'd be on him in an instant. And he couldn't just walk by them and wish them a good evening. Behind him he heard a truck approaching, slowing as it neared the *Guardias*. One of them held out his gauntleted hand, and the truck slowed and stopped, obscuring Rosales from their view. As they talked to the driver of the truck (it was an old one, Rosales's mind registered, and full of cattle), their booted feet resting on the running boards, Rosales moved fast.

He ran to the truck, vaulted over the wooden slats of its rear gate, and landed among the cows. He crawled forward, under cow bellies and over cow turds, and buried himself in a thin bed of straw at the forward wall of the compartment. Scarcely breathing, he lay there, praying that the *Guardias* would not want to dirty their elegant uniforms by an inspection of the truck's contents.

In a moment the truck lurched forward, and Rosales took a deep breath. He did not dare to peek through the slats of the compartment to see whether the *Guardias* were preparing to follow them, and so remained in his bed of straw, looking up at the faces of the black cows that gazed down at him without curiosity. Well, Rosales thought, this is no Seat, but it's not so bad. He even felt rather at home in his straw, and the powerful barnyard smell brought him pleasant recollections of his childhood in Poqueira. At least they're not goats, he thought;

85

*that* odor would be almost insupportable in such close quarters.

The lurching about of the old truck made him drowsy, even in the cold, and it did not immediately occur to him to wonder where he was headed. He dimly heard the sounds of a city, and assumed they were passing through Castellón. *Perhaps by morning we'll be in the true south, beyond Valencia.*

Some time later he awoke. It was dark, probably quite late at night. He wanted to smoke, thought better of it, and climbed slowly out of his straw. There were no sounds of traffic around them, and the truck seemed to be laboring generally uphill, along a winding road. They were off the coast road, he realized, and heading inland. *Not so bad; maybe we're heading down through La Mancha.* If so, by daylight they could be in the Sierra Morena, at the very edge of Andalucía. The cows were standing silently around him, occasionally pressing him against the slats where he leaned. He looked ahead, around the cab of the truck. The road on which they were traveling was indeed no great thoroughfare; it was of gravel, narrow and rutted. Here and there along the sides of the road were patches of old snow. And now that he was out of his straw hiding place, Rosales felt cold, colder than he had been since the Pyrenees.

Presently the truck came to a crossroads, and slowed to a stop. Rosales craned his head forward to read a sign that stood by the road they were taking. *Jesú.* It said: A TERUEL 38 KM. All night long, as he had shivered peacefully with his cows, this whore's-breath of a *camión* had been carrying him to the northwest, straight back toward the godforsaken terrain of Aragón. *What*

86

*kind of God is it who would take him to Teruel, a place that not even Satan himself would willingly pass through?* "Teruel," he said aloud, slumping back into his straw. "Can there still be such a place, after what we did to it?" He saw the wet muzzle of a cow just in front of his face. Viciously he lashed out his right hand and struck at it. The hurt and astounded animal leapt back and gave a short bellow, then stood solidly, its four legs planted wide apart, and gazed down at the furious human who lay there, swearing oaths at the Almighty.

---

Teruel had never been a place of beauty, not even before the war. Another gray and cheerless Aragonese city, its only real claim to distinction was that it regularly recorded the coldest winter temperatures on the Iberian peninsula. It sits on a high plateau surrounded by bleak and rocky ridges, the most precipitous of which is on the west side of the city. It is called *La Muela*, the Tooth, of Teruel. After the defeat at Belchite, the Republican army resolved to regroup to the south and attack Teruel; and on December 15, 1937, the assault began. Since Enrique Lister's Eleventh Division was still considered the most disciplined and best-led element of the army, it was assigned the most difficult sector of attack: *La Muela*. In spite of falling snow, and a temperature that was rapidly dropping toward zero, by evening Lister's troops had reached the top of *La Muela*, and were looking down on the rooftops of Teruel. The encirclement was completed by the following dawn, and the Republicans brought up their meager artillery to begin the systematic destruction of the city below them.

But Teruel's four thousand defenders, half of whom were civilians, refused to surrender. Lister and the other commanders sent companies of their men on daily forays into the city. This fighting was the most vicious of the war. After it was all over, the victorious Nationalist general told a correspondent: "Of course it was terrible, *hombre*. There were brave Spaniards fighting on both sides."

Sergeant Sebastián Rosales, El Lobo, promoted after Belchite, was quick to learn what the staff officers referred to as the tactics of urban warfare. The Wolf now was in the streets of Teruel. Whenever his platoon came to a house from which enemy sniping was coming, El Lobo ordered his men to surround that house. Then, under covering rifle and machine-gun fire, he and a couple of his *veteranos* rushed to the doors and windows of the house and lobbed in hand grenades. As soon as the shrapnel from these grenades ceased tearing through the rooms of the house, El Lobo kicked open the door and, followed by his men, rushed in to shoot anyone still alive within the building. Many civilians died. El Lobo's orders were to destroy the resistance of Teruel. Sebastián Rosales, called El Lobo, eighteen years of age, was a remarkable exemplar of the kind of professional soldier Lister and the other leaders were hoping to create out of the rag-tag militia that the Republican army had been in the first months of the war. El Lobo and his men were becoming fighting machines for Lister.

And they succeeded. The Nationalist army, headed as usual by the German Condor Legion, rushed to the defense of Teruel, sweeping down from the northwest.

They pushed the Republican forces back steadily, but the ring around Teruel did not break. The weather continued to worsen, but this worked as much to the disadvantage of the Nationalists as to the Republicans who were closing in ever closer on the city. On New Year's Eve came the worst storm of the year: Over a meter of snow fell, the thermometers dropped to eighteen degrees below zero, the roads to Teruel froze over, and nothing—neither men nor material—could move.

Throughout the four-day blizzard, El Lobo and his men hung on to the tip of *La Muela*. Four months earlier, at Belchite, he had watched his men collapse from heat and thirst; now he watched as they began to freeze. There was no way to light fires for warmth or for cooking; there were no dry clothes to be exchanged for their soaked and icy uniforms; and there was no way to evacuate to the south men who were suffering from frostbite. Between Teruel and Valencia, 168 kilometers to the southeast, six hundred vehicles—including the ambulances and trucks that might have evacuated the wounded and freezing—were snowbound, and often abandoned where they stood by their crews.

Here it was that El Lobo learned to become a surgeon. One morning, as he made his way along the line of trenches occupied by his platoon, he came upon a young boy from Málaga, one of those southerners who, like El Lobo, had been in the war from its first days. The boy was huddled in his trench, conscious but in great pain.

"What's wrong, *hombrecito?*" asked El Lobo. "Are you wounded?"

The boy shook his head, not looking up. El Lobo was angry. "What will you do when the *fascistas* reach your position? Where is your rifle?" The boy continued to shake his head. El Lobo groped around in the snow that reached to the boy's knees, and found his Mauser. Its action was, of course, frozen solid.

"Get up. Get up, *maricón*. Stand there and hold your rifle next to your skin until you can work the bolt again. *¿Eres hombre o bebé?* When the boy did not move, El Lobo grabbed him around his chest and pulled him to his feet. The boy screamed and collapsed, his woolen Balaclava hood twisted sideways about his head, so that his face was obscured. El Lobo called to the soldiers in the next trench back: "Get us some sort of *médico* up here. I have a man who needs one."

Within minutes one of the older men, an ex-shepherd from the mountains of León, had crawled forward through the snow and dropped into the trench with El Lobo and the unconscious boy. Without speaking, he looked at his sergeant, then down at the boy. After a second he nodded to himself, then said to El Lobo, "Look, my sergeant, there is no *médico* here. So I am going to give you a lesson in the practice of surgery. And if this weather lasts, and the Nationalists don't get us first, you will soon become an expert in the kind of work I am going to show you."

As El Lobo watched, the shepherd squatted beside the boy and began to remove his boots and leggings—a task of some difficulty, since ice had encased the boy's lower limbs almost to the knees, and since the hands of the shepherd were themselves blue and stiff with cold. Once the boy's legs were bare, and his trousers pulled up to his knees, the shepherd looked up at El Lobo and said, matter-of-factly, "This is frostbite, my young sergeant. Do you see the whiteness of the feet, and the bright redness of the legs above the whiteness?" El Lobo nodded.

"We must amputate these legs above the redness. If we do not, this child will surely die of gangrene. Even if we do amputate, he will probably die of shock from the amputation. If he does not die, then he must be evacuated immediately. What do you say, Lobito?"

El Lobo shrugged. "Who is to evacuate him, *pastor?* Do you see any ambulances among us?" He pulled at his long nose, staring abstractedly at the boy's ruined legs. "All right, here is my decision. We amputate. If he does not die immediately, we pass him back through the trenches until he reaches one of the emergency aid stations below us—if there *are* such stations."

"*A sus órdenes, señor médico,*" said the shepherd. "Take out your bayonet, clean it as best you can in the snow, and do as I do." He stood quickly, and called back to the trench from which he had come: "Tomás! Reach into my pack and bring me my knife with the sawblade, and my sewing kit."

A minute later a young private dropped into their trench, carrying in his gloved hand the items the shepherd had requested. He stared at the legs of the unconscious soldier, crossed himself as he realized what was about to occur, then turned and crawled quickly back to his position. For a division of Communists and atheists, Rosales thought to himself, the lessons of the priests stay with us always. He could not remember, though, when he had last crossed himself.

"Here is how we do it, Lobito," resumed the shepherd. "It is really quite easy." He lifted the boy's right leg, raised his knife, and made a rapid incision around the leg, just above the knee. "First one does this, then one makes three vertical cuts of the skin, up the thigh." As he did so, the boy's leg began to twitch, and his hands reached reflexively down to stop what was being done to him. "Hold him, Lobito: It's easier if he can be kept still."

El Lobo crouched half atop the boy's midsection, pinioning his arms above his head. "How did you learn this sort of thing, *pastor?*" he asked. "Are all the shepherds of León so educated?"

The shepherd, now occupied with peeling the healthy skin back above the boy's knee, and cutting away the flesh to expose the femur, laughed harshly. "I have done this more than once, Lobito, when autumn snows have caught us in the mountains before we could get our flocks to the lowlands for winter grazing. And why is this so foreign to you? Don't you come from the Sierra Nevada, the highest mountains in Spain? Is no one ever frozen there?"

"Above my village are peaks so high the snow never leaves them," answered El Lobo. "But my people have sense enough not to lie about in the snow for days."

"Of course, the wisdom of the Andalúz is famous throughout Spain. I was not thinking clearly, my sergeant." The shepherd had now cleared the flesh from the thigh bone. He picked up his sawbladed knife, and began to move it back and forth across the bone, rapidly and with great pressure. "This is the hardest part," he observed. "It is like sawing through wet tree limbs. However"—and he held up the leg, severed above the knee—"it can be done. The rest is easy: work for a seamstress." He quickly tied off the artery, folded down around the stump of the leg, from which little blood was flowing, the flaps of skin he had pared back earlier. "Kindly hand me the needle and thread Tomás brought me, and I shall make a neat conclusion to our operation."

El Lobo turned to reach for the needle. As he did so, he pulled the young soldier's woolen helmet around so as to see his face. His eyes were open, but his face had about it that stillness, that absolute stillness, which one finds only in the dead. "Forget it, *pastor*, your sheep is finished," he said.

The shepherd rose from the boy's side and took a deep breath. "Too bad, Lobito," he said. "You never got your turn. But at least you have had the lesson, and will know what to do next time. And if we stay on this hill another night, there will be many next times." He wiped the blade of his knife on the clean snow at the top of the trench, and prepared to return to his position. "Kick snow over this one," he said, pointing down at the dead boy, "and wait for the others, *señor médico*."

After the shepherd had left, El Lobo leaned against the forward wall of the trench, trying vainly to see any signs of the army that had to be below them, waiting for the snow and sleet to cease, so that they might begin their assault against *La Muela*. Let them come soon, he thought; I would rather be what they call me, a killer, than a surgeon. This war was truly amazing. If one lived long enough, one could learn a great deal about the things men can do to one another. Four months ago I was instructed in how to be an executioner. Now I am a physician. But if there were a God, that he should require me only to be a soldier. "All right, *Dios mío*," he said aloud, smiling up into the storm. "If I cross myself, will you lift the weather and resume the attack?" He crossed himself.

But the weather did not lift, not for another two weeks. No one knows exactly how many Spaniards, Republicans and Nationalists alike, froze to death in the hills around Teruel. On January 8, 1938, the city finally fell to the Republicans, and the civilian population of the city, what was left of it, was evacuated. Then the snows began to lift, and the Nationalists launched their counterattack. By the end of the month the Republicans were driven from *La Muela* down into the city, where they held out as stubbornly as their enemy had done before them. On February 7, an attack by Nationalist cavalry, one of the few such of the war, pierced the Republican perimeter, causing Lister and his fellow generals to pull to the southern outskirts of the city. And, by February 20, Teruel was once again in Nationalist hands. It was a great victory for Franco, who bestowed numerous citations for bravery upon the city itself. The remains of the Republican army were able to escape before the road to Valencia was cut off, but more than twenty-one thousand prisoners were taken, along with a vast amount of matériel—weapons, munitions, and ambulances. When the winter snows melted, ten thousand Republican corpses were discovered in and around the city. *La Muela* itself contained more than two thousand, many of whom had died not from combat, but from cold.

El Lobo had never tried to practice his surgical knowledge. It was easier to let his men die where they were, and let the snow bury them. As he fled south toward Valencia with Lister's army, he began to think of his primary vocation not as that of soldier but as that of survivor. *Let all these die*, he thought, looking around him at the column of troops straggling down the swampy road: *I will last; I will live to go home.*

# Chapter 3

So now, while the truck was still halted at the crossroads, Rosales made his decision. His mind, still full of the horrors of Teruel, would not let him even think of returning there. He crawled slowly back under the placid cows and slipped soundlessly off the tailgate. A thicket of *espino*, hawthorn, grew near the road behind the truck: a place to hide until the truck had gone on. Shielding his face from the brambles, Rosales crouched low, and waited. The first faint light of day was coming now from the Levante, behind him. Shivering, and letting his jaw hang slack to keep his teeth from chattering, he thought briefly and with some regret of how much more pleasant it would have been to continue southward along the crowded coast road, through Valencia and Alicante down to the south coast, his coast.

* * *

He had the fondest memories of his one brief stay in Valencia. To him it had seemed the liveliest, most beautiful city imaginable. Old Inés had laughed at his praise of Valencia. She had been born in Sevilla, and for her the only Spanish cities with any *gracia* at all were those of Andalucía: Sevilla of course, and Córdoba, Granada, and Málaga. Rosales had found this a reasonable judgment, although of these he had seen only Granada—once, as a boy—and Málaga—and that only after it had been reduced to rubble in early 1937. He had arrived in Valencia in the spring of 1937, a wounded veteran and an authentic war hero. The wound itself, from a bullet that had struck his thigh and temporarily paralyzed his leg, was inconsequential enough by the time his evacuation train had reached Valencia for him to be declared an ambulatory patient. He was free to spend his days and evenings away from the former convent that had been made into a hospital after the retreat from Málaga. So, with his new bronze medal of the Spanish Republic pinned to the chest of his *mono,* his blue overalls, his red-and-black neckerchief tied around his neck, and his anarchist's cap cocked low on his forehead, he had gone into Valencia.

Surrounding the city were large *huertas,* irrigated fields, brimming over with oranges, lemons, and grapefruit, all of a lushness he had never seen in the Alpujarras. The scent of orange blossoms filled the streets of the city. Flower stalls were set up everywhere, and the *valencianos* were of a gaiety and optimism that he found a little hard to reconcile with the scenes of war he carried in his head. As a soldier, a wounded hero, he had free use of movies and streetcars, both great novelties to him. Whenever he went into a café, the most beautiful women he had ever seen—great plump Levantine girls, all breasts and behinds—would gather around his table, laughing and flirting. On his first night away from the convent he had lost both his bronze medal and his virginity to a lovely and patriotic *valenciana* with blond hair and enormous brown eyes. All he remembered now of this event was that she had taken him to the beach at Nazaret, and that he had been ashamed to admit to her that he could not swim. Probably he had told her that the wound in his leg would not allow him to swim, and that they had better rest on the beach lest he become tired. Sebastián Rosales, fifty-four years old and crouching like a timid animal in a hawthorn thicket some kilometers south of Teruel, laughed silently at himself at seventeen, the celebrated El Lobo, playing at being a man on the beaches of Valencia. And wished that he were there this morning, out of these unspeakable mountains. He would not require a woman, now: What he wanted most at this moment was warmth, food, sleep, and perhaps even a bath.

The two men who had been in the cab of the truck climbed down to the road, leaving the motor running. Ten meters from where Rosales hid, they urinated at the edge of the road, smoked, and walked up and down for some minutes, stamping their feet to keep their circulation going in the thin, frigid air of dawn. Some minutes later they stepped back into the truck, slammed their doors shut, and resumed their descent into Teruel. When he could no longer hear the sound of the motor,

Rosales emerged from the brambles, his face and hands bleeding slightly from the thorns that had scratched him. He walked over to the shoulder of the road that branched off southward from the one the truck had taken, sat down, and thought of what lay before him.

Somewhere to the south, presumably along this road, was Utiel, on the Madrid–Valencia highway. Beyond that, another day's walk away, was the city of Albacete, on the edge of the *meseta*, the tableland, called La Mancha. From there it would not be more than a couple of hundred kilometers to the Sierra Morena and Andalucía. *Luck and shrewdness. I can do it, with these things plus a little discipline. Take inventory. Recite to yourself what you have, and think of what else you will require.*

He touched his bayonet, its blade warm next to his chest. He hefted the *bota* he had taken from the shepherd's cave: It was perhaps half full, sufficient to give him enough warmth and strength to reach Utiel, at least. He lit a cigarette, and then as he did so counted the matches that remained in the little box the *yanqui* had given him. A penknife. A note for a thousand pesetas. A pair of shoes that did not fit well, but that should see him home to Poqueira. As for himself and his clothes, not much to admire. No chance for a bath. Normally this would not have bothered him greatly. Washing was something one did before the Sunday *paseo*. Or when ill. Even so, there were limits to the amount of dirt that a man of dignity should accumulate. Something would have to be done before long about himself and the clothes he wore.

"*Un páramo verdadero,*" he murmured sourly to himself, looking about him in the early daylight: "A real wasteland." There was no way he could live off *this* land, as he could in the south. Here there were only steep hillsides of clay sandstone, interrupted occasionally by eroded pillars of *caliza*, limestone. The road south lay along the high ground; on either side the earth fell away sharply into deep *cuencas*, dry riverbeds. On the leeward sides of the hills were occasional small groves of scarlet and pin oak, leafless and stunted. Here and there, where the barren soil permitted, were clumps of *chaparral*, oak thickets grown out close to the ground, of no use to man. Any tree that reached a height of more than five meters was bent grotesquely eastward, forced over by the wind that blew almost ceaselessly from the Serranía de Cuenca, barely visible now on the western horizon. This is no place for the living, Rosales thought, rising to his feet and gathering his belongings about him; the only thing to do with such a place is to get out of it, as quickly as possible. He lifted the shepherd's *bota* above his head, squeezed the goatskin bag, and held his mouth open to receive the thin stream of wine that spurted out. He lowered the *bota*, screwed the top on to its neck, wiped his mouth, and announced aloud: "*Bueno, he desayunado; ahora me marcho:* Okay, I've had breakfast; now I get going."

To walk in mountainous terrain is a natural thing for one from the Alpujarras, where the only flat spaces are those that are made by men, for use as plazas, marketplaces, playgrounds. Sebastián Rosales did not appear to be walking rapidly, but he was—his pace was such that only one raised in mountains could have kept up with him. His pace never varied from hour to hour: He simply marched along, arms swinging slightly, shoulders a little stooped, head bent somewhat downward. He walked uphill with the same stride he used going downhill. His mind, except as it registered those things his senses discovered, was blank, empty of reflection. After a time he became aware that he was climbing another mountain range—the Sierra de Javalambre—but all this meant to him was thinner air, sharper wind, perhaps twenty kilometers more covered. His legs ached, and his right one—the wounded one—asked to be allowed to limp. This request he ignored, refusing to alter his stride. When the sun was above his head, and his belly began rumbling, he stopped, removed the blanket roll and *bota* from around his shoulders, and stretched out beside the road for a mouthful of wine and one of the American's Ducados. He allowed himself a siesta of perhaps fifteen minutes, never shutting his ears to the possible approach of a car—of which there was none. The sky at noon was clear and blue; when he opened his eyes he could see a particularly high mountain far to the northwest, its peak covered with snow. Not once did he see any sign of life: From horizon to horizon, he was alone. Except for the whistling of the ever-present wind, the only sounds he heard were those made by himself. He was far from unhappy: This silence, this sense of vastness, were among his chief reasons for returning to Spain. In fact, he realized, it was the land and the sky, much more than the people, that were drawing him back.

After his siesta he resumed his march, aware that the gravel road was now descending gradually. By midafternoon he heard the day's first signs of life: sheepbells, cattle lowing, and human voices. Almost hidden in a valley down and to his right was a tiny *pueblo* of considerable poverty. *Should I skirt it?* No: Such a place is too small and too poor to justify a police force of any kind. Indeed, it was hardly a town at all. On either side of the road were five or six houses made of clay blocks plastered over with innumerable coats of lime, with roofs of branches wound around with strands of esparto grass. No threat to him here, certainly. *I am hungry.* Rosales raised his head, straightened his shoulders, and marched on, looking from one side of the road to the other for signs of life.

He saw a pair of children, barefoot, scurrying away from him to hide behind one of the houses. The shutter of a window opened slightly, then closed again as he turned toward it. Somewhere a goat bleated. He saw a small stream of smoke rising from a hole in the roof of one house, and walked slowly over to the door, a thing of boards coated with clay. He knocked. Nothing.

"*Hola,*" he called out. "*Muy buenas tardes. ¿Hay alguien?*" Still nothing. "I am a simple traveler, wishing only to buy a little food and wine, or whatever this good town offers," he tried again. After a long moment, the door opened slightly, and a very old woman, so small and stooped she could gaze no higher than Rosales's chest, peered out.

"*Muy buenas,*" she mumbled. "The men are in the fields at this hour. We have nothing. There is a larger *pueblo* just along the road where one can buy things. *Adiós.*" She was about to shut the door when Rosales stopped her.

"Please, *señora,* I wish only a piece of bread and some wine. Or goat's milk. I heard a goat. Surely you have

102

milk. I can pay, or barter. You would not turn a stranger away?" The woman would have tried again to close the door, but she was thrust aside by someone else within. The door opened wider, and now before Rosales was a man of even greater age than the old woman. He was leaning on a handmade crutch, and Rosales noticed even as the man stood braced in the doorframe that he was scarcely in control of his body. One side of him, from his face to his feet, seemed slack and dead. Still, the man was not without something like authority. He nodded to Rosales, and said, with the half of his mouth that still functioned, "We are as you see us. The old woman is right. What little we have, we need."

"Do you need a penknife? Or some cigarettes? I have these things." Hurriedly, Rosales dug them from his jacket pockets. "And would be glad to exchange them for a little to eat and drink. I have come far today without eating, and must go farther. I place myself in your hands." He held out the knife and the cigarettes for the cripple to see.

The door closed. He heard the man's voice calling to a child, but was unable to understand what was being said. He stood before the door, still and expressionless, for some minutes. The sun was much lower in the sky, he noticed. How far had he come today? Twenty-five kilometers, perhaps.

Then around the corner of the house crept a small girl, carrying something in her apron. She stopped some distance from Rosales, never looking at him, and laid on the earth before her a slab of goat cheese, a fistful of dark bread, and a small corked bottle of wine. Then she ran behind the house again, without glancing back.

The door opened again, and the cripple stood there as

before. "Give us the knife and the cigarettes, and this is yours. It is all we have." And it probably is, too, thought Rosales; someone in this godforsaken *pueblecito* will go hungry tonight. "The knife you may have," he said, "but it would be a cruelty to take all my cigarettes from me. I'll give you five, and some matches." The cripple shrugged with the one shoulder he could move, and nodded. Rosales held out the knife and the cigarettes to him. He did not move. "I'll put them here, in the yard, and take the food. And I give you my thanks, *señor*. It is a Christian act for the poor to share with the poor." Rosales did so, then turned back to the cripple. The door was closed. There was nothing to do but gather up the food and wine, and walk on away from the town. *To live like this; to live like this.*

He ate as he walked along, not wanting to use up any more of the daylight hours than was necessary. The cheese was bad and the bread almost inedible, but Rosales ate. He tasted the wine, then replaced the cork in the little bottle. He would save it for tonight, to drink as his supper wherever he could find shelter.

He stopped just before sunset, cold again but not so cold as the night before: We're coming down now from these mountains, he thought, looking about him for a place to spend the night. Some distance away, uphill to the left, was a forest of ilex, surrounded by a row of limestone outcroppings. It looked like a good place to hide. *Who would have the energy to pursue me in so luckless a place as this?* There he prepared to pass his night, his head propped against a smooth edge of stone, his body wrapped in his wife's blanket, dozing a little and taking occasional pulls on the little wine bottle the child had laid at his feet. Not exactly the beach at Valencia, he smiled to himself, half asleep; but better than the way they live in that *pueblecito* back there.

Something woke him. Quickly and sharply, he came on guard the moment his eyes opened. And once again, as in the shepherd's cave, he knew immediately that he was not alone. But this time it was not a rabbit. A small man, dressed in beret and corduroy trousers and jacket, was perched on a large flat stone a few meters from where Rosales was lying. Rosales did not move, his hand on the hilt of the bayonet, waiting.

The man smiled at him and nodded pleasantly. "*Buenos días, señor*. You have slept well. Please don't be alarmed: I am here as a friend."

Rosales lay still. "Who are you? What do you want?"

The little man nodded again. "I am called Paco, and I am from the village you passed through yesterday—Alpuente. They told me I could expect you along here; and, as you see, there was no trouble guessing where you'd be. As for what I want from you: only nothing, *hombre*. I go in my cart to Utiel, and I would be glad of your company, if that suits you."

Warily, Rosales rose to his feet. He sensed no danger from this person, but he was angry with himself for having been taken by surprise. So far as he could tell, the man had touched none of his belongings. The *bota* still lay beside him, as did the little wine bottle. Quickly he glanced over his shoulder. On the road behind him was a small wagon, to which were hitched two scrawny mules, idly flicking their ears and tails at the flies that never left these mountains, not even in winter. On the bed of the wagon were several parcels wrapped in damp cloth and bound up with cord.

"It is Saturday," said Paco de Alpuente, "and I am carrying cheese to the *gran mercado* in Utiel. As you may have guessed, little goes on in my *pueblo*, and I should be happy to spend a few hours along the way in conversation. In Alpuente we are poor, but we are not all as silent or sour as the old couple you accosted yesterday. They are my parents, incidentally, and the child with them was my daughter. You frightened them badly, I might add, but you treated them with great courtesy, for which I am grateful. You could have simply pushed your way in and taken what they had. It was not necessary for you to leave your knife and the cigarettes behind for them." The little man rose and hopped down from his stone. "Shall we be going?"

"As you will, and thanks," said Rosales. *This one thus far shows as much eagerness to talk as the* yanqui *and the* zaragozanos *from Frankfurt put together. Ah, well, empty spaces make some silent, while they make others jabber. I am no one to choose his company, just now.* He gathered his things, urinated against a tree, then hurried to catch up with the little man, who was already climbing aboard the wagon.

"Who taught you to move quietly?" Rosales asked the peasant, when he had seated himself on the bench beside him. "I am not usually so easy to surprise." It gave him a certain security to notice that he was almost two heads taller than this Paco.

"We are a quiet people in these mountains, to begin with," Paco answered. "And the war, and what followed after, taught me to walk quietly and wait patiently. You are not from here, clearly. *Andaluz*, I'd say. Right?"

"Right."

"Might one ask whether you are a veteran of the war? I do not wish to intrude."

"I was a man, then," Rosales answered, still on guard. "Like most who were men, I fought."

"For an *andaluz*, you're not very talkative. Look: I've told you my name. You know my *pueblo*, such as it is. Now I'll tell you this: I fought for the Republic, and then I came home. I hid in these mountains through all the years of reprisals, and now I poke my head out of Alpuente just often enough to sell cheese in Utiel on Saturdays. I have a few drinks in a bar where they know me, then I go home. There, that's my whole life. What do you have to say to that?"

Rosales relaxed a fraction, weighing the chances that this inquisitive man might be some sort of informer, hoping to make a little money, or just curry favor, by turning him in to the *Guardia* in Utiel. Men with big mouths should be spoken to as if they were stones, as they said in the Alpujarras.

"Rosales, from Andalucía. I, too, was in the wrong army. I have been away, but now I go home." He intended to say no more than this, and did not.

"Very well, Rosales from Andalucía. I will respect your secretiveness. You are wiser than I, I'm sure. Let us ride in peace, and view the beautiful scenery of my *patria chica*. It is truly a magnificent terrain, is it not?"

"Very distinctive, yes," said Rosales politely: It would never do to insult a man's home land, no matter how mean and primitive it was.

The little peasant laughed. "Rosales, the tactful *andaluz*. As a simple fact, no vulture with honor would deign to shit on this land." Rosales said nothing: If this Paco wanted to insult his own *patria chica*, that was for him to do, not Rosales. He could not imagine an Alpujarreño speaking in such a way as this peasant. It entered his mind that he had not even *seen* a vulture since he began his trek from the crossroad south of Teruel the day before. It was a poor land indeed that could not even bring vultures to it.

The wagon jogged along over the rutted road, and the little man kept up his chatter, to which he did not seem to expect Rosales to respond. Slowly they moved through the morning toward Utiel, at a pace perhaps only twice as fast as Rosales could have walked. They saw no one along the way, not even a shepherd. Only once did they stop. Beside a narrow stream Paco reined in the mules, hopped down from his seat on the wagon, and announced to Rosales: "Now we rest for a spell, and eat and drink a little something. Come on, *hombre*, get down and stretch."

"I have nothing to eat," said Rosales.

"Then let us have a couple of those famous cigarettes of yours, and you can share more of Alpuente's good wine and cheese. And here in this stream is water you can drink, without charge." Paco pulled from beneath the seat a small basket woven of esparto grass, and beckoned to Rosales. "Come on, *andaluz*," he insisted. "You behave more like one of those arrogant goddamn *castellanos* than the true son of the south I'm sure you are. Relax, *hombre*."

Rosales did climb down then, and stalked slowly over to the stream. The water was clear, cold, and coursing swiftly over the light sand and pebbles that lay on the bottom. The day was quite warm, now, warm enough for him to have removed his jacket had he not been afraid that Paco would see the outlines of the bayonet that hung from its wire thread beneath his shirt. He knelt and was about to drink when he saw his reflection in the clear water of the stream. "*¡Qué animal, qué bruto!*" he almost exclaimed. His beard had become almost full, now, except in the places that the German barbed wire had marked him. Without his beret, which he was going to use to scoop up the water, his head seemed all gray fur, matted and filthy. Only his close-set black eyes and his long nose made him recognizable to himself. You are a thing to frighten children, he murmured to himself as he dipped the beret into the water and raised it to his lips. When he had drunk enough, he splashed water on his head and arms, then stood and walked over to where the little peasant was sitting, a bottle of wine and chunks of his bread and cheese spread on a cloth before him.

By four o'clock the wagon was close enough to Utiel for them to hear the traffic on the Valencia–Madrid highway. Rosales, who had been lulled by the emptiness of the gravel road they had come down that day, began to worry. Where there is traffic, there will be *policía. And policía look for men with no papers.* Utiel might be a quiet market town, or it might not. He wondered whether it would be wisest to hop down now from the wagon, and make his way on foot around Utiel, to seek the road to Albacete that lay to its south. As he was pondering these things, he was preparing to shoulder again his blanket and *bota*, and the little peasant noticed this uneasy activity.

"Forget it, *amigo*," he said to Rosales. "Utiel is a safe

town. Even so mysterious a personage as yourself will excite no curiosity. It was with the Republic until the end of the war, and no one would think of questioning your politics. Come on, *hombre:* Utiel is a few cafés and stores, a granary, a movie house, two service stations, and a *fonda* where one can eat and sleep for next to nothing. Stay with me: We'll go to the market, sell the cheese, and then relax a little. Anyway, this is 1973, remember? Not 1939."

Rosales grunted, remembering that he had no papers of any kind. Any fool of a constable or deputy could stop me, and I'd be a prisoner by nightfall, he thought to himself. But he was tired and hungry, with still a great distance to cover; and if he watched himself carefully, perhaps a few hours in Utiel, with maybe a bed in a *fonda,* would be safe enough. "All right, Paco de Alpuente," he announced, "show me this Utiel."

It was as Paco had said: Utiel was not much. Through its center ran the busy highway, full of cars, trucks, and buses carrying tourists and travelers. By the town plaza was the open-air *mercado,* full now of peasants from the surrounding countryside, selling whatever poor stuff they had brought down from their mountain villages. He helped Paco unload the cheeses from the wagon, then walked about in the crowds of shoppers, happy at hearing in his ears only the sound of many people speaking Spanish. He felt conspicuous, because of his height and his new beard; but it did not seem to him that anyone gave him a glance of more than casual interest.

The crowds at the *mercado* dwindled away by eight o'clock, when the people of Utiel began going back to their homes for their dinner. Rosales found Paco at his spot in the dusty square, loading onto the wagon those cheeses he had not sold. Paco smiled at him. "So, Rosales, now we have a little money, and I am sure you have enough thirst to join me at a café for a *copita* of something. Then we can eat, and bed down at the *fonda* at the edge of town. Okay?" Rosales nodded.

Together they stood at the oaken bar of a dirt-floored café two blocks back from the highway. It was the sort of café that would not be used by travelers through the town, but by men like themselves—poor, dirty, and thirsty. There were three small tables, a pair of pale light bulbs, a door inscribed: ORINARIO, and the bar itself. Behind it stood the owner, a squat and saturnine man, and a boy who assisted him. On the wall behind the bar was a row of bottles of *coñacs* and sherries, a small icebox containing beer and Fanta, and two casks of wine; one marked: TINTO, the other: BLANCO. A roll of flypaper hung from the cord of one of the light bulbs. Taped to the side of the owner's wooden cash register was a calendar, on which there was a full-color print, much flyblown, of a plump girl wearing a sailor's hat and a bathing suit of a propriety suitable perhaps in 1940. Paco had ordered them each a glass of *aguardiente*, fiery and cheap. There was little conversation in the bar, which suited Rosales. He was dizzy after a single swallow from his glass, and would not have wished to speak. Paco, however, was expansive. He apparently knew the other men who stood at the bar, and joked with them about all manner of things—their scrawny cattle, their failing virility, their undoubted cuckoldry, the primitive quality of their *pueblos*, and the poor seed that had evidently gone into the making of their children—until Rosales felt sure that a fight was about to erupt. Certainly, men never spoke thus in the Alpujarras except when deliberately provoking trouble. The last thing he wanted was a Saturday-night fight in Utiel, so he prodded Paco in the ribs, and announced to the bartender, "I'll pay for these, and say good night to my friend here, and to all my *compatriotas* in this place."

The men at the bar, and those who sat at the tables playing *mus* or *tute* with the greasy cards the boy had brought them, looked up in surprise. Rosales reached in his trouser pocket and pulled out his thousand-peseta note, which he placed on the bar before him. The young boy, after a moment's hesitation, picked up the note and handed it to the bartender. Paco for once was speechless, staring in amazement at the money that the bartender was clutching in his fist, reluctant apparently to place it in his cash register. The men in the bar muttered their thanks, then fell silent, looking everywhere but in the direction of Rosales.

It was not until the bartender brought his change to Rosales—seven one-hundred peseta notes and two twenty-five peseta coins—that Paco regained his voice. "*Hombre*," he whispered, "this is not necessary. Here we are all poor. Now these men will feel obliged to buy you drinks for the rest of the night, and this they cannot afford to do. You are shaming us."

"And what was your talk doing to them, Paco?" Rosales asked. "You were asking for trouble, and I wished only peace and quiet. Now I must go. A thousand thanks, and good night."

"What kind of trouble, *coño*," Paco shouted. "These are my friends. They know me, and among friends there are no offenses. Where have you been, that you have forgotten how friends speak to one another?"

Rosales drew back from the bar, turning toward the door of the café. "Here men speak differently to one another, clearly. I have forgotten much, and I beg you to forgive me. Where I come from, such insults as yours are not taken so lightly, as jokes. *Vaya con Dios*," he concluded formally, and pushed his way through the curtain of yellow plastic strings that hung in the doorway.

*What did I do wrong?* He should not have brought out his money, he knew, nor embarrassed the men in the bar by obligating them to him, a stranger. He walked rapidly through the darkened streets of Utiel, all thoughts of a good meal and a night's sleep in the *fonda* gone from his mind. Before he turned toward the center of the town, where he hoped to find a sign pointing to the Albacete road, he looked back and saw Paco, small and sad, in the doorway of the bar. Rosales hesitated. *Call to the little man? Offer to buy him supper? Perhaps even joke a little?* But he said nothing, and after a moment Paco withdrew into the bar.

Suddenly Rosales felt very old and tired. This being among strangers was very wearing, much harder on one than walking through these mountains. He thought with some sorrow of the road out of Utiel, and the long journey still ahead of him. He did not want to go any farther tonight. He wanted a meal and a place to sleep. *I'll find this* fonda *of Paco's, and perhaps I'll see him there later.*

\* \* \*

113

The *fonda* was, predictably, at the edge of the poorest part of the town. There were no lights on the dirt path that led to it, but he made it out by a sign above its entryway: VENTA DE CABALLOS. If this were the right place, then it was not much even as *fondas* went: just a *venta*, a place where one might lodge his horse or mule, eat a simple supper, and bed down for the night on a cotton mat filled with straw. But it would do, Rosales thought, walking across the stone floor of the patio toward an ewer of water that had been placed in a corner near the far wall, by the stables. Drinking slowly from a tin dipper, he looked at this *venta* with some approval. Four men were squatting around a brazier on which their supper was cooking: a large copper pot full of *olla podrida*, a stew made of whatever the landlord had been able to gather—some sort of meat (goat, Rosales's nose told him) and vegetables, probably potatoes, cabbage, and the inevitable *garbanzos*, chickpeas. After a day in which he had eaten only Paco's poor *manchego* cheese, Rosales found himself eager to join the men around this brazier. He sought out the owner, exchanged greetings, paid him two of his twenty-five peseta coins for his food and lodgings, and was given a large wooden spoon for the meal. He squatted with the other men around the pot of *olla*, nodded to them, then fixed his eyes on the simmering stew. He was glad to note that these men, whoever they were, seemed no more inclined to conversation than he. This talking business still troubled him: All his life he had, as an *andaluz*, been expected to be glib, eloquent, witty, a chatterer. But people were not like that in the Alpujarras, whatever they might be like in the rest of the region. There men kept their reserve and decorum, never speaking frivolously, not even during the fiesta of San Sebastián, their patron saint, or the holidays of the *matanzas*, the times of the pig killings, when no one went to the fields, but stayed in the villages to celebrate the slaughter. *If an* alpujarreño *has something to say, he says it; if not, he keeps silent*.

When the pot had simmered long enough, the landlord came over with his own spoon, said only "*Empecemos*": Let's begin, and each man dipped his spoon into the stew. They ate rapidly but not greedily, each careful to observe the invisible boundaries of his portion of the bowl. When there was nothing left but a watery sauce at the bottom, the landlord's wife, as saturnine as the men, walked out of the inn carrying a loaf of bread and a long knife. Holding the bread against her breast, she cut thick slices for each of the men, with which they sopped up the sauce of the *olla*. Rosales, like the other men, handed his spoon to the woman, then followed the landlord to a far corner of the stables, away from the horses and mules, and was given his straw-filled mattress. More content now, but still wary, he lay down near the stable door, made a brief visual reconnaissance of the ways he might escape most quickly if the need arose, then spread his blanket over him and closed his eyes. He was kept awake for perhaps a half hour by the sighs and farts of his companions, and by the rustling of their mattresses; but soon he fell into his usual deep and dreamless sleep. His last waking thought was of Paco. Why had he not appeared? Was this perhaps not the *fonda* of which he had spoken? Or was he still at the café, drunk by now and talking about his mysterious passenger to anyone who would listen? Rosales knew that one did not have to wear a uniform to be some kind of policeman, and it seemed probable that Utiel would have its informers, eager to carry information to the *Guardia. To hell with it. Tonight I sleep. If they want me, let them look for me.*

At dawn he arose with the others, drank a mug of *café con leche* brought him by the landlord, and watched as the men brought their animals out of their stalls. From the landlord he bought, with his remaining change, a slab of salted pork and a large piece of the bread from the night before. The man made a bundle of this food for Rosales, wrapping it in newspaper and tying it with string. When the other men led their animals out through the gate of the *venta*, Rosales moved with them, as if part of their company. As they neared the central plaza of Utiel, he touched one of the men on the arm and asked for the road to Albacete.

"Take the Madrid highway three kilometers to Caudete, then south until you encounter the Requena road. Do you walk?" The man did not seem curious, but businesslike. Rosales nodded. "It's a hundred kilometers to Albacete. You have a long day before you, *viejo*."

Rosales smiled briefly at the man. "I walk fast," he said, "and at my age time is not so important."

He found the highway with ease, then walked away from it through the scrub and shale until he could no longer see it. He set a westward course that he judged would parallel the highway, and commenced his rapid stride. The land was a little flatter now, as he moved toward the immense steppe of La Mancha, and he felt reasonably sure of coming close to Albacete by dark.

Once clear of the outskirts of Utiel, he climbed back onto the Albacete road. It was hard-topped, and the walking was easy. No more than five or six times an hour did he encounter traffic—a truck or two, heading for the factories in Albacete, and an occasional tractor pulling carts laden with straw or with esparto grass. No one stopped for him, which was, he thought, just as well. He had had enough of human company for a while.

By late morning he had crossed the bridge over the Río Cabriel, and had left the Sierra de Rubial behind him to the west. The December sun was warm and brassy, and the air of the steppe was so clear that he could see farther than he would have imagined possible. The sky above him was a deep blue, and the three or four clouds that hung above him, billowing and fleecy, seemed perfectly motionless, their shapes unchanging from hour to hour. All around him were great stretches of barren land: red sand dunes sparsely covered with esparto and chapparal, rocky hillsides topped with oaks and pines, and the occasional deep *arroyo* where some river had once flowed.

Before noon, though, he reached irrigated land, and found himself walking through enormous olive groves, the rows of which opened like fans to him as he strode rapidly along. These groves belonged to rich men, he reflected; many of the fields stretched in all directions, as far as he could see. To him it was all quite beautiful, especially when a breeze ruffled through the groves, turning up the silver undersides of the olive leaves. If we had won our war, he reflected, such groves were to have been taken from the landowners and parceled out to the peasants whose families had been working for those landowners for centuries, never earning enough to fill their bellies or clothe their children. Would this really have happened, as the political leaders had promised? Rosales had his doubts: Where there is great wealth, it is not natural for men to wish to share it. The owners would exploit, and the peasants be exploited. This had always been so, and Rosales, even as a young man during the war, had been too cynical to believe that any revolution would change things for the better.

He had never known any rich men, if one excepted the few *granadinos* who owned land in the Alpujarras, and rented it out to the villagers. These city men would visit their farms infrequently, coming into the mountains only for weekend vacations or to collect their rent from the men who oversaw their land. Rosales had, as a child, hung about the enormous automobiles of these *granadinos*, marveling at their sleek opulence; and once or twice he had stood in the doorways of the cafés in Poqueira, watching these men and their families eating the tremendous meals they had ordered served them on tables set up in the gardens outside. It did not seem likely to him then, nor did it now, that any social change could force these proud, fat men to exchange their wealth for his poverty. Not that, strictly speaking, he had ever regarded himself as poor: In the Alpujarras there was little money, but no one went cold or hungry—except for those few shameless ones who refused to work. So far as he had been concerned, and he had never found any reason to change his mind, politics and ideologies were subjects for café conversation merely, not things to act on, let alone go to war over. But then he *had* gone, hadn't he? At the first signal, he had joined the *Confederación Nacional de Trabajo*, the Anarcho-Syndicalist Trade Union, lined up in his overalls and his *alpargatas*, his rope-soled sandals, with the other men and boys of Poqueira, and marched off to join the militia, to fight for social progress in Spain, and to put down the fascist uprising launched by the generals and the reactionaries. It had never occurred to him to choose *not* to go. A man went, that was all. Only the weak and the cowardly stayed home.

All he had ever wanted was to grow up in Poqueira, work his land, court the lissome Ana María and then marry her, get several children on her, and live out his life. The concept of a nation called "Spain" was alien to him. He knew that he was a Spaniard, and the young *maestro* who conducted the school in Poqueira had shown him maps of the country, with a place called "Madrid" at its center, and with high mountains in the north beyond which was a country *not* called "Spain," but "France." Yet he had never been out of the Alpujarras until 1936, except once to visit the city of Granada, soft and fragrant, full of the sound of fountains splashing and the scent of jasmine; and it was very hard for him to imagine a world that was not bordered on the north by the Sierra Nevada, and on the south by the Mediterranean. Rosales thought now, as he marched along through kilometer after kilometer of olive groves, that he had been robbed of thirty-seven years of his life—his life in the Alpujarras—by some stupid *idea*, some *cause*. What a stupidity. Again he realized how much he preferred the land to the people. There were no causes and ideas in the land. It took people,

people and their damned *thinking*, to come up with reasons for men to kill one another.

Shaking his head, and calling an end to this long conversation with himself, he stopped for *almuerzo*, his midday meal, on the northern edge of the town of Casas Ibáñez, at a spot where an olive grove ended and a field of grape vines began. The day had become quite warm, and he was conscious of carrying too many burdens for a man with far to go. He would rest at the edge of the grove, eat the bread and pork he had bought at the *venta* that morning, finish the little wine bottle he carried in his jacket pocket, and thus reduce his inventory for traveling. He did not bother to hide, now, from passersby. Let them see him: He was like any other man, a peasant on his way to anywhere at all. An old man passed by on the back of a donkey, a large clump of esparto tied to the animal's small rump. Rosales waved and called "*Muy buenas*" to the man, who raised his hand in greeting.

As he lay in the midday December sun, propped against the trunk of an olive tree that was perhaps two hundred years old, Sebastián Rosales ceased to think of himself as a refugee, an exile, or a criminal in flight. He was no different from anyone else, he had done no one harm, nor did he intend to. So long as he kept away from heavily populated areas, so long as he stayed with his own kind, what was there to fear? He would go on his way, avoiding trouble, remaining cautious as always —but without fear. The holiday season was approaching (what precisely *was* the date? he wondered), and not even the *Guardia Civil* would be actively seeking discord at this time of year. Perhaps he had been too suspicious: What danger really threatened him, after all? And even if he *were* stopped and questioned, he could represent himself as simply a stupid old man, on his way from staying with relatives in, say, Zaragoza to his home in— where?—some town near Granada, where his children and grandchildren were expecting him for the fiestas of *la Navidad*. What could be more innocent? Full of a new sense of contentment, Rosales pulled his beret down over his eyes, resolved not to worry about reaching Albacete that day, and fell asleep.

When he awoke, the sun was setting. The heat of the day, as well as the salty pork he had eaten for lunch, had given him a real thirst. He did not want to finish what was left of the wine in his *bota*—and he knew from long experience that wine after a siesta was bad for the head—so he stood and looked around for the irrigation ditch that must lie along the edge of the vineyard before him. Though the final harvest was over a month past, there were still a few gray and puckered grapes on the plants near the road. He plucked a few, wiped them against the sleeve of his jacket to rid them of the thick powder that covered them, and put them, five or six at a time, in his mouth. They were even more bitter than he expected, and contained almost no moisture. The irrigation ditch, when he found it, was almost completely dry, nothing but a line of cracked and peeling mud. Disappointed, he lifted the *bota* and took a long pull from it. The tartness of the grapes was still not gone from his mouth, but perhaps he would find a place in Casas Ibáñez where he could rinse his mouth properly.

At the entrance to the town was a service station, with a pair of attendants lounging about, wearing blue *monos*, staring without interest at the empty oil cans and wads of soggy paper that had accumulated around them during the day. Rosales approached them, smiling amiably. "*Hola, amigos*," he said, touching his beret. "*Buen tiempo, no?*"

One of the attendants looked briefly at Rosales. "*Hola, barbudo*," bearded one. It's good weather if you like it this way." He looked away.

Rosales continued smiling. "Of course it's good: It's hot in the sun and cold in the shadow. One can find what weather he desires on such a day."

The attendant who had spoken touched lightly the leather change purse he wore at his belt. "Look, *viejo*," he said, "if you want money, forget it. If there is a loose coin in this asshole of a *pueblo*, which I doubt, you'll find it in town, not here. Get going."

Rosales's benevolent mood evaporated. *A pair of greasy little pimps.* His hand touched the outline of the bayonet beneath his shirt. "You misunderstand me, *caballeros*," he said with irony. "I need no money. I wanted only to ask directions to an inn of some kind, where I might eat and sleep. However, if you wish to insult me . . ." He stood quite still, ready for anything, staring straight ahead at an advertisement for Michelin tires that was pasted to the large front window of the station. The merry little rubber man made of Michelin tires smiled back at him from the placard.

"Okay, old man, okay," said the attendant. "No offense. But you won't get in a hotel looking like that, not even in Casas Ibáñez. Why don't you stop at a *peluquería* first, and have a shave? Then you'll be ready to join the *paseo*, and maybe even find a little *coño* for yourself."

Rosales spat, not exactly at the man's feet, but not exactly anywhere else, either. He did not want a fight, but life contained moments when fights were not to be avoided. *But I must get home.* To fight would be foolish. He turned abruptly and began walking into the town. The attendants were silent.

Dizzy with anger and insult, Rosales made himself march toward the center of this *pueblo* as if on parade in the old days. There were many people in the streets, coming out from their siestas to saunter through the town for an hour or so before dinnertime. The evening was cool, almost chilly, and most of the men of Casas Ibáñez were wearing jackets, or topcoats. The older women were wrapped in heavy shawls, and looked thick and shapeless next to the young girls of the village, who seemed to Rosales to be dressed with remarkable smartness. They walked together in shrill bunches, arm in arm, conspicuously unaware of the young men who, in their own bunches, lurched along behind them, hoping by extravagant acts of buffoonery to attract some girl's glance. In spite of his anger Rosales smiled at this, remembering how similarly the girls and boys of Poqueira had behaved in his day, when throughout the long Sunday afternoons they would parade back and forth on the road from their *pueblo* to the neighboring town of Bubión, two kilometers below.

Then he sensed trouble, quite suddenly, as though by smell. At the far edge of the plaza were two *Guardias*, resplendent in their evening dress uniforms, sauntering benignly through the crowd, speaking to no one but each other, yet never ceasing to cast their eyes over the peaceful scene, looking for trouble. The *Guardias*, Rosales recalled, were never posted to duty in their own *pueblos:* They were always from somewhere else. This kept them from the dangers of friendship or familiarity of a sort with the citizens over whom they watched. It must be a lonely thing to be one of those, he thought, even as he looked around anxiously for a way to escape their gaze. If they saw him, they would not know who he was, but they would certainly know immediately that he did not belong to this *pueblo*. His cheerful optimism of a few hours before had suddenly drained from him. He ducked into the doorway of a bar, trying to decide what to do.

Dizzy again, he leaned against the counter, shoulder to shoulder with the other men who stood there, talking loudly about crops, politics, sex, and about whatever bad things they knew about whatever man was not there to defend himself. In a corner of the bar was a television, its volume turned down. On its screen was some sort of domestic drama enacted by people who could not have been Spanish, judging from their dress and behavior. In the five seconds Rosales watched the screen, a thin woman with too much makeup on had hit a fat man (her husband? her father?) with a pie. Around the two of them ran another couple, swinging at one another with pillows. A comedy, perhaps, thought Rosales, wondering momentarily why the sound of the television was reduced. "*Una caña,*" he said to the bartender, not knowing whether he really wanted a glass of beer, but supposing that he could not very well stand at the bar without asking for anything at all. The bartender put the glass in front of him, and slid a dish of peanuts to within his reach. Not daring to look behind him, lest the

*Guardias* should at that moment be entering the bar, Rosales bowed his head over his glass of beer. For the first time, he heard music. Out of the corner of his left eye he saw a small jukebox, all chrome and plastic. From it was issuing the same horrible sort of noise that his daughters in France loved so, only now the words, of an incredible insipidity, were sung in Spanish, not French. It seemed even worse, so.

"*¿Otra caña más?*" asked the bartender. Rosales nodded, not raising his eyes. When the new glass was before him, he cleared his throat, which was still dry and parched (*Am I that afraid?*), and spoke as loudly as he dared to the bartender. "Can you give me the name of a place where I might eat and sleep in this town, please?" His voice sounded hoarse and weak—an old man's voice.

"A cheap place?" asked the bartender, perhaps with a little irony, as he looked for the first time at Rosales.

"I am not particular," Rosales answered, "but I am able to pay."

"What, then?" asked the bartender, a little impatiently. "Hotel, *fonda, pensión*, room—what?"

"A small room, perhaps," Rosales murmured, "with maybe a quiet restaurant nearby. I would wish to eat early and go to bed soon. And might I have a glass of water, now, please?"

The bartender moved away again, then returned with the water. "You wish to pay now for the *cañas, señor?*"

Rosales pulled the seven crumpled hundred-peseta notes from his trouser pocket and gave one to the man, who, satisfied from what he had seen that Rosales could pay for some sort of food and lodging, anyway, now declared: "Turn right outside, go down the next street to Calle Pozuelo, number 11, and tell them I sent you.

They are friends of mine, and will give you food and a bed for very little. Tell them Manolo sent you."

Manolo scooped away the glasses, the dish, and the three pesetas that Rosales left as a tip from the change he had been given. Before Rosales could thank him, he was at the far end of the bar, turning up the volume of the television, where now a *yanqui* cowboy was talking to a beautiful woman in a bar much larger and grander than this one.

At the doorway he took a deep breath, knew himself to appear highly suspicious, not to say menacing, and stepped out into the street. The crowds were still there, but the *Guardias* had moved on. Quickly he turned down the side street, and headed for the house of Manolo's friends. He was as thirsty as ever, and his dizziness had not left him. *Something is wrong with me.*

He knocked at what he hoped was the correct door. A tall man, taller even than Rosales, answered almost immediately (Had Manolo called ahead?), and invited him into the tiny foyer of the house. On the walls around him Rosales saw a calendar, an oleograph of a saint, and a portrait of a general from some earlier war than his. "I was told by Manolo that you might have a room where I might sleep," he said to the man. His voice sounded faint and faraway to him, and he prepared to repeat what he had just said, more loudly, when the man answered him. "I might have such a room. The price is one hundred pesetas."

"Good," said Rosales, trying to speak with authority. "And could there be supper and perhaps breakfast, too?"

"For fifty pesetas more, of course we can feed you—if you eat what we eat." The man had closed the door behind Rosales, who noticed suddenly how hot he was becoming. Probably, he thought, there must be an *estufa*, an electric space heater, burning in some nearby room. "I should be happy to pay that much, and I thank you."

"Do you wish to eat now, with us, or do you prefer to rest first, and wash a little, perhaps?" the tall man asked. Rosales understood that he was being requested to clean himself up before presenting himself at the man's table, so he replied: "If I might wash and lay my things in my room first, that would be best."

"Good enough," said the man. But he did not move from the foyer. Rosales stood looking at the man for some seconds before he realized that the man expected him to pay in advance. Embarrassed at his own slowness, he dug once again into his pocket, and paid. The man then turned and led him down a narrow hallway, past several closed doors, to a room at the rear of the house. In it were a bed and a basin with two taps. "The toilet is outside, just past the door there," said his host, pointing. He left Rosales at the entrance to his room, and walked back toward the front of the house.

Had it been only a week since he had last slept in a real bed? This one was not much—a brass bedstead, a sagging mattress with a gray cotton cloth buttoned around it, a lumpy pillow, and a blanket not much better than the one he carried over his shoulder, but Rosales wanted almost irresistibly to lie down and sleep. Discipline, he told himself: Hold on. Wash first. Eat something. Then you can sleep—*if* you have decided you can trust this place.

On his sink was a bar of soap—a good sign, and a

piece of luck he had not expected—and when he turned on both taps, one of them poured cold water, while from the other came a slow trickle of water that was, if not quite hot, at least warm enough to help in breaking loose some of the dirt from his face and hands. There was no mirror above the basin, which did not displease him. He stripped to his waist, being careful to hide his bayonet beneath the pillow on the bed, and did what he could to clean himself. He thought of shaving, but realized that he was too weak and shaky just now to try, especially with only the bayonet as his razor. There was no towel: He dried himself with his shirt, put it and his jacket back on, slipped the bayonet on its wire around his neck again, settled his beret firmly on his head, and went out into the hallway in search of his supper.

The tall man evidently heard his footsteps, for he opened one of the doors Rosales had passed earlier and nodded that he should enter. He seemed to be looking rather carefully at Rosales, but his expression showed neither like nor dislike. Fine, thought Rosales. Let's keep it businesslike. He walked into a small dining room and stood, waiting for further directions from his host. "Please sit," the man said. "The cook will bring the supper to us in just a minute." Rosales looked at the table. On it were two deep plates, two small plastic glasses, knives, spoons, and forks, and two paper napkins. Either he was the only guest, or this was not a place that regularly took in boarders. He sat where the man indicated, wondering whether he should behave as one did in cities, and remove his beret. In Poqueira it would have been a rudeness to do so, but he could tell nothing about the customs of such a place as this. Before he could decide what to do, the door to the kitchen opened, and a very small and ugly woman entered, carrying in both hands a steaming bowl of *sopa de pescado*, fish soup, which she placed on the table between the two men. Rosales said good evening to her, and when she turned to answer his greeting he saw with some dismay that she had a cast in one eye. Quickly he looked down at his plate, placed his hands in his lap, and crossed his fingers. *No me mata, Mal Ojo*, he muttered to himself: Don't kill me, Evil Eye.

The woman brought a bottle of white wine and a loaf of bread, then left the two men alone. The host ladled soup into Rosales's plate, poured him his wine, and they began to eat. The man still had said nothing.

The soup was probably quite good, Rosales thought, but difficult for him to eat. His hands were shaking so that he could scarcely raise his spoon to his mouth; and the strong smell of the fish, which was not one he could identify, filled him with waves of nausea. A cold sweat broke out across his face. Carefully putting his spoon in his plate, he wiped his face with his napkin. Perhaps if I wait just a second, all this foolishness will pass. I *must* eat, or I'll *really* be ill. He cleared his throat.

The tall man, who had been watching Rosales, spoke up at last. "Does the soup not please you? I'm afraid it's all we have."

"On the contrary, I like it very much. It is just that I am a little tired, and need only to compose myself for a moment before eating." Rosales tried to sound sincere. "Please tell your cook that I like it extremely."

"That's my sister. She has not married." I'm not surprised to hear *that*, thought Rosales. A man would have to be an idiot to marry a woman with the Evil Eye. "We live here alone, she and I," the man went on, steadily spooning soup into his mouth. Then: "Are you married, *señor?*"

"Yes."

"How many children?"

A fog had moved in across Rosales's mind, and he had trouble answering. Finally he said, in his strangely thin new voice, "Two daughters. Some grandchildren."

"How many?"

Rosales tried to think. "Four, perhaps, or five. It is difficult to know."

The man raised an eyebrow, but said nothing to this. "I have never married. I was to have done so, but my *novia* did not want to share a house with an unmarried sister-in-law, so that was that."

Rosales tried a piece of the bread, and found to his relief that he was able to chew and swallow it. He drank a little of the wine. In a moment, he thought, I'll see again about the soup. He knew that he must make some effort at conversation. What could he find to say? Well, hell, anything, *some*thing: "Is there much work in this *pueblo?* Does one live well here?" That wasn't so bad, he reflected: No harm in questions like that. He lifted his spoon and tried the soup again, this time managing to swallow a little.

But his questions had touched his host in a sensitive place. For the first time he showed some animation. "Work!" he exclaimed. "Of course there's work, if one is a *campesino,* and is content with his sheep and cattle. Or if one has *enchufe,* connections. But for an educated man with no *enchufe,* there is nothing. Do you know what I do?"

Rosales shook his head, sorry to have agitated the man, but glad to have taken his attention away from his attempts to eat his soup.

"Listen," said the man. "I'll tell you what I do. But first, look at this." He rose hurriedly from the table and threw open the door into the next room. Rosales saw shelves of books, more books than he had ever seen together in one place. There was a desk filled with papers, and an enormous old typewriter. The man went into this room, and returned immediately with a framed certificate of some sort. "Can you read this?" he demanded of Rosales.

"I can read a little Spanish, but this does not seem to be written in Spanish." Rosales squinted at the certificate the man had thrust in his face. It was very formal and elegant, with many signatures and with a seal of red wax in its bottom right-hand corner.

"It's written in Latin, *señor*," said the man, "and I am probably the only man in Casas Ibáñez who can read what it says. I am an *abogado licenciado*, a qualified lawyer, a graduate of the *Facultad de Leyes* of the University of Valencia. But I have never practiced, not once in five years. Do you know why I haven't?"

Rosales shook his head. Should he try another spoonful of the soup?

"I'll tell you why. I do not belong to *la gente conocida*, the known people, of the *pueblo*. There are other lawyers here, lazy little *señoritos* who bought their diplomas and who do nothing but sit in the cafés all day. But they belong to the families of category in Casas Ibáñez, so they have all the business, and I have none. It is all handled very efficiently, as such things always are in this country. Where are you from?"

This sudden question startled Rosales, who was already put off-guard from his host's bitter outbursts. "Poqueira," he answered without thinking.

"And where is that? It sounds Galician, but you're no *gallego*, are you?" The man did indeed sound like an *abogado*, thought Rosales, who had never known one, but had always heard that they were a brusque and quick lot, able to confuse simple men with shrewd questions. He tried to compose himself, to keep a sense of reticence and discretion, but he was too weak now to do so. "'In the Alpujarras, in the province of Granada. It is a small place," he said apologetically. "There's no reason for your Honor to have heard of it."

"Are there lawyers there?"

"Oh, no, *señor*. There is a *juez municipal*, a justice of the peace, who handles disputes. For real lawyers, one has to go down to Órgiva, in the valley." People in the Alpujarras, he remembered, were fond of threatening to take one another to court over one thing or another, usually rights to irrigation ditches or the boundaries of farms; but nothing much ever came of such threats.

"Then you are fortunate. I wish I had never heard of the profession. I should be a knife sharpener, or a *limpiabotas*, a bootblack," the man said, his voice heavy with sarcasm. "Then I would not be cursed with being a thoughtful man. Do you know how I live?" Again Rosales shook his head. This was all very tiring for him, and he thought with some longing of the bed in his room.

"I have a noble profession, *señor*. I sit all day at a table in the plaza with my typewriter and write letters for all the *analfabetos* of the *pueblo*. The stupid people of Casas Ibáñez come to me to dictate their important business correspondence. And their disgusting and insipid love letters. I write down what they tell me, and they pay me. *That* is my profession—that and renting a room now and then to such as you. What do you think of that, my old gentleman?" The man sat down again at his place, his anger making him tremble almost as badly as Rosales.

Rosales tried hard to think of a polite phrase. Finally he said, shrugging, "A man lives as he has to, *señor*. Life is hard. Happiness is granted to few."

"You are a born disciple of Séneca, *viejo*, a true Spaniard: made for abstinence and toil, a natural stoic." The man gazed at Rosales with mock admiration.

Rosales, sick as he was, felt a touch of the old arrogance in himself. Quietly, he answered the furious man: "I am a simple peasant, *señor*, and I cannot follow much of what you say. But I have learned that it is an unmanly thing to complain of one's lot. One does what one must."

"Of course, *señor* stoic, you are right. But if one is cursed with the gifts of thoughtfulness and ambition, then to be as resigned as you is very hard." The man's anger was subsiding now into something like self-pity. Rosales finished his wine, and made as if to rise. But his dizziness held him in his chair.

"I am sorry, *viejo*. I have spoken rudely to you." The man bent his head over his plate, staring apparently at the lumps of now-cold fish that lay in it. "But there are times when it is difficult to reconcile myself. I would leave this *pueblo* tomorrow, and return to Valencia. But I have this house, and my sister . . ." He fell silent.

Rosales rose from the table, holding on to the back of his chair for support. "Forgive me for leaving early, *señor*," he said to his host. "But I am not quite well, and have far to go tomorrow. Good night to you and your sister."

The man did not raise his head. "Sleep well, *viejo*," he said softly. "My sister will serve you your breakfast in the morning."

Leaning his shoulder against the wall of the hallway, Rosales stumbled to his room. He closed the door, and turned toward his bed. Something is wrong with me, he told himself again, and fainted, falling crosswise onto the bed.

# *Chapter 4*

How long he lay unconscious, Rosales did not know. It could have been for five seconds, or five minutes, or half the night. But when he regained his senses, he felt anything but rested. His head hung forward over the edge of the bed, and was throbbing with an intensity he found hard to believe. Cramps grabbed at his belly, causing him to draw his knees up almost to his chin. The nausea and dizziness had not abated. He was about to vomit, he realized, and pulled himself to his feet to grope for the sink that was somewhere in the darkness of his room. He found it just in time. Clutching his arms around his midsection, he threw up in a series of contorting heaves all that he had eaten and drunk that day—fish, bread, wine, beer, even remnants of the pork he had bought the previous morning from the landlord at the *venta*. When he had finished, he turned on the cold tap, rinsed away the mess as best he could in the dark, and then held his head under the faucet. Except for his war wounds and their aftereffects, he had never in all his fifty-four years known what it was to be ill; and it occurred to him now that he was surely dying.

Before he could lie down to contemplate this certainty, the cramps commenced again, and he knew that he would have to find his way outside to the toilet bowl his host had told him was there. He opened the door to his room. The hallway was dark. Reeling from pain and dizziness, he turned to the right and crept to the rear of the house. There he found a door. Let it not be locked, he prayed, lest I shit in my trousers where I stand. There was a latch, but he was able to pull it open and stumble out into the walled garden behind the house. He made out a small shed in a corner of the yard, and headed for it as fast as he could, doubled over with cramps and urgency, tugging at his belt as he went. His buttocks had no sooner touched the seat than his sphincter muscle relaxed, letting out what seemed to him whole liters of the most noxious filth he could imagine. The war had shown him what dysentery looked and smelled like. In the last months, after the Ebro especially, more than one of his men had died from it, puking and shitting as vilely as he himself was now doing. Rosales had not had much compassion for these men at the time. If he had thought anything, he had been rather contemptuous of men who died so, lacking all dignity and respect for others.

He leaned his sweating head against the wall of the shed, gasping, and thought briefly of an etching someone had shown him during the retreat from Cataluña, when the treasures of the Prado Museum in Madrid were being taken for safeguarding away from the war zone into France. It had been by an Aragonese, Goya, and was entitled *Edad con desgracias:* Age with Misfortunes. In it an old man, his nightshirt pulled up to his waist, had fallen over on his chamber pot, the contents of which had poured back over him. Rosales had laughed at the expression of horror and disgust on the face of the old man. I will not die so, he swore now to himself: I will not be an object for mockery. He found a roll of paper, wiped himself, stood, hoisted his trousers up and buckled them about him, and finally reached up and pulled the chain of the toilet.

This will pass, he thought. I will rest until tomorrow, eat a little something, and be on my way. *I will die when I am ready to die, on my own terms, in my own way— and certainly not in a stranger's house, in a town I do not know.* Walking a little steadier now, Rosales returned to his room. His thirst was extreme. He felt around for his *bota*, and swallowed a mouthful of the wine. Then he removed his clothes, replaced the bayonet beneath his pillow, and stretched himself out under the blanket. He was still dizzy, and his head still ached; but the nausea and the cramps were gone, at least for the moment. He touched his forehead, and knew he had a considerable fever. Good, he thought; let it burn this sickness out of me. He slid into sleep in this fashion, remembering as he did so his boyhood in Poqueira, when he and his friends would spend the day at a pond above the town, splashing each other with the icy mountain water that poured down in torrents from the Sierra Nevada. He would never have dreamed then that this "Spain" of which he was a citizen was in large part a great desert, with wine more plentiful than water.

He heard a knocking, and struggled up to consciousness to respond to it. His eyes opened, then closed quickly as they reacted to the pain of daylight. Where was he? Why did he feel such great weakness? Taking a deep breath, he called out "*Adelante*," and waited to see what would happen.

The knocking ceased, and he could hear the door to his room opening. With great effort, he turned his head toward the door, and encountered the skewed eyes of the unfortunate sister of his lawyer landlord. He crossed his fingers again, under his blanket, and tried to smile. "*Buenos días, señorita*," he said, as pleasantly as he could, all the memories of his illness, and last night's misfortunes, coming back to him. "I'm afraid I have overslept. Give me just a few minutes to dress myself, and I'll be ready for breakfast."

The woman opened the door a little more. She was carrying a tray, with coffee and a *bollo* on it. "Here is your breakfast, *señor*," she said timidly, "but I think you are not well. Forgive me, but I heard you during the night." She blushed at this admission, and Rosales turned his head away in shame, thinking of the noises he had made.

"I was a little ill, that is true," he said, closing his eyes again. "But I feel much better now. Perhaps if you were to leave the tray here, I might eat my breakfast as I dress." The woman nodded, set the tray beside Rosales's bed, and withdrew, closing the door softly behind her. When she had gone, Rosales sat up, reached beneath the pillow for the bayonet, and hung it around his neck. He swung his feet slowly over the side of the bed, and felt around him for his trousers and shirt. The shirt he could manage, though the buttoning was hard, but getting his trousers back on was something else. As soon as he stood, all of yesterday's dizziness returned, and he fell back upon the bed, the trousers in a heap around his feet. Though he felt no desire for any breakfast, he waited a moment for his head to clear, then reached down beside the bed for the large cup of coffee. He swallowed a little of it, then tried a piece of the *bollo*. The nausea came back as before, and once again he pulled himself to the sink, dragging his trousers as he went. This is foolish: I must stop this, he said to himself, as he stood before the basin, leaning with his hands on the wall. He resolved to rest a few minutes more. He stumbled back to the bed, fell across it, and drew the blanket up to his chest.

When he opened his eyes again, he counted three people around the bed: the sister, looking quite frightened; his host, staring at him with great concern; and another, older man, wearing a dark suit and a necktie. He tried to sit up, but could not; his weakness held him to the mattress. The older man, the stranger, reached over and touched Rosales's forehead, then glanced at the lawyer. "Who is this man?" he asked. "How long has he been here, and how long has he been this way?"

"I don't know who he is, *señor médico*: a stranger, an *andaluz* on his way home to his family. He came yesterday, for the night only. He was not this way last night, perhaps just a little tired." The lawyer was agitated, and it seemed to Rosales that he was considerably annoyed with him. The sister hung back by the door, as if ready to flee at any provocation at all.

"The man needs to be in a hospital, clearly," said the doctor. "I will call ahead to Albacete, and order an ambulance. Has he any money?"

Before the lawyer could answer, Rosales sat up. "No." His voice was stronger than it had been for many hours. "I will go to no hospital. Let me rest only another few hours, then I will be quite well enough to travel on my own." Hospitals, he knew, were for the dying, and he would fight these men before he let them take him to one.

The doctor peered down into Rosales's eyes. "*Viejo*," he said, "either you have dysentery, or you have poisoned yourself somehow. This young lady says you have extreme nausea and diarrhea." Beneath his beard, Rosales blushed with shame. "I can give you some medicine now that will help you temporarily, but you *must* go into the hospital in Albacete. You are dangerously dehydrated. Do you understand what that means?" Rosales shook his head, reaching one hand slowly up to the strand of wire around his neck. I know only that I will go to no hospital, he thought.

The doctor stood up and looked at the lawyer. "I will send for the ambulance. Be sure that he is put into it when it comes. Is that clear?" The lawyer nodded, his eyes full of anxiety. "In the meantime, give him these pills, and as much water as he can hold down." The doctor moved past the sister into the hall, not looking back at Rosales. "Have him ready, *hombre*," he said to the lawyer. "The ambulance will be here within the hour. *Hasta luego*."

Rosales watched the lawyer follow the doctor to the front door. Never had he felt so helpless. What good was a man if he could not even get himself properly into his trousers?

The lawyer returned to the room, and seated himself at the foot of Rosales's bed. He sat silently for a moment, with his hands clasped in his lap. Then he spoke: "All right, *viejo*. Do you understand my predicament?"

"What predicament, *señor*? It seems to me that *I* am the one in difficulty, here." Rosales felt his anger giving him strength.

"Look, *andaluz*, I am responsible for you, legally speaking. I took you in. I did not ask to see your papers. Do you *have* any papers, by the way?" Rosales was silent.

"I thought not," said the lawyer. "Look: you've got to leave here, now. Before the ambulance comes, understand?"

"To do so is my fondest wish," said Rosales fervently. "Help me up, and get me into the street, and we will be well rid of one another."

"No, *hombre*. I can't let you out to stagger around the *pueblo* and be picked up. They'd trace you right to my door, and then I'd be ruined. I have to get you out of town." He thought a moment, then said, "All right. You want to go to Andalucía. How much money do you have?"

Rosales thought quickly, then replied, "Two hundred pesetas only, *señor*. But I—"

"Good, then," the lawyer interrupted. "We'll give you this medicine, get you dressed, and my cousin will take the evening off from his café and drive you all the way to Jaén. We can tell the doctor you sneaked out before the ambulance arrived. Will that suit you?"

"*Ojalá*": *May God grant it.*

The lawyer stood then, and called to his sister. Together they tugged Rosales to the side of his bed, and
wrestled him into his trousers. The sister knelt at his feet
and tied on his shoes. While the lawyer called his cousin,
the sister gave the pills—several large brown ones—to
Rosales, and scurried around the room gathering up Rosales's belongings. Then she and the lawyer held Rosales
up and walked him to the front door of their house.
Within minutes the cousin—Manolo, it was, from the
café of the evening before—arrived, in an old pickup
truck. He looked on with curiosity as the lawyer and the
sister lifted Rosales into the rear of the truck, propped
his head on his blanket roll, and returned to the front of
their house. The lawyer waved Manolo on, but the sister
cried for him to wait. She ran inside the house, and returned in a few seconds with a large flask of water and a
fat, round *bollo*, wrapped in a paper napkin. She handed
these to Rosales and said, "*Adiós, abuelo*, grandfather.
*Vaya con Dios.*" Rosales, fingers crossed, nodded to her,
and the truck set off out of Casas Ibáñez.

Mostly, now, he slept, as Manolo's truck rattled along
through the cool evening toward Albacete. The pills he
had taken before leaving Casas Ibáñez must have contained some sort of opiate, he suspected, because he felt
when awake nothing more than a mild kind of euphoria,
and was content to lie as he was, face up to the night sky
full of stars, dreaming of his boyhood in the southern
mountains.

Vaguely, he regretted not being alert enough to observe Albacete as they passed through it. Here he had

spent a couple of good months during the war, after his convalescence in Valencia. The Anarchist militia with which he had fought since the siege of Ronda in 1936 had been gathered there, to be incorporated into Enrique Lister's famous Fifth Regiment, as a part of the regular Republican army. Though some of his fellow militiamen were, as ardent members of the FAI, the Anarchist Secret Society, resentful of being turned into members of a Communist-led regiment, this change was welcome to Rosales. The Anarchists were good fighters when they chose to be; but by both temperament and ideology they resisted being led, much preferring to enter or withdraw from combat as the mood struck them. Rosales admired this sort of aggressive independence, but he was intelligent enough, even at seventeen, to realize that the rebel army was not going to be defeated by bands of militia who organized their campaigns by caprice. So he had traded in with willingness his Anarchist costume— *mono*, neckerchief, and tassled cap—for the clumsy brown uniform of the Fifth Regiment, and passed his days at their camp near Albacete happily learning close-order drill, the proper conduct of a platoon, company, and battalion in situations of offense and defense, and the handling of weapons. Mentally, he resisted only the political indoctrination by the commissars, one of whom was assigned to each company of Lister's regiment. He attended the required lectures, and tried to answer correctly the questions put to his class by the commissar; but for him all this was only words, not much different really from the religious instruction he had suffered, with the same silent cynicism, in Poqueira.

For the rest of it, he had made a model soldier—and a

privileged one, at that: His reputation as El Lobo, the youth who had fought with such distinction at Ronda and at Málaga, still clung to him. In and around Albacete were camps full of the newly arrived International Brigades, and Rosales heard many tales of their often bizarre conduct—companies full of eager but untrained *extranjeros* from God knows where, led by men who sometimes had military experience, but who were more often given positions of authority because of mere ideological enthusiasm. Their companies were infiltrated with spies from Russian secret services, informers who could, if they chose, precipitate midnight trials and executions at dawn of men whose only fault might be ignorance of party doctrine. From these dangerous adventurers he had, as the young *cabo* called El Lobo, kept apart. What he wanted to learn was how to fight in a real army; and membership in Lister's Fifth Regiment gave him all he needed in the sort of instruction he most desired. Albacete itself had not been much of a place—a flat and characterless city, totally devoid of *ambiente*, known only for its chief industry, the manufacture of knives—but his months there had been happy ones, and he wished now that he were strong enough to sit up in the back of Manolo's truck and look around him as they drove through it. But for the time being, at least, he was unable even to lift his head from the blanket roll that was serving as his pillow. They drove through Albacete without stopping, and Rosales, dreaming away in the rear of the truck, never saw it.

When daylight awoke him next, they were already far along on the road south to Úbeda. The effect of the pills was wearing off, his great thirst had returned, and he knew that he must make Manolo stop the truck to let him lower his trousers and squat for a few minutes in the ditch that ran along the side of the road. With the flask of water the lawyer's sister had given him, he reached behind him and rapped on the glass window at the rear of the cab. Manolo turned around; Rosales pointed to the roadside, then turned his thumb downward. The truck stopped, and Rosales tried to lift himself back to the tailgate, but was still too weak to do more than thrash about on the truck's floor. Manolo appeared at the tailgate, lowered it, and reached in to grab Rosales's feet. He pulled strongly once, and the sick man came sliding out onto the shoulder of the road. Manolo caught him before he hit the ground, and, putting Rosales's arm over his shoulders, walked him over to the ditch.

"Thank you," said Rosales, "I can help myself from this point." He made himself stand while Manolo walked back to the truck, then lowered his trousers and squatted in the ditch. When he had finished, he wiped himself with clumps of grass that were growing within reach of his hands, then stood again, pulling up his trousers as he did so. *Good enough: I am at least still man enough to shit without help.* But when he tried to walk back to the truck, his knees buckled and he sat down on the shoulder of the road, so that Manolo had to return to his side, and lift him back into his makeshift bed. "Take it slow, *viejo*," Manolo said. "Drink something if you can, and chew on a piece of that *bollo* there. An old man as knocked out as you has got to take care of himself. I can't have you dying on me out here, can I?" Clearly, thought Rosales, this Manolo is not a bad man; he's only a little preoccupied. And this transporting of a smelly old man cannot be any great pleasure for him, especially if that smelly old man looks as if he might die any moment. He drank a little of the wine in his *bota*—not much left, he noticed—and ate half of the *bollo*. No nausea, yet, he thought. That's a good sign, surely. He fell asleep again as the truck resumed its journey toward Andalucía.

Some time later, he awoke to find Manolo looking down at him over the side of the truck. When he saw that Rosales's eyes were open, he asked, in a friendly enough manner, "How are we now, *abuelo?* Still with us?"

"Still here," Rosales smiled. "Are we in Jaén?"

"*Hombre*, no," answered Manolo. "In Alcaraz, only. I thought I'd stop long enough here to buy gas, and to get a little breakfast. We're by a café. Can I bring you out something?"

"If you would have them fill this for me," Rosales said, holding the *bota* out to Manolo, "and perhaps a little bread or cheese. I'll pay you, of course."

"Of course, *viejo*. I'll just be a moment."

Rosales lay dozing in the morning sun, then, more confident every hour that he would recover. If they were already in Alcaraz, they'd surely be in Úbeda by evening, and on the Jaén road by dark. From there it would be only a day's walk to Granada, where he could take the bus that went each day or so up into the Alpujarras. He'd be in Poqueira well before *Navidad*, without doubt.

"Hey, *hombre*, come look at this!" a voice shouted quite close to him. Startled, he lifted his head off his blanket roll and looked toward the sound. A young man was standing by the truck, beckoning to someone. In a matter of seconds, Rosales and the truck were surrounded by a pack of men, women, and even children, who had to climb on the bumpers to look inside. "Holy Mother," someone said, "what is this truck? A hearse? Look what it contains."

"It's alive," someone else said. "Look at its eyes." Rosales tried to sit up, to speak to these gawkers. "Get away," he croaked. "Leave me in peace, *sinvergüenzas*."

"It speaks!" exclaimed a woman merrily. "And look at the way it rolls its eyes!"

"Is it one of the Three Kings, Mama?" asked a little girl. General merriment, as the crowd grew. "Well, it might be," insisted the child. "Look at his beard." The laughter increased.

Rosales's head felt clearer than it had since he had become ill. Shaking more from rage than from fever, he sat up, and tried to grab the throat of the man who had discovered him. The man slapped his hand away, laughing. Another man leaned in quite close to Rosales and said, mockingly, "Give us your blessing, San Nicolás." Rosales spat into the man's face, then fell back, snarling and panting. He reached for the wire necklace that carried his bayonet, but his fingers were too unsteady for him to draw it over his head.

"It's angry," someone said. "Maybe it hasn't been fed today."

"Let someone bring him some *tapas*," a woman's voice said. "See if they have any chicken heads in the café."

Rosales turned onto his belly, then lifted himself slowly to a kneeling position, with his head hanging below his shoulders. All right, God I've never prayed to, he said silently; if you exist, give me strength to kill one of these vultures, at least. As he knelt there, waiting for the strength to murder, the crowd suddenly began falling back. He heard the voice of Manolo nearby. "Come on," the voice said, "what kind of people are there in the *pueblo* of Alcaraz? This is a sick old man, an *abuelo* who is trying to reach his home in Andalucía for the holidays. Leave him alone. What are you trying to do, attract the *policía?*"

"Where there is shit, there come the flies," said a voice, still full of laughter.

"And you're the shit, and your mothers, and your daughters," Rosales tried to shout. "I would not let my hog fuck the women of this town, for pride and fear of disease. What kind of *maricones* are you to mock a man so? I shit in the mouths of your mothers, I—"

"Stop it, *viejo*," said Manolo. "Save your strength. The show is over. Stop yelling before *you* bring the *policía*, and I have to explain what you're doing in the back of my truck." Rosales stopped his tirade, and realized that the other voices had ceased. He breathed deeply, and let himself fall over on his side. He felt blinded by shame. *That this should happen to me*. He did not even notice when Manolo put beside his head the refilled *bota* and a package of various sorts of food.

As the truck moved along toward Úbeda, Rosales realized that there must never again be the chance for such humiliating scenes as the one in Alcaraz. Before he could deal with humans again, he must have his strength back. The next time Manolo stopped the truck, he would es-

148

cape into the hills, and stay there until he was himself again, no matter how many days it took. He drank for several seconds from the *bota*, ate the rest of the now-stale *bollo* the sister had given him, and lay back with his new package of food under his arm. He wedged two hundred of his remaining pesetas under a block of wood that lay near his blanket roll, then composed himself to sleep again until he saw an opportunity to escape.

The moment came an hour or so later, when Manolo stopped the truck again. He walked back to look down once more at Rosales. "Well, *viejo*," he said. "Just ahead lies the *pueblo* of Puente de Génave. I'd like to stop there for a quick coffee. Can I count on your lying still, and not creating a scene such as the one we went through in Alcaraz?"

Rosales looked up at Manolo. "I created no scene back there, except by lying still, allowing myself to be gawked at by that filthy *canalla*. What else was I to have done?" He paused to regain his breath. "Look: Why don't you leave the truck on the edge of town, away from people's eyes, and walk in to your café? No one will bother me here, nor even see me. That way there will be no scenes, and I can rest in peace."

Manolo thought a moment, then nodded at Rosales. "All right," he said. "I'll only be a few minutes. Let me pull a few meters along on a side road, away from the sight of anyone who might pass by. I'll leave you here alone. But for the love of God, if anyone approaches the truck, see if you can contrive to appear asleep. I don't want to have to come running back to rescue the good people of this village from your ferocity." He smiled at Rosales, tapped him on the shoulder, and returned to the driver's seat of the truck. Moments later he turned off the highway onto a dirt road that was hardly more than a path across a field, and parked. He looked back at his passenger, winked at him, then set off for the village.

Rosales counted to a hundred, then pulled himself to his knees. Manolo was nowhere in sight. Around him on all sides were tall hills covered with thyme and lavender. They appeared to be parked beside the town's garbage dump, tall mounds of refuse partially covered with earth and overgrown with weeds. Beside the dump was a shallow *barranco* that wandered upward. Rosales's eyes followed it all the way to the top of the highest hill above the town, where, in sharp outline against the clear blue sky, was a ruined *castillo*, an old fortress that looked from this distance to be abandoned. "*¡Qué buena suerte!*": the perfect hiding place. It was perhaps only a kilometer away, but the hill on which the *castillo* stood was steep and high—an easy ten-minute climb for El Lobo, but an obstacle of almost insuperable difficulty for the emaciated Rosales. Still, he thought, eyeing the fortified walls with their crenelations that looked like rotting teeth, the several cylindrical towers that rose up in the midst of the battlements, and the crumbling keep that towered above the whole fortress, this is where I must go. The *castillo* looked as though no human had been near it for centuries, perhaps not since Christians and *moros* had fought over it in the campaigns of the *Reconquista* he had learned about in school. There it stood, its limestone bricks gleaming red in the midday sun; and he knew he must reach it.

He tossed the blanket roll and the package of food over

the side of the truck, hung the *bota* over his shoulder, and, cradling the still-unused flask of water under one arm, lifted his legs with painful slowness over the side of the truck that faced away from the road. He fell to the earth, and lay there panting for a moment, until his head cleared. Then, on all fours, he moved around beside the truck collecting his possessions and arranging them about his body so that he could manage their transportation. He rested a final moment, then crawled to the base of the *barranco*. It was filled with sharp rocks, and everywhere were brambles that he would need to avoid in his ascent. Looking up at the fortress, he paused for a second, fighting the urge to lie still, to rest. *Get up, you great disgrace.* He stood. When he did not fall, he took a deep breath, glanced back at the truck, and began his climb up the *barranco*.

For perhaps a hundred meters he trudged upward, walking carefully over the rocky bed of the gulley: To fall down now, before he was out of sight of Manolo's truck, might be to fail in his escape. The *castillo* loomed above him, deceptively close in the pure, thin air. Blackness began to obscure his peripheral vision—a prelude to fainting, he knew. Still he walked on, until his knees began to tremble so that he had to kneel and lower his head onto the earth. The sandy soil was warm, and the strong odor of thyme helped to revive him. He drank a little water from his flask, then got to his feet again. When he turned to look behind him, he could no longer see the truck. To the south was Puente de Génave spread out below him, a small village made up mostly of one-story buildings with white walls and tawny, tiled roofs. The church, an ugly gray box of a building, squatted in the center of the town. The air was so clear that even at this distance Rosales could see the pigeons that hovered around its belfry.

Another half hour, and he was lying in the shadow cast by the walls of the fortress. Some time back he had heard a voice far beneath him: Manolo, surely, returned from the town and calling out for him. Then the sound of the truck's motor reached him, and he knew he could relax. Manolo had given up his search (probably not much of a search at that, Rosales smiled to himself), and headed back toward Casas Ibáñez. He felt something like gratitude toward the young man, and his sense of honor made him hope that Manolo would find his two hundred pesetas under the block of wood, and not think that he had been cheated. He began to feel chilled in the shadows of the fortress. His heart leapt: *The southern sun: in its light one baked, but in shadow one froze.* Rosales forced himself to his feet to look for a way through the walls into the inner court. There would be no difficulty in this: Openings gaped at every few paces; and, following a trail of sheep droppings, he crawled over a mound of fallen stones and entered the heart of the *castillo*.

It was as quiet and empty as he had hoped. He propped himself against a wall that was warmed by the sun, and looked around the court for signs of human presence. Here and there were empty food cans, long since rusted. In one corner was a small circle of stones, with a few charred pieces of wood still in it. Shepherds come here, he thought; but probably only to allow their flock to graze on the grass of the courtyard, and not to stay for long. And, judging from the length of the grass, no sheep had been here for weeks. He took a long drink from his flask of water, and fell asleep.

Awakening when the shadows of late afternoon fell across the wall against which he was propped, Rosales resolved to explore the interior of the *castillo*, to find a place of both security and comfort where he could set up housekeeping until his strength returned sufficiently for him to resume his journey. He needed a room, or at least a niche, above ground level. *For these are the foothills of the Sierra Morena, after all, where there might be wolves.* It had to be where the morning sun would strike it early, to take away the chill he knew the night would bring; and it had to be near an exit from the fortress that would allow him to escape quickly in the event of some shepherd's intrusion.

At the entrance to the keep he found what he wanted: a dark, shallow entryway opening to the east, elevated three or four steps above the level of the court. Only a couple of meters from the wall of the keep was a small break in the battlements through which he could easily crawl if he had to. The reserves of strength that had let him make his escape from Manolo and his truck were nearly gone now; and, encumbered as he was by his belongings, he needed the best part of an hour to crawl to the hiding place he had chosen. Only occasionally did he feel the cramps and the nausea, but any real exertion of energy instantly brought back the dizziness and the blackening vision, forcing him to lie flat in the grass for long minutes. By the time he was stretched out on his blanket, which he had spread on the cold stone floor of the entryway, there was almost no light left. He knew he should eat, but the prospect of opening the packet of food Manolo had given him made him sick at the thought. He drank more water, pulled a corner of the blanket over his body, and lay back. Tomorrow he would eat, hungry or not. Now he would sleep. Occasionally the evening breeze brought faint sounds from the village far below him, and once he thought he heard a sheep bell in the distant hills. He might have been alone in the world. When he could no longer see the ragged outline of the *castillo's* walls against the night sky, he slept, feeling more secure than he had since leaving the Pyrenees.

The morning brought no sun. Rosales awoke shivering, and crawled to the edge of the entryway to look at the sky. It was full of dark clouds, moving rapidly past him in a southerly direction. Wind whistled through the breaches in the fortress wall. As he knelt there, with his face turned upward, he felt an occasional spatter of cold rain. For a moment he experienced his *campesino's* ingrained detestation of being caught out in a storm, but as he became more awake he realized that the rain would be a blessing to him, even if it should turn to snow: No one from Puente de Génave would be walking in the hills today, and he could spend the next few hours resting, and perhaps teaching a little discipline to his belly and bowels. "Fifty-four," he said aloud, and thought: Where I come from, a strong man lives to eighty. He was tired of this *viejo* business. He was no old man, and would not be one for many years. Crawling back to his shelter in the entryway, he pictured his old age as it should be in Poqueira.

In the morning he would drink his *café con leche* and eat some bread with jam in the kitchen, brought to him by Ana María, his daughters, and his daughters-in-law. He would discuss the day's work to be done by the younger men of the family, who would listen deferentially to his advice. At eleven he would visit his favorite café, and sit on the terrace with his friends, drinking a little wine and discussing crops, politics, and the decadence of the young. At one o'clock his grandchildren would come for him, to escort him home for lunch. He would sit at the head of the table in the kitchen, and dispense wisdom to his family. Then would come the long siesta, until perhaps five o'clock, after which he would slowly climb up the steep path to the café, and join his friends for *montilla*, dominoes, and more discussion. At eight, his grandchildren would call again for him, and bring him down to supper: perhaps a bit of *tortilla* and a vegetable or two. He and his sons would talk until bedtime, as the women cleaned up and put the children to bed. By ten he himself would be in his own bed, full of satisfaction for a day well and decorously filled, Ana María's warm body beside him. *This* was how a man should grow old; and Rosales promised himself now, as the rain began to pour down on the ruined *castillo* and he sat huddled in his filthy clothes in the crumbling entryway, that he would soon reclaim for himself as much of his rightful old age as he could. That he had no idea of whether he had any relatives left in his own *pueblo* did not, at the moment, concern him much. Let him only reach Poqueira, and things would arrange themselves in the desired order.

* * *

For now, he had to eat, hungry or not. After much fumbling, he succeeded in opening his package of food. Manolo had been generous and thoughtful, he discovered: Once he had pulled the string from around the package, it opened to reveal a pair of oranges; some slices of *serrano* ham, from his own region; two tins of anchovies; and a pair of sugared rolls. These last he ate at once, washing them down with wine from his *bota*. He felt stronger immediately. I am not old, he told himself, only a little ill and perhaps dirtier than I ought to be. Wrapping himself in his blanket, he slept for another few hours.

The rain had not ceased when he next awoke. With no sun to serve as his clock, he could not tell how long he had slept; but there was still enough light for him to begin an examination of his clothes. They would not do, he saw immediately: Cold or no cold, illness or no illness, some laundering must be done. He pulled off his socks, trousers, and shirt as he had done in the Pyrenees, took a deep breath, and, full of distaste for the feel of rain on his naked body, dragged all his clothes except for his vinyl jacket out onto the grass of the courtyard, where he spread them out to soak. He crawled back into his hiding pace, zipped himself into his jacket, wrapped the blanket around his legs and midsection, and waited for the rain to wash away the days of filth and smell of sickness from his clothes. To warm himself while he waited, he smoked the last of the American's cigarettes, and, as an afterthought, set fire to the thin paper in which his food had been wrapped. It burned for perhaps ten seconds, and warmed him not at all. The bayonet felt icy against his skin. He lifted the wire necklace over his head, and laid the bayonet by his side, after first drying the blade off with the blanket to prevent rust.

Fortunately, the rain lifted at nightfall, and the moon came out, bringing an eerie light to the courtyard and the battlements that surrounded it. A perfect night for ghosts, he thought, imagining the shades of countless dark *moros*, dancing in their white *djellabahs* on the parapets of the *castillo*. For the first time since the war, Rosales crossed himself.

He was much too cold and wet to sleep, and cursed himself for his vanity: Here he was, ill and in hiding in strange terrain, with no fire to warm him, and clad only in a beret, a flimsy jacket, and a blanket that did more to hold in the dampness than to keep it out. Why should he have worried about the state of his clothes? He took some small pleasure in the thought that old Inés was not here to see him in such a ridiculous condition, and drank more wine from his *bota*. With luck, he told himself, the morning sun would quickly dry his clothes, and he could be on his way by noon. For now, there was nothing to do but shiver and try to think of better times. The beach at Valencia, for instance. Finally, in spite of the cold and the dampness, Rosales slept.

The sun was already well above the horizon when he awoke. He drank the last of the water in the flask the ugly sister had given him and, using the sharp point of the bayonet, peeled one of the oranges, taking great care to lose none of its juice. Whatever his disease had been, it was—in spite of his having gone to sleep half soaked from the rain—clearly a thing of the past. His belly rumbled with healthy hunger. He folded a large piece of ham, thrust it into his mouth, and chewed it rapidly. He belched, full of contentment. As always in the south, dryness returned soon after the storm. He could still see droplets of water on the grass of the courtyard, but nowhere else around him were there any other signs that the day before had been stormy. He knew that by midday at the latest his clothes would be dry enough to wear again, and decided to try out his strength by a brief tour of the fortress.

His legs still had little of their old resiliency, but they no longer trembled when he walked. Slowly and carefully, he climbed the remnants of a stairway that wound around the keep. From the top of the tower he could see, far to the west, the gray outlines of the Sierra Morena. Somewhere over there was Jaén, the northernmost city of Andalucía. Below him, standing out with such sharpness that he could discern individual tiles on the roofs of the houses, was Puente de Génave. The people of the village were moving about busily, looking from here like a large colony of black ants. From time to time he could hear the sounds of automobiles, and looked for the road leading westward out of the town. There it was, bordered by tall plane trees, wandering through the hills toward Úbeda, past more enormous *fincas*, estates, of olive and almond groves. The amount of irrigation necessary to give water to such groves must be, he thought, prodigious, because rains like yesterday's were rare, even at this time of year, and moisture would not linger very long in the sandy, near-sterile soil of the steppes. Where there were no groves, the terrain below him was like a desert: sand, clay, and limestone, heavily eroded in many places into deep *barrancos* like the one he had ascended day before yesterday. Even the Río Génave, curling along beside the north edge of the town, was hardly more than a trickle. Briefly, he thought of the lushness of southern France, and recalled how cloying, how *feminine* it had always seemed to him. *This* was a country for men whose pride was founded in adversity, men who knew how to endure. *"Aquí estoy yo": Here am I, Here I stand, where I belong, as a man in charge of himself, needing nothing, wanting nothing.* And so he was, standing there—dressed only in his beret, his jacket, and another man's shoes. He was Sebastián Rosales, *hidalgo*, master—for the moment—of this *castillo*, and of all the terrain below him.

In this mood of exaltation, he walked down the steps of the tower, stumbling only once in his descent, to the courtyard. It was time to dress himself in his newly clean clothes, pack up, and be on his way. His shirt, trousers, and socks were quite dry by now, even warm. As he put them on, he thought of how he could best reach the road from Jaén to Granada. He was still too weak to count on covering much distance by walking, not today anyway. Though he dreaded the idea of more rides with strangers, kind or unkind, he knew that his best chance lay in climbing through these hills north of Puente de Génave, then descending onto the road beyond the town, where he might find a truck or wagon to carry him farther along his way.

But walking in the rarefied air of the hills was more difficult than Rosales expected. Every fifteen minutes or so he had to stop, lean over, and wait until his breathing returned to normal. Then he would continue, careful always to keep the town off his left shoulder, until he was quite sure he was well past its outskirts. No more humiliating encounters with filling-station pimps, he warned himself. After an hour's walking, he turned down toward the road, reached it, and sat down upon his blanket roll to wait for a ride. Here, in the more hospitable south, he did not have to wait long. A gasoline truck stopped, a long face topped by a beret peered out at him, and a voice said, full of the lilt of Andalucía, "*¿Adónde vas, amigo?*"

"Jaén," Rosales answered, smiling.

"Will Úbeda help?" the driver asked.

"Anything will help," said Rosales, and pulled himself into the cab.

An hour later he was in Úbeda; and with two more rides, by early evening he was standing on the highway just south of Jaén, facing toward Granada. The only thing to mar his happiness at such rapid progress was that the road seemed as full of various kinds of police as the coast road near Castellón had been, days before. As he stood in the doorway of a café, eating a hard-boiled egg and drinking a bottle of San Miguel beer, he counted four green Land Rovers, two personnel carriers full of political police in their gray uniforms, and three pairs of *Guardias Civiles* on motorcycles. In addition to these, there was a small convoy of army trucks, each containing soldiers wearing the German helmets that were a holdover from the Civil War. He could not guess the reason for activity, unless perhaps there was to be a parade in Granada honoring *Navidad*.

As he was draining the last of his beer from the bottle,

a large maroon automobile of great elegance came to a halt beside the café, and a young man dressed in gray flannel trousers, short suede boots, and a leather jacket leapt from the driver's seat and pushed past him into the café, not bothering to speak. In the passenger's seat was a young woman of real beauty, wearing a jacket of some sort of fur. She was lying back against the seat, her long black hair spread around the headrest. Her eyes, Rosales saw, were closed, and she was smiling faintly. As the young man, carrying in his hand a bottle of *Ciento-Tres* brandy, brushed by him on his way out, Rosales, on impulse, and expecting to be refused, said to him: "I go to Granada, *señor*. Is there room for me with you?"

"No," answered the young man, not even looking back at Rosales. Evidently, he was in a great hurry. Rosales shrugged—he hadn't really been expecting much, here—when the girl opened her eyes, looked at him, then turned to the young man, who was already beside her in the car, ready to turn on the ignition. "Let him come with us, Claudio. We have room for him, and he might be fun. More fun than you, anyway."

Claudio looked at Rosales, then at the girl. "Shit," he said, without much emphasis. Then: "Get in, *barbudo*," bearded one, "but quickly. A woman this expensive requires lots of playthings." The girl smiled, and closed her eyes again. Rosales climbed into the small rear of the sleek automobile (surely it could not be Spanish, he thought, in spite of the Madrid license plates he had noticed as the car had pulled up beside him; perhaps English, or Italian) and moved his rough hands over the smooth leather of the seats. *Hombre*, he told himself, you must be riding with nobility. On the seat beside him was a suitcase of tan leather, on which were two tennis racquets, things he had seen only in illustrations in the fashion magazines his daughters had brought to his home in Cambó.

Once he had this formidable vehicle hurtling down the highway at a speed that left Rosales nearly breathless, hanging on tightly to the straps that hung above the rear doors, the young man spun open the top of the brandy bottle with one hand, lifted it to his mouth for a long moment, then passed it to the girl. She drank from the bottle, too. Rosales was shocked. *Women do not drink, except perhaps for a little sherry and wine with meals.* Then she turned in the seat and offered the bottle to Rosales. He raised one hand in polite refusal. "Thank you, *señora*," he said, "but I have recently been ill, and should not take anything strong."

"Come on, don Graybeard," the girl smiled. "This settles one's stomach. This settles everything, in fact. Right, Claudio?" Claudio said nothing, his glum face fixed on the road ahead of them. When the girl persisted, Rosales took a large swallow from the bottle, and was immediately queasy. "*Gracias, señora*," he gasped, hoping that he would not disgrace himself by becoming sick.

"It's *señorita*," the girl said, with a glance at Claudio. "But to you I am Isabelita. And this hero, this movie star of a man beside me, is Claudio. Doesn't he look like a movie star?"

"I am sure he does, *señorita*, though I have never seen one—or a movie either, as far as that goes—not for the last thirty years, anyway." Claudio still said nothing. At this rate, Rosales thought nervously, we'll be in Granada by suppertime, if this movie star doesn't kill us first.

Why, he wondered, was Claudio tolerating the obvious mockery of this girl? In the Alpujarras, in the rare instances when a girl spoke so to her mate, she could expect to be soundly beaten. Evidently, the rich and noble of the world had different customs.

The girl turned on the radio of the car, and Rosales was forced to listen to more of the same cacophonous hideousness, the modern *yé-yé* music, that he had heard in the café in Casas Ibáñez. She turned the volume up full, and began to make dancing motions, swinging about in the car seat.

Claudio reached over and snapped off the sound, then returned his gloved hand to the polished wooden steering wheel of the car. "*Puta*," he muttered to the girl: Cunt. Rosales blinked his eyes in consternation. Could a man really call his woman such a name? But Isabelita only laughed.

To distract the pair from what must surely erupt into a vicious fight, Rosales cleared his throat and asked politely, "Might you be going for your vacations on the south coast? I have noticed these things here, which are for the *tenis*, no?"

The girl turned in her seat so that, propped up on her knees, she could peer back at Rosales. Her eyes were black, and her skin of a purity that he had never seen, except in infants. She wore a great deal of makeup, however.

Very solemnly, she spoke to Rosales, "Do you smoke, don Graybeard?"

"Of course, *señorita*. What man does not smoke?"

"Of course. Shall we offer don Graybeard a *porro*, Claudio?"

163

"Idiot," spat Claudio. "The roads full of cops, all the country in an uproar, and you want to get out a joint. Nothing of that, do you hear? *Nothing*, until we reach Marbella."

Still hoping to calm things down (if this madman loses his temper, we'll surely crash, he thought), Rosales said, "I have noticed that it is as you say, *señor:* The *policía* are everywhere on the road today. Is there some special event taking place?"

At this, even Claudio smiled; and Isabelita laughed gaily. "You haven't heard anything about what happened in Madrid day before yesterday, *viejo?*" Claudio asked.

"What goes on in cities has never been any concern of mine, *señor*."

"It may be now," Claudio smiled grimly. "The police you have seen are searching every quarter of the country for a bunch of assassins. Do you know who Admiral Carrero-Blanco is? Or was, rather?"

The name meant nothing to Rosales, but the idea of a widespread police search for any reason at all filled him with alarm. He shook his head.

"Carrero-Blanco," explained Claudio, his eyes fixing on Rosales in the rear-view mirror for an instant, "was Franco's number-two boy, his favorite, the man who was to have taken over the reins after the *Caudillo's* death. Except that day before yesterday, in the middle of Madrid, someone set off a bomb beneath the street under his staff car, as he was leaving Mass."

Isabelita giggled. "The old *cabrón* was sitting in the back of his car in his blue uniform, and got blown three hundred meters into the air, right over the cathedral and onto the roof of an apartment building. The fastest *ascención* since the Blessed Virgin's, it was. I wish I'd seen it, don't you, Claudio?"

"I wish you'd drink yourself to sleep, and shut up until Marbella," said Claudio. "Can you imagine the trouble this is going to cause, from the top on down? Goddamn Basques."

"Was it the Basques who did it, *señor?*" asked Rosales. If so, he wondered, then why weren't the police chasing around in the Vascongadas after the assassins, instead of running around down here in Andalucía?

"The Basques *say* they did it, and one assumes, since they're so clever, that the killers are halfway across the Pyrenees by now. But maybe the police figure that the Basques are clever enough to run south, not north. For all we know, they're already sitting in the Sierra Nevada, happy and safe as pigs." Claudio glanced back at Rosales. "*Now* do you understand about the *policía, hombre?* And where have *you* been hiding out, that you hadn't heard about this monstrous thing?"

Isabelita, still on her knees looking over the back of her seat at Rosales, the brandy bottle in one of her hands, said somberly to Claudio, "*I* think this is the man they're after, Claudito. Doesn't he look like an assassin to you? To me he looks *exactly* like an assassin."

"I have never been in Madrid, *señorita,*" Rosales protested, only partially convinced that the girl was joking. "I have been in La Mancha, in the hills, for the past week. And I am no assassin."

"Assassin," the girl repeated. "Look at him, Claudio, look at that face. Don Graybeard, you're a killer if I ever saw one. If I put my hand back to you, would you bite it?" As if afraid, she slowly stretched out her hand toward Rosales's mouth, a look of great apprehension on her lovely face.

Her fingers just touched his beard, as Rosales tried to draw his head back, when Claudio yelled, "Hang on!" and pressed his foot on the brake. The car swerved, skidded, and finally came to a halt not ten meters from a wooden barrier that had been thrown across the road. Lights flashed on, and Rosales, momentarily blinded by the glare, was aware of the figures of several men approaching the car. Operating purely on reflex action, he threw open the left rear door, dove out of the car onto the road, and, doubled over, ran in zigzag fashion for the shelter of a pine forest that began almost at road's edge.

"Halt!" he heard a voice cry once. Then a submachine gun somewhere behind him began firing, well to the left of the direction in which he was running through the woods. He threw himself to the ground, as bullets struck the trees just over his head. He hesitated a second, then leapt to his feet and ran to the left. Now the bullets—and surely more than one gun was firing, now—were off to his right. He ran on, falling, picking himself up, and dodging through the pines until his breath began giving out. After perhaps two minutes, the firing stopped. Had Claudio convinced the police that Rosales was no assassin, but simply an old peasant? Or were the police now tracking him through the forest, deliberately holding fire? He looked to his left: A few hundred meters across a clearing was a large *pantano*, a dammed-up lake. No escape that way: The moon was almost full, and he'd be as visible as in daylight. He turned to the east, and began running, more slowly now,

166

careful to preserve what energy he had left. There was no more firing; and, when he paused to rest, and held his breath, he could hear no sounds of men coming behind him. He began to walk, still eastward.

He crossed a footbridge over a small canal, and found himself on a dirt road that seemed to curve slowly to the southeast. All right, he thought. Not even the *Guardia* would be stupid enough to set a barrier across this burro's path. *I'll follow it where it takes me, as long as it goes south.*

The road did go south, fifteen kilometers through a series of small and dismal towns with gravel streets, shuttered windows, and no character at all. Even their Moorish names were ugly to him: Güevéjar, Nívar, Alfacar, Víznar—the kinds of places, he thought wryly, where the village idiot was elected *alcalde*, and governed well. But the road through them took him generally southward, so he continued on. By midnight he had reached the northern limits of Granada. Far beyond the hills of the city he could see, white in the light of the moon, the snow-covered peaks of the Sierra Nevada, the highest mountains in Spain. And just beyond them lay the towns of the Alpujarras. The surge of adrenaline that had carried him this far had left him as weak now as he had been when he reached the *castillo* above Puente de Génave, but exhilaration still filled him at the sight of these mountains. One night in Granada, a long and bumpy bus ride toward the coast, and he'd be home.

What could one do for the night in Granada? He followed the highway that ran around the northern edge of the city, saw a sign to the right pointing to something called the Albaicín, and descended into a labyrinthine network of narrow streets, windows covered with iron grills, and the stench that comes only from hundreds of years of poor people living too close to one another. This was not the Granada, so full of *gracia*, that he remembered from the one summer day, long ago, when his father had taken him there for market day. In the Granada he remembered, one could breathe, but here! Rosales's quick nose took in the smells of urine, shit of several varieties, sweat, garlic and rancid olive oil, and small animals that had been dead for some time. Even though it was well after midnight, the streets of the Albaicín were clogged with shouting men, women, and children. As he stood in the corner of a cobblestone *placeta*, he watched a group of large pink tourists being hounded up a street toward their bus by packs of small, fat women and slight, thin young men. The complexions of the pursuers were of the dusty hue that Rosales recognized as belonging to gypsies. So that's what this Albaicín was, he thought: a *barrio gitano*, a gypsy quarter. *No wonder there is all this noise, and all this filth.*

In each of the Alpujarreño *pueblos* there had been one or two gypsy families, and he had been taught from childhood that wherever there was theft or violence, the gypsies were sure to be around. They were all beggars, too, artful and ironic. But they had a sense of honor that was keener even than that of the "true" Spaniards who lived in the villages. A gypsy man would kill without forethought or remorse anyone who damaged—or even threatened to damage—the purity of one of his women.

So now Rosales watched, half amused and half appalled by the manner in which these gypsies alternately whined over and bullied these Germans, or whatever they were, who were trying to board their bus without losing their cameras and wallets. He laughed, remembering the gypsies who had fought in the militia with him during the war. When they chose to kill, they had killed with a cold-blooded ease that amazed him; when they chose to run, they had run in utter abandon, flinging down their weapons and deserting their comrades as they went. Altogether, he thought, an amusing and dangerous people. These he would not choose as his company for the night.

But there was something compelling about this Albaicín, something that started him off ever further into its depths. For one thing, there was genuine merriment here, once one got away from the streets that were apparently set aside for the fleecing of tourists. For the first time since returning to Spain, he heard guitars, and the clacking of *castañuelas*, coming from behind the white-washed walls that shielded patios from the filth of the street. People were singing, people were drinking, people were laughing. Bands of dark-eyed young girls in short dresses and lace shawls were walking through the streets, ignoring the December chill and exchanging ribald insults with the young men who pursued them. By no means were all of these people gypsies, either: Many were true *andaluces* like himself, speaking with his accent, and lacking only his fundamental seriousness. As tired as he was, he would have liked to join in the fun, to drink a little wine and hear a little music; but people seemed to shy away from him, sobering momentarily into something like silence as he passed by. Was it simply that these people of the Albaicín were a closed community, who would not open their activities to include any outsider, even if he were another *andaluz;* or was there something special about him, something that repelled these lively people? Ah, well. He shrugged. To all of these rejoicers I must look like a ghost, and a dirty old one at that. But this will pass; it is only the misfortune of a few days.

Following the sound of the music, he turned into a small street that seemed to end in darkness a few meters along. He stopped quickly. He sensed that he was not alone. Moving slowly, as if entering a cave, he felt his way across the cobblestones, one hand held before him against the darkness. Someone struck a match, illuminating the narrowness of the alley. The light blinded him momentarily. It was as if they had been waiting for him there. *All right, here it comes. This is the real thing, much worse than the* policía *on the highway from Jaén.* He stopped where he was, his whole body sending him danger signals. *Hold still: Wait for whatever it is to declare itself first.*

"*Muy buenas noches, señor.*" A young man's voice. "Could we trouble you for a cigarette?"

"*Muy buenas,*" Rosales answered, out of an old fear. "I would gladly share my cigarettes with you, but I have none." He moved only his eyes as they came closer to him.

"Then perhaps you might give us a taste from the *bota* you carry," said another voice. How many were there?

"Again, I am sorry, but there is only enough for myself."

170

"See if the *barbudo* has a little change, Barrillos," another one said, evidently speaking to the one who had asked for a cigarette. *Barrillos: that has to be a nickname. Not even a gypsy would be truly named "Pimples."*

"I have no money to speak of, *caballeros*, not enough to make a fight worthwhile," Rosales said. He could see their shapes quite close to him, now. There were at least five of them. *Like all gypsies: tough guys in groups.*

"Who talks of fighting, *viejo?*" asked Barrillos. "We talk only of a loan." His booted foot lashed out with a quickness Rosales could not counter. It hit him precisely where his ribs joined above his gut. He sat down, unable to move or breathe. While the others watched, Barrillos took the *bota* from Rosales and tossed it over his own shoulder, then reached into Rosales's pockets to see what money he might have. The young gypsy straightened up after a moment, pushed Rosales's beret over to a rakish angle on his forehead, and said, "That's it, a few *duros*, no real money." They left Rosales sitting there, and moved past him, laughing, into the lighted street from which he had entered the alleyway.

Rosales pulled himself to his feet, ignoring the sharp pain in his gut, and lifted the bayonet from around his neck. Holding it next to his side, with the blade pointing downward, he made his plan. Barrillos and his friends had turned left, uphill: He would go down this dark street, turn right, and stalk them until he found the correct place.

In fifteen minutes, turning in and out of the twisted streets of the Albaicín, he caught sight of them, standing under the bright light of another *placeta*, talking and laughing with some girls. They were passing his *bota* around, each—the girls, too—drinking from it. He stood in the darkness of a pile of rubble for perhaps half an hour, until the young men moved on. He moved with them, keeping in the shadows, waiting for his chance.

After another few moments of his stalking, two of the band separated from the others, moving back down the street. Three of the young men were left, including Barrillos, who still carried Rosales's *bota* over his shoulder. Rosales stood in the darkness of his side street, and softly called, *"Hola, Barrillos, ven acá momentito"*: Come here a second, Pimples. Barrillos heard him, and moved to the edge of the dark street. Rosales stepped forward, pressed his hand over the gypsy's mouth, swung the bayonet up into his belly, and let him fall, a look of profound surprise on his face. As he did so, the bayonet pulled free, and Rosales bent over, placed it across Barrillos's neck, and stepped on it to keep him from crying out. When he was sure the gypsy was dead, he reached down and pulled his *bota* free, then turned and walked swiftly away down the dark street, wiping the blade of the bayonet on his trousers as he went. *I am still El Lobo: No man shames me.*

How to get out of the Albaicín was a problem, especially when he had to worry about running into Barrillos's friends at any turn he took. He found that if he headed uphill wherever he could, and kept always on his right the brightly lit Moorish castle that he vaguely remembered from school was one of the architectural glories of Spain, he would move away from the heart of the Albaicín. The crowds were still thick, and he hoped that a tall, bearded man such as he would not stand out among all the others, most of whom were much shorter and certainly more prosperous-looking.

* * *

Then, quite suddenly, the urge to escape left him. The business with Barrillos had indeed reawakened something in him of the days when he was El Lobo, and not some aging fugitive. He had no money, but he still had in his jacket pockets the tins of anchovies that Manolo had bought him days ago in Casas Ibáñez. Before he ran any farther, he would eat. When he passed a tiny bar, he entered, tapped on the counter, and looked boldly around the room for the proprietor. "Look you," he said when the man came. "I have a proposition. Open one of these tins for me, and give me a half bottle of wine for the other." As an afterthought, he added, "As a favor, of course."

The proprietor, a large man, looked at Rosales for a moment, then said, "Of course." He opened one tin of the anchovies very quickly, and then hurried for a small bottle of red wine, which he uncorked with great dexterity before Rosales.

"Pour the wine into the *bota*, please," said Rosales, leaning against the bar and peering idly around the room.

"Of course," the proprietor responded. Then he added, "The *bota* is nearly empty, still. Would you like me to fill it?"

"I have no money," said Rosales. "Will an orange buy me more wine?"

"Of course, *señor*," said the man, who probably had less than no need for a week-old orange.

As he left the bar, Rosales wondered a little at the extreme politeness of the proprietor—until he looked down at his right hand and saw that he was still carrying his bayonet, and that he had as yet by no means wiped all the blood of the gypsy from its blade. That accounts for the great courtesy of the proprietor, he thought, laughing: *There is nothing like a little blood to improve people's manners*. He returned the bayonet to its place, hanging by its wire around his neck.

Eventually he found himself at the top of the Albaicín, looking across its now-dark streets to the walls and towers of the Moorish castle, still brightly lit on its hill beyond the old quarter. Wondering where he could find the place where he could get the bus south in the morning, he sauntered back along the road that circled the northern edge of Granada. He reasoned that this route would take him into the center of the city, where he could find a park to sleep in until morning. He saw a sign that pointed down a broad, paved street: CENTRO CIUDAD. Good enough: He'd follow the direction indicated, and ask directions as he needed to. The night had grown much colder, and his breath fogged before him as he walked, more than ever aware of his fatigue. He thought no longer of his recent illness, and reasoned only that a man had a right to be tired who had in one day been fired upon by police and then stabbed a gypsy to death. Well, he would find a place to rest soon, and then tomorrow there would be the long bus ride, when he could sleep in peace until he reached Poqueira.

Suddenly he stopped walking, and stood quite still at a corner, oblivious to the diminishing street noises around him. Fool, he said to himself: idiot. Are you going to take a bus tomorrow out on the main highway south?

How far would you get before you encountered another roadblock? He pictured the bus, halted in the road while a pair of *Guardias Civiles* moved down its aisle, checking papers and looking at faces. That would be the end of him, without a doubt: even if the *Guardia* should not suspect him of having blown up that admiral in Madrid, they would nonetheless by morning be on the lookout for a bearded man who had stabbed another man in Granada. *Even if the victim had been only a gypsy.*

There would be no bus for him, Rosales knew; no easy ride south to the Alpujarras. *Mierda: How was I even going to pay for the ride—offer the driver my bayonet?* As he stood on the empty street corner, it came to him that the only way home now lay straight over the Sierra Nevada, past the peaks he had seen that afternoon lifting themselves high over the city of Granada. For a moment, the enormity of the journey ahead of him filled him with something very like despair—but only for a moment. Then he straightened, gazed in the direction of the Sierra, and grinned his mirthless grin.

# Chapter 5

The streets of Granada were almost deserted now, as Rosales looked for a way out of the city that would take him across the Río Genil and into the foothills of the Sierra Nevada. He walked several blocks along the Calle de Elvira, a street that paralleled the city's Gran Vía, seeing only an occasional *sereno*, the night watchman who keeps the keys to apartment buildings, and, for a tip, admits those who return home after their building is locked up for the night. From one of these he got directions to the Carrera de Genil, which he could follow to the edge of the city. The *sereno*, an old man in a gray uniform much too large for him, laughed when Rosales asked whether there were still a muleteers' trail up into the mountains that he might follow past the peak of Veleta into the valleys of the Alpujarras.

"Come on, *hombre*," said the *sereno*, "how long have you been away?"

"Thirty-seven years, more or less," Rosales answered.

The *sereno* thought for a moment, made some computations on his fingers, then glanced knowingly at Rosales. "So, *compadre*, let me guess: You left in the early days of the war, and have stayed away since then. I don't suppose I need to ask why?"

"I have been busy elsewhere, that's why," said Rosales, too tired to be lured into conversation with the old man. "I asked about the trail through the Sierra. Is it still there?"

"Yes and no," answered the old man. "Yes, it's still there; but no, it's not a trail." He smiled toothlessly at Rosales.

Rosales refused to play. This old man was evidently what the rest of Spain believed all *andaluces* to be like: silly, given to foolish riddles, unable to give a straight answer to a straight question. "All right, old one," he said, trying to curb his impatience, "see if you can understand this. I am tired, too tired for games. I need to sleep for a couple of hours if I can find a bench in a park, and then I intend to go across the mountains. Help me, or don't help me. It's cold, and it's late. I would pay you money for the truth, but I have none. What do you say?"

"Were you in the war?" The *sereno* was still smiling. Wearily, Rosales nodded.

"On which side?"

"The wrong one, of course."

"Why do you call it the 'wrong' one?"

"Because the side that loses is always the wrong one,

*cabrón*. What game do you play now?"

Still smiling, the old *sereno* took him by the arm and pulled him closer. He winked at Rosales, laid his index finger along his thin nose, and whispered hoarsely: "Because I was a prisoner of the Nationalists for six years after the war. That mule path you talk of is a well-paved *carretera* now, reaching almost to Veleta. I know—my fellow prisoners and I built it for the greater glory of the *Generalísimo*, and for the even greater glory of *el turismo*. You will find the going easy as far as Veleta, and you will pass great hotels, ski resorts, and even a government *parador* on your way there. You can walk in style and even luxury as far as Veleta, *compadre*."

Amazed, Rosales stared at the old man. Could this be true? "And beyond Veleta, what is there?" he asked.

"Nothing, so far as I know," shrugged the *sereno*. "Probably only the old path, covered now by the winter snow. The government ran out of money, or too many prisoners starved or froze in the construction of the road, or anything. Who knows why things start or stop in this country?"

The old man might be a fool, but Rosales believed him. Perhaps I can even trust him, he thought. "All right," he said, "tomorrow I'll walk up your *carretera*, and worry about finding my own way after that. For now, where can I sleep?"

Still holding Rosales's arm, the *sereno* pulled him into the darkened entryway of an apartment building, fumbled for several minutes with the chain of keys he carried on his belt, and finally succeeded in unlocking the large door into the *foyer* of the building. "Whose army were you with, *veterano?*" he asked, guiding Rosales into the building.

"I was in the militia, first CNT, then FAI; then I was with Lister and Modesto until the end." Rosales was too tired and cold to do anything but tell the truth.

The *sereno* was happy. He threw out his chest, stood at attention, and announced: "*I* was with El Campesino, a *real* general, a man with *cojones* like this." And he spread out his arms as if to encompass a pair of watermelons. Rosales remembered the famous El Campesino as a fat, posturing ass, a joke general who believed the flattery of the Russians who really led his army, allowing him to command only nominally, for propaganda value. But he nodded to the old *sereno*, his attitude signaling great respect. "Were you perhaps at Teruel, then?" he asked.

"Was I not, *hombre?* It was a great victory for our side, and earned great honor for El Campesino. Were you there, too?"

"I was," answered Rosales, remembering no great victory or honor at Teruel for anyone. The *sereno*, very grave now, shook his hand.

"Look, *compadre:* sleep in here, on a couch, until early morning, when I go off duty. Then I'll wake you, and point out the way to the *carretera* we built." He patted Rosales on the back, winked again, and gave the old salute. Feeling foolish, Rosales returned it, clenching his fist and raising it above his head. Now at least I can sleep, he thought. This old man is too stupid to be an informer. As soon as the *sereno* had gone out and locked the door they had come through, he found a long sofa covered in plastic made to resemble cowhide, and lay out upon it, not bothering to unroll his blanket or to put his bayonet where he could use it quickly.

Perhaps three hours later, he heard the *sereno* jangling

his key ring outside the door. Rosales felt worse now than he had before sleeping. The extent of his fatigue and weakness was such, he realized, that he would need whole days and nights of rest before his old strength returned. But today he would go over the mountains, and worry about resting when he had reached Poqueira.

Still half asleep, he followed the old man (why do I think of him as an old man? Rosales wondered: He's probably not many years older than me) down the still-empty street, hardly bothering to look around him at this famous city of which he had heard so much in his childhood. In the cold dawn light, Granada was no more beautiful than Zaragoza had been: The buildings were gray and cheerless, the shop windows were shuttered, and the few people who were moving about in the streets looked as surly and disagreeable as any Aragonese.

They came to a broad boulevard, at the end of which was a fountain from which no water flowed. Down the center of the boulevard was a wide strip of sparse lawn, on which had been erected ferris wheels, merry-go-rounds, and booths where souvenirs and carnival food would be sold. "For the fiesta of *Navidad*, you know?" said the *sereno*, nudging Rosales.

By the empty fountain, the old man stopped Rosales. "Listen, *veterano;* just ahead is the Río Genil. Turn left here, and go along the Paseo for a few hundred meters, and you'll see a sign to the Sierra. It's thirty-five kilometers to Veleta, but you'll be able to get a ride easily once the day begins. There are always tourists, and the *urbanización* goes on every day it doesn't snow, so that there'll be plenty of trucks. Are you all right, now?"

Rosales had to say that no, he was not all right. "I'll tell you the truth, *amigo*," he said: "I have no money, and the work I have before me would be easier if I had a few pesetas for some coffee and perhaps a little *coñac*."

The *sereno* waved his arm at Rosales. "Forgive me for making you ask," he said, reaching for his leather change purse. He handed Rosales two twenty-five peseta coins—probably as much as he'd made in tips during the night, Rosales suspected—and looked insulted when Rosales tried to give back one of the coins. "Consider it a loan only, *amigo*. When you return to Granada, we can have a meal together. Go now to that café, and fortify yourself—and hope for no snow on the mountains."

Rosales shook the *sereno's* hand once again, regretting his harsh thoughts of the night before.

"One last thing," the old man said, as Rosales had begun to walk away. "Are you Alpujarreño, by any chance?"

"*Claro, hombre, claro que sí,*" answered Rosales eagerly. "Do you know the Alpujarras?"

"No, of course not," said the *sereno*. "Who would go there? Nor have I ever known anyone from the place. I asked only because of curiosity: One hears such strange things about the Alpujarras—how old it is, how remote, how . . . how *different* people are there. More like *moros* than *cristianos*, they say."

Rosales smiled. "All we are is people, *amigo*. We work hard, keep to ourselves, raise our families. Perhaps we do not talk so much as those from other places; but we live and die much the same as everyone else. Only quieter." The two nodded again at one another, and Rosales headed for the café the *sereno* had suggested.

After his coffee, his roll, and a glass of Fundador, he returned to the Paseo and began his long walk. A truck stopped when he waved to it, and took him several kilometers along the way, until it turned off just as the road crossed the Genil. The road upward, the one built by the *sereno* and his fellow prisoners, was steep and winding, but well-engineered. As he began to move along Rosales glanced upward from time to time. Early morning fog was close about him, and he could see no farther than the next bend in the road. Soon there was fog below him, too, and he seemed to be climbing along a road that led from nowhere into nothing. The fog was chilly, but he walked rapidly enough to keep himself warm. From time to time he would hear an automobile horn honking behind him, and would leap away from the road and hide behind one of the young pine trees that had been planted there recently, in what was apparently some sort of government plan for reforestation. If there is *urbanización* ahead, he reasoned, there will be *policía*. There could be no question of any more rides.

By midmorning, he had reached the snowline. The road was kept clear, obviously, by plows, but the hills were spackled with old and dirt-encrusted snow, and blades of ice hung from the granite rocks through which the road had been blasted. The air was much thinner, now, and Rosales often had to stop and crouch down, panting and waiting for oxygen to return to his bloodstream. Occasionally he drank a drop of wine from his *bota*.

Then the fog began to thin, and finally burnt away altogether. There, directly above him and seemingly quite close, was the peak of Veleta, a triangular piece of snow-covered rock that stood out above the lesser, more rounded mountains of the Sierra. Beyond Veleta, he knew, the muleteers' old path wound near Mulhacén, even higher than Veleta, but not so dramatic. Would the path still be there? Surely: Such things did not change. This was the top of Spain, and in a few hours he would be looking down on the green southern slopes of the Sierra. But for now, when he peered into the valleys on this side of the range, all was snow, rock, and dirt; and far down the slopes of Veleta was an enormous building under construction. This was, he assumed, the ski resort of which the *sereno* had spoken. Still ahead of him, and probably quite near, was the *parador*, the government inn the old man had mentioned. He did not relish the thought of walking past it in daylight, but he did not want to have to spend another night on this side of the Sierra.

He would have to take his chances. He could imagine that anyone who did see him would wonder why an old *campesino* should be trudging along up this isolated road that led nowhere, and tried once again to invent a story that might sound credible. Nothing came to his mind. Maybe they'll just think I'm crazy, he thought, smiling, and leave me alone.

The *parador*, when he reached it, was not directly on the road, but off to the left and down a driveway. There seemed a good chance of getting past it unobserved, so he quickened his pace and kept on the road. Not that he really had much choice in this: The prisoners had built the road along the crest of a narrow ridge only a few

183

hundred meters across; and the drops on either side of this ridge were so sharp and deep that he would have had to be a skilled climber to leave the ridge at all. The snow by the side of the road, when he stepped off to test it, was icy but not deep. It reached only to the calves of his legs.

Above the *parador* was another bulding with a large dome atop it. Whatever it was, it was certainly closed for the winter, for he saw no signs of any recent activity around it. He came next to a shrine of some sort—a small roofed structure made of flat stones piled into four corner pillars. He paused here for a moment, and sat on the stone floor of the shrine, looking back in the direction from which he had come.

Directly below him was the *parador*, with smoke coming from one of its chimneys, and with several foreign cars parked at its entrance. He watched as a man, evidently a tourist, walked with some trepidation from the *parador* toward the precipice that lay behind it. He had a camera, and was trying to brace his legs so as to hold himself still in the fierce wind that came down from the peaks above him. But he had no luck, and finally fell backward into the snow, dropping the camera. Rosales chuckled as the man groped in the snow for the thing, then tottered back to the warmth of the *parador*.

As Rosales raised his eyes to the north, he saw first the Río Genil he had crossed that morning and beyond it, more than thirty kilometers away, the entire city of Granada, laid out beneath him as if it were a place on a map. He could make out with ease that famous *moro* fortress, and, off to its right, the congested streets of the

Albaicín. He wondered idly what was being done about the gypsy he had killed. Were his friends searching the quarter for Rosales now? Had they gone to the *policía*, who were perhaps already fanning out across the whole city, looking for the murderer? He thought not—the death of a gypsy was not likely to be of any great concern to the *policía*—but one could never be sure.

Beyond Granada, stretching out as far as his eyes could see to the north and west, was the great *vega*, the fertile plain, full of wheat fields and olive groves, that covered all of northern Andalucía from Jaén to the mountains above Málaga in the west. Just below the horizon he could see the outlines of the large lake where the roadblock had been set up yesterday. To its southeast, he knew, lay the sorry little towns he had escaped through on his way to Granada. As he watched, the sun's rays fell full upon the *moro* fortress, and its long walls and tall, rectangular towers gleamed with a dusty redness that seemed to him quite beautiful. Perhaps, he thought as he rose to resume his climb, this Granada was not always so ugly a place as it had seemed last night.

Four hundred meters farther along, the road ended abruptly. Just to his left, and not far above him, was the top of Veleta, brilliantly white against the cloudless blue sky. If he could find the old trail, and if it were not covered with snow, he could expect to see the Alpujarras by sundown.

In spite of the crusty snow, he could still move along with some speed. From time to time he came upon patches of stony soil from which the wind had cleared the snow. He suspected that the trail lay along here, and proceeded with confidence, noting with pleasure that he was now going downhill, very gradually but definitely.

An hour later the shadows were lengthening rapidly in the valleys far below him on his right, and he knew that he could not hope to reach Poqueira by nightfall, and that he would have to find some sort of shelter up here. If a wind should come up, or if the temperature were to drop suddenly, as it often did in these mountains, then he could easily freeze during the night.

He remembered that the heights of the Sierra Nevada were the home of what the Alpujarreños called the *cabra montés*, the elusive mountain goats who were supposedly of such great rarity that it had been forbidden to hunt them. The men of Poqueira *had* hunted these goats, though, going after them with old single-barreled shotguns, and occasionally bringing one of the wide-horned beasts home, to be smuggled past the *Guardia Civil* into their homes, where their wives and children could rejoice over the feast the goat would make for them. He had gone on such hunts with his father, when he was old enough to keep silent and help with the stalking. If he could find one of the *cabra montés'* caves, Rosales thought, he would be safe for the night. He began to look for places where shelves of rock stood out above the snow; if there were caves to be found, they should be in such places.

Far off to the right, and down a steep slope, he saw what he wanted—a tall outcropping of granite, inaccessible except from above. Trudging through the snow, as evening descended quickly, it took him over an hour to reach the place. Just as he had hoped, there was a cave, large enough for him to crawl into and deep enough for protection against the wind. To get to the cave he had to climb down along the perilously narrow track that the goats used to reach their home. He kept his back to the rock wall, and edged slowly downward until he arrived at the entrance to the cave. To his relief, it was empty, though it smelled mightily of its owners, who might be in the vicinity, watching from a safe distance the invasion of their sanctuary by the human.

He thought of the possibility of a fire, as being something that would serve not only to warm him but also to diminish the goat smell, but he was much too high in the mountains to find anything but moss and lichens if he were to climb up from his cave and go out into the snow again. So he contented himself with using his blanket as a curtain over the mouth of the cave, by stuffing wads of it into niches and cracks around the mouth until almost none of the night air could enter. The smell was almost more than he could abide. But at least he would not freeze. His hunger he regarded as irrelevant. There was still the *bota*, and tomorrow there would be plenty to eat in Poqueira.

Usually Rosales was able to will himself to sleep, simply by closing his eyes and emptying his mind. But tonight his mind insisted on turning to frightening things, things he had heard in his youth about these mountains, and his eyes would not close.

Very near him, he knew, must be the Laguna de las Yeguas, the Lagoon of the Mares. This was dangerous territory, and no shepherd or hunter in the old days would have ventured near the lagoon after dark. It was deep, so deep, the *alpujarreños* believed, that it was fed from caves that ran clear to the Mediterranean. No one ever fished in its black waters, even though large numbers of fat trout were said to leap in them, as if daring one to have a try; for there were evil spirits in the depths of the lagoon who waited for humans to come near the water's edge, so that they might grab them and pull them under forever.

The high regions of the Sierra were also, remembered the wide-awake Rosales, the home of the dreaded *mantequero*, a monster shaped like a man who fed only on *manteca*, the body fat of humans. Occasionally one of these *mantequeros* would creep down into a village at night to steal a small child, whose soft flesh it especially preferred (Rosales's mother had often terrified him by reminding him of this whenever he had stayed out too late with his friends, playing in the thick forest below Poqueira); but for the most part the monsters stayed high in the mountains, hoping to waylay shepherds, muleteers carrying sacks of grain over the Sierra to Granada, or the men who fished in the mountain streams of the area. What foolishness this all was, Rosales told himself, huddling against the wall of the cave and not really believing that it was foolishness. People from the villages *had* disappeared among these peaks, and surely not *all* of them had been the victims of the bandits who had lived up here in the old days, preying on travelers who came along the high trail during the summer months, when no snow blocked this shortest route to Granada. Their priests and schoolteachers scoffed at the *alpujarreños* who believed in such creatures as the *mantequeros*, but every village had its *bruja*, or conjure woman, who could contradict the educated cynics very

188

convincingly. It was almost dawn before Rosales dozed off, so carefully was he listening for whatever might be moving around outside his cave.

He was glad to find, when he awoke and pulled the blanket away from the entrance to the cave, that the day was as clear and sunny as yesterday had been. Far down to his right was the Laguna de las Yeguas, large and dark and—to him—ominous. Everything else around him, as far as he could see, narrowing his eyes in the bright glare of morning, was snow and rock. He drank from his *bota*, again noted and then disregarded his hunger, rolled the blanket once more over his shoulder, and climbed out of the mouth of the cave and up the narrow goat path to the top of the rock face. The cold night on the rough floor of the cave had left him so stiff that the climb was very nearly more than he could manage, and his fingers were too numb to be of much use in helping him cling to any projections from the rock face. If he fell (the distance was not great, perhaps a matter of fifteen meters) on snow, he would probably not be hurt; but if he slipped where there was only rock below him, and broke a limb or injured something internal, then he would surely die, of cold and exposure. Staying alive meant keeping in motion. So he climbed very cautiously, and breathed heavily with relief when he finally stood at the top of the rock face, numb fingers bleeding and stiff knees trembling.

After several hours of struggling along through the impacted snow, falling often as he slipped on ice or as his feet broke through the surface of the snow, tripping him up, Rosales lifted his eyes from what he hoped was the trail of the muleteers, and saw what he had dreamed of for thirty-seven years. *Como nidos de águilas,* he said to himself, exulting.

Far below him, just beneath the snowline, standing out in sharp white detail against the green and brown of the folded hills, were three of the villages of the Alpujarras. "*Como nidos de águilas,*" he said again: like nests of eagles. First was his own *pueblo,* Poqueira; then Bubión, then Pampaneira. He squatted down, in no hurry to lose this moment. There, at the precise center of Poqueira, was the church tower, as it had always been since the days when these villages had all belonged to the *moros,* and the church had been a mosque. Spreading out around the tower were the houses of the town, with their walls of small stones, covered over with white lime, and their flat roofs, gray with the dirt that the *moros* had pounded onto them as insulation from cold and heat, snow, rain, and sun. Poqueira was exactly as he had remembered it—no smaller, no larger. The only change he could detect from this height above the towns was that the road which had always joined them, and then continued down the mountainside to the city of Órgiva, was now paved, where in the old days it had been of dirt only.

He looked beyond the valley where the city of Órgiva would be, and ran his eyes over the two small ranges that separated the Alpujarras from the coast. Barren and snow-topped, scarred since ancient times by the lead mines dug into them, they had never seemed anything but ugly to Rosales; and so they seemed now. Beyond them, he knew, was the coast road, hugging the edges of

the sharp cliffs that rose from the sea between Málaga to
the west and Almería to the east. He could see a faint
strip of blue almost on the horizon—the Mediterranean,
with a large tanker passing now along it, only a tiny
black sliver on the blue band. And in the farthest distance he could see the Rif Mountains of Morocco, as
vague as smoke even on so clear a day as this one.

It was not until he began shivering that Rosales
thought of moving on. This was a sight a man could
look at forever. He would not reach Poqueira before
dark, even with the easier walking he would have once
he got below the snowline; and he did not relish the idea
of another night spent like the last one. So he rose, took
a look back at Veleta, which was now just another,
slightly higher, point in the jagged outline of the Sierra
Nevada, and then began the last leg of his journey home,
moving at his old pace, which seemed almost leisurely,
but which ate up the kilometers almost as swiftly as if he
were trotting. He felt young now, almost like the seventeen-year-old Sebastián Rosales who had marched so
bravely out of Poqueira in July 1936. Grinning, he
thought of those days as he walked, those days when the
war had seemed a possible thing.

———

Almost every able-bodied man in Poqueira had joined
with the village stewards of the CNT as soon as they
called for volunteers to fight the fascists who had re-
belled against the Republic. With fifty of his fellow villagers, Rosales had marched down the road to Órgiva,

where they were issued their rifles and belts with ammunition pouches. There was no ammunition, and few of the volunteers would have known how to fire these strange Mausers even if there had been; but no one worried. When they reached the front they would surely be given what they needed in order to defeat the rebel army. Then they were put into trucks and buses that the CNT had commandeered, and headed west along the coast road to Málaga, where they turned inland and drove over the rugged Serranía to Ronda, which, they were told, was about to be attacked by the forces of a General Varela, who had in his command two regiments of the *Tercio*—the Spanish Foreign Legion—and nine mechanized battalions of Italian Black Shirts. Against these, the Republic had been able to gather together perhaps two thousand militiamen, mostly peasants like Rosales or workers from Málaga, or even fishermen from the towns along the coast that had already been overrun by the Nationalists, who were moving swiftly eastward, encountering little real resistance as they came.

The men from Poqueira were put in a battalion led by Anarchists from the hills around Ronda. This did not please the *alpujarreños*, whose own brand of Anarchism was rather less extreme than that of these *forasteros* from Ronda, but they had little choice. If they wanted ammunition and instruction, they had to put themselves under the authority of the men of FAI, the Iberian Anarchist Federation. So they did so, and Rosales now had as his battalion commander a man named Pedro López, who had been a manufacturer of pork sausages in his home town of Montejaque, somewhere to the west of Ronda.

He had served as Montejaque's *alcalde*, mayor, as well, and was skilled in leading men. Rosales liked him immediately, and tried with extra diligence to master the basic combat techniques that López and his assistants hoped to teach their men before the arrival of the Nationalists.

Rosales was tall and strong and quick to learn, and López noticed very soon this mountain boy, who had an air of cold aggressiveness about him that promised good things in battle. When the enemy was rumored to be only a few kilometers west of Ronda, López walked one evening around the ancient *plaza de toros* of the city, where his battalion was bivouacked, and asked for volunteers to go out at night into the hills on a reconnaissance mission to locate the enemy. Rosales raised his hand immediately, was given three clips of ammunition and a pair of hand grenades, and sent off with thirty other men across the tall bridge that lay across the deep gorge that split through the center of Ronda, and into the hills to the west.

Two evenings later four of the men returned, and one of them was Rosales, walking with a somewhat aloof and distracted manner a few steps ahead of the other three. They reported to Pedro López what had happened, the oldest among them doing the talking. Of the original band of thirty, fully half had deserted while still in sight of Ronda, heading off in all directions but west. The other fifteen had continued as ordered, walking toward the enemy lines that could not be far away.

At some point during the preceding day they had climbed over a particularly rocky hill to find themselves looking down at what seemed to them the largest army in the world: thousands of men, dozens of tanks, armored cars, and howitzers, even cavalry—all facing toward them, all preparing to move at any minute.

The fifteen Republicans, inexperienced in the techniques of reconnoitering, were seen immediately, and before they could turn and run back over the crest of the hill, bullets began to spatter about them, kicking up tiny spouts of sand and caroming off the rock behind which they were leaping for shelter. At least four of the fifteen fell immediately, dead or dying. As the survivors lay as flat as they could behind whatever rocks they were able to crawl to, they heard the sound of men running toward them.

The one of the four who was doing the recounting to Pedro López paused in his tale here, and looked at Rosales, who so far had said nothing. "All right, *compadre*, go on with your telling: How did you get out of there?" asked López.

"Señor López, it was—"

"Comrade Pedro," López corrected him. "*What* was it?"

"Comrade Pedro," the man continued, "all we thought of was running, straight down the hill and back in the direction we'd come from. And we started to do so. But *this* one"—he indicated Rosales, who seemed to be paying little attention to the reporting—"stood up and yelled at us. He called us idiots, and told us we'd all be shot like rabbits if we just jumped and ran. He said: 'Do as I tell you. Not many are pursuing us, maybe a dozen. Five of you come over here with me, and the rest crawl quickly over there, to the left. Get down, and wait. When they come between us, we all open fire on them, from both sides. *Then* we run, but not straight downhill like rabbits. We run over *there*, to that next hill to the south, and we hide until dark. Then we return to Ronda.'"

López looked at Rosales appraisingly for a moment, then turned back to the man who had been speaking. "And is this what you did?" he asked.

"*Sí, señor*—Comrade Pedro. They came between us over the crest of the hill, as that one, the boy there, said they would. And we opened fire on them, and they on us. But we had surprised them, and they all died, while only five of us did. When the shooting stopped, we ran for the hill as this one here had said to do. They shot at us from below as we ran, from the valley below, and killed two and wounded another. We ran to the next hill—"

"What about the wounded man?" López asked this of Rosales, who looked coolly at him.

"We left him there. We had our mission to complete." Rosales gazed at his commanding officer without expression.

"You were right, of course," answered López, looking at this tall boy, wondering what to make of him. "So then you waited until dark, and returned to Ronda. I congratulate all of you, especially you, *niño*. What's your name?"

"Sebastián Rosales, *a sus órdenes, compañero*."

"Do you know what you remind me of, Comrade Sebastián?" López asked. Rosales said nothing.

"You look like a young wolf, and apparently you know how to fight like one. How old are you, may I ask?"

"Seventeen, as of six months ago."

"Well, *niño*, as far as I'm concerned your name with us here is now 'El Lobo.' We don't have any medals to give, but we can give names. Now you and your friends try to be as specific as you can about the enormous army you saw from your hill, and then you can rest."

And so he had become El Lobo, and before long only the men from Poqueira called him anything else. They were, of course, beaten out of Ronda that September by the *Tercio* and the Black Shirts, and fell back toward Málaga, clinging to the bare and windy hillsides of the Serranía and trying to keep ahead of the cavalry and the Italian tanks. López used El Lobo as a kind of flanker, one who ran along the ridges of the passes through which they were retreating, seeking out and thwarting ambushes by Moroccans from the *Tercio*, men who were as skilled as any in the hit-and-run techniques of guerrilla warfare. By the time the Republican defenders of Ronda had reached the coast, at the town of San Pedro de Alcántara, El Lobo had demonstrated a half-dozen times the skill that he had learned from his father when they had hunted goats in the Sierra Nevada: With one or two men to help him, he could find enemy troops hidden in the heights above the road his army was moving south along, stalk the enemy if they were not too great in number, and, with the great advantage of leaping at them from behind and above, kill them, or at least drive them away from their vantage points. His technique, under ideal conditions, was to creep with his men as close as he could to the *moros* without being detected. Then they would each throw a grenade into the midst of the group below them, wait for the shrapnel to cease

196

flying but not for the clouds of dust and sand to clear, and then move in on the position with rifles and bayonets. Most of his fighting was a matter of seconds, not minutes or hours; and he killed with an efficiency and remorselessness that made him respected, but feared, too, by his comrades.

Once or twice he wondered a little about the source of this special talent of his. In all his childhood, he had seen nothing more violent than the ritual *matanzas* in Poqueira, when the pigs to be slaughtered would be yanked upward by ropes tied around their hind feet, their throats were slit, and basins put beneath them to catch the blood for pudding. There had been, of course, the hunting with his father, but until the actual shooting of the goat or rabbit that kind of hunting had been a quick and almost gentle thing. He had seldom fought, either with his own friends or with "strangers" from Bubión, two kilometers down the mountainside. It was just that he had a sort of vocation for this kind of thing, he concluded. He was good at it; it came easy. Some men carved wood; some played the guitar; he killed. His comrades rarely spoke of fear. Like sex at this stage of his life, this was something that he knew existed, but of which he had no experience. Nor of anger, either. The men he killed where the enemy, simply—bodies to be destroyed, weapons to be silenced. War, even in retreat, was not so difficult, if one were careful and reasonably prudent, and, above all, silent.

In Málaga and what happened afterward, however, El Lobo had learned anger and hatred; and when he did so, it was not only against his enemies that he directed these

197

emotions, but against his own side, too. The details of strategy interested him almost not at all, but even a seventeen-year-old peasant from the Alpujarras could see that there was no need for Málaga to have fallen, nor for there to have been the disgraceful rout after its fall. When he and the defenders of Ronda had fought their way to the coast, there was nothing left of Republican territory except a strip thirty kilometers wide, running from the fishing village of Estepona to east of Motril, the coastal town due south of Granada. Málaga was at the center of this narrow corridor, and it did not take a military genius to see that it could withstand a siege at least long enough for reinforcements to arrive from Almería, Valencia, or even from Madrid. When El Lobo reached Málaga, there were forty thousand Republican troops in and around the city—militia of various kinds, as well as units of the regular army. Moreover, there was a large civilian population, furious at having been bombed for weeks by German and Italian planes, and shelled from offshore by Nationalist ships and by the German pocket battleship *Graf Spee*. Madrid was holding out against *its* siege because the people of the city had been issued weapons, and were manning the barricades beside the army and the militia. In Málaga, though, the Republican provincial commander refused to arm his civilians, and in fact could scarcely bring himself to employ his militia, so contemptuous of them was he. So the front narrowed daily, until by the beginning of February, Málaga was very nearly encircled, and the provincial commander had left by staff car along the only escape route left open: the *corniche* road along the sea to Almería, some two hundred kilometers to the east.

Although they could have done so, the Nationalists did not cut this road, preferring an evacuation of Málaga to the fight of desperation that would take place if they tried to capture the city entire. Thus El Lobo found himself for the first time in this war losing, not because of the enemy's superiority of numbers and matériel, but because of his own leaders' stupidity. And this angered him. His own battalion left Málaga on February 7, unable to keep its formations intact because it had to jostle with civilian evacuees for space on the coast road. He found this shameful, and for the first time his aggressiveness lost the coolness that Pedro López had noticed in Ronda. There they had suffered a military defeat, and left the city only when beaten out of it. But here there was fighting still to be done, and El Lobo's battalion had barely reached the eastern outskirts of Málaga before they heard the first sounds of machine gun and rifle fire in the western suburbs—evidence that the conquerors of the city intended to kill any men left there. That so beautiful a city as Málaga must have been was now largely rubble was unfortunate to El Lobo, but not tragic. But to lose needlessly was worse than tragic, especially with the knowledge that civilians were at this moment being put to death simply for having been *malagueños*. El Lobo did not lose his outward composure, which was to him an essential sign of his manhood; but from this time on he would kill with something like pleasure, and he never respected another leader until that man had fought until combat was no longer possible. Bravery, endurance, and contempt for cowardice were for him now the only virtues, the only abstractions that he recognized at this time, in this place. It made life in wartime very simple, except for the few bad moments like when he executed the two men at Belchite. At such times it was hard to know which was bravery, and which was cowardice. But usually in war there was not so much complexity.

Between Málaga and Almería there were perhaps sixty thousand refugees, packed so tightly along the road that staff cars and ambulances could barely make their way in either direction. In Almería were several battalions from the International Brigades, hoping to rush to the defense of Málaga, but there was no way their trucks could move through the masses of refugees streaming at them, so they gave up and returned to Albacete or Valencia.

At the other end of the road, near Málaga, El Lobo at first assumed that his leaders would mount some sort of rear-guard action, in order to hold back the Nationalist advance until the road cleared enough for reinforcements to be able to reach them. But no rear-guard action materialized. The regular units of the Republican army were off somewhere in the north, probably between Antequera and Loja, and had evidently left nothing of themselves behind near Málaga—except for the bedraggled remnants of a cavalry troop, which was moving along among the refugees. Their horses were almost exhausted and covered with mud. Few of the troopers were riding their mounts; most walked beside them, having given their place in their saddles to old women and children.

As for the militia, it had melted completely into the mob. El Lobo could find almost none of the men of his battalion. Pedro López had vanished. It occurred to El Lobo that he might try to round up a few dozen militiamen and set up a last line of defense, hiding in the scrub and cactus in the hills above the road. Whenever he saw a militiaman (who would be identifiable only by his possession of a rifle carried anyhow), he would stop him, and try to turn him back, or ask him to wait by the side of the road until he could be joined by other men who could fight. But every man El Lobo tried to stop either ignored him or laughed at him. He was an idiot, they told him. What could a few rifles do against a whole division of Nationalists, spearheaded by the dreaded Italian tanks? Anyway, they told him, they were too tired to fight anymore for now; maybe later, in Almería . . . So El Lobo plodded along with the rest, full of silent anger.

All around him were gray-faced old people, most of the women in dirty black dresses, with their feet bare and their heads covered with shawls. Old men sat silently by the side of the road, staring vacantly at the procession. No one in Málaga had had enough to eat for months, and El Lobo saw the signs of malnutrition and starvation all around him—especially in the very old and in the thousands of children who trudged along with them, as silently as their elders. Their feet were bleeding from the hours of walking over gravel, and the eyes of many of them were almost shut with pus and gum. A few lucky ones rode mules or burros; three or four slumped atop each forlorn animal. But almost no one cried, almost no one spoke.

Many of the refugees would never reach Almería, El Lobo knew. Already there were many little clusters along the roadside of those who were too weak to go on, or who had simply given up from fatigue and despair.

With nothing to eat or drink, they would not last much longer.

Near dawn of his second day on the trek, as he sat under a palm tree trying to warm himself at a small fire he had built, he saw a commotion on the road ahead of him. A truck of some sort, with a large red cross painted on its side, was trying to nudge its way through the throngs of refugees, who were clinging to its sides, banging on its windows and crying to the men inside. As El Lobo watched, the truck stopped, then began to back and fill until it was facing back toward Almería. The driver, a civilian and evidently some sort of foreigner, got out and walked to the rear of the truck, looking quite harassed and distressed by the women who crowded around him, tugging at his arms to gain his attention, and crying for him to notice the children they were carrying. The man threw open the rear doors of the truck, leapt up into it, and began lifting babies and the children most obviously ill in beside him. Soon the truck was packed full, but people continued to gather at its rear, crying to the foreigner for help. The man looked frantically around him, trying to say in Spanish that there was no more room. His companion came around to help him push the people away. An old man thrust himself to the front of the pack, carrying in his arms a young boy who was unconscious, clearly burning with a high fever. "He's dying," the old man said, tears running down his dusty face. "You must get him out of here, *compadre*. I ask this not for myself, but for the boy. Mother of God, you must take him."

The foreigners looked at one another, shrugged, and

lifted the dying boy into the packed truck. As they were doing this, a young woman, healthier-looking than most, took advantage of their preoccupation to crawl into the truck. A second later the foreigners discovered her presence, and began to tug at her wrists and ankles until, try as she might to claw at the sides of the truck, they had her outside. She stood there screaming at them as they tried to indicate they had room for only the ill and the children. Suddenly she lifted up her black skirt and pointed to her belly: Obviously, she was pregnant. The foreigners, remorse on their faces, relented and began to help her back into the truck. Her screams turned to cries of gratitude, and she blessed the two men, one of whom reached down to pull her in, while the other stood on the ground below her, trying to help her lift her heavy body. In her relief at being saved, she could not restrain her bladder. Her urine poured over the shoulders of the foreigner below her. No one laughed.

With some difficulty, the two men closed the rear doors of the truck, and returned to their seats in front— to find them crowded with children, each trying to look as small as possible. Finally the truck drove off slowly through the crowd that had gathered around it, and the commotion died down. Women who had not succeeded in getting their children aboard had fallen by the side of the road, sobbing helplessly, as their children stood or sat by them, not understanding.

The sun was fully up now, and El Lobo looked south-ward toward the sea. There, only a few kilometers off-shore, were the warships that were following them as they continued their march. From time to time, as if engaged in target practice, they would lob a shell at the coast. Occasionally a shell would burst along the road, killing many refugees in a geyser of smoke and flame.

Then, at noon, the German and Italian planes appeared overhead, sweeping low over the column of refugees. "Get down!" El Lobo yelled, diving for the ditch by the road. But the civilians, numb with fatigue and panic, only stood where they were, staring dumbly upward at the planes. After one pass the planes circled widely out to sea, then returned, their machine guns firing into the crowd. Too late, the refugees realized what was happening to them, and threw themselves down, covering their heads with their hands. When the planes—there must have been five of them—returned for another pass, El Lobo, almost blinded with rage and frustration, stood up in his ditch, ran onto the road, and began firing his Mauser at the attackers, working the bolt of the rifle as fast as his hands could move. The planes were so low that he could see the faces of the leather-helmeted pilots as they passed, and it seemed to him that they were laughing. El Lobo turned to look after them, and saw smoke and flame begin to billow from the nacelle of an engine: He had hit one, he knew, and he yelled again, this time with exultation.

Suddenly he was flung to the ground with great force, and a loud roaring noise filled his ears. He attempted to rise, but one leg refused to function. He pulled himself to the ditch and lay very still, trying to stay conscious. He had been hit, and it seemed to him of the utmost importance to learn the nature of his injury at once. There was no pain, as yet. He pulled himself onto his back, and began to run his hands over his body and limbs. Blood was spreading out rapidly over his right trouser leg. Quickly he unbuckled his belt and lowered his trousers. A bullet from one of the planes had torn through his thigh, making a ragged wound that El Lobo knew would be fatal if it were not attended to promptly. He was already quite dizzy from loss of blood, and calling out for help took almost more energy than he possessed. The road was littered with bodies, looking like so many untidy bundles of laundry, and people were only now beginning to climb out of the ditch, or to creep from behind the palm trees that grew along the road. He called again, and saw an old woman look his way. Then he fainted.

When he awoke, he found himself on an improvised litter, being carried along by two militiamen, their rifles slung over their shoulders. He lifted his head to look down at his leg. Someone had tied a length of gray rag around his thigh above the wound, and there did not seem to be as much blood as before.

"Awake, *niño*?" asked one of the men.

"Where is my rifle?" El Lobo asked in return, feeling around him on the litter.

"Fuck your rifle. Did you think we'd carry that, too? You're no light thing, you know. Lie back and go to sleep, before we put you down and leave you for the Italians." The man was serious, El Lobo saw. He said no more, and lay back, falling asleep almost instantly.

Some time later he was aware of voices, and opened his eyes to see a group of men standing by his litter, which the militiamen had put on the ground at the roadside. "Are you the one who shot the airplane back there?" someone asked.

El Lobo nodded, vaguely recalling what he had done.

"Then we have a present for you," the voice said. "Look at this."

El Lobo raised himself up on the litter, tried to focus his eyes, and saw that one of the men in the group was wearing a pilot's helmet and a strange uniform. His face and hands had been burned, and his dark eyes were wide with fear. He stared at El Lobo.

"This is the one you got, *niño*," said a man. "His plane crashed on the road back there, and we got him out before it burned. He's yours. What do you want us to do with him?"

"What do I care, *hombre?*" murmured El Lobo. "You can have him."

"Good, then," said one of the men. Smiling, he turned to the Italian pilot, who seemed to know that his fate had been decided. He glanced with terror at the peasants who surrounded him, and let himself be nudged away by them toward a palm grove some meters away. Ten minutes later one of the peasants returned to where El Lobo lay. Smiling affably, he held out toward El Lobo a small sickle, the kind one used to crop esparto grass. It was gleaming with blood. "You approve, *niño?*" the man asked. El Lobo nodded, feeling nothing much but the desire to sleep.

He lay by the road for the rest of the day, fully expecting to die, or to be left behind by the last of the refugees; but when night fell he heard the sound of a truck motor, saw a pair of dimmed headlights, and watched as a battered old ambulance pulled up beside him. The men with him lifted him inside the ambulance, which was almost filled with other wounded men and women, and then hopped on the fenders and roof of the vehicle. "Okay, let's go," one of them cried, slapping his hand on the side of the ambulance. "Take us to Almería. And drive carefully: You are carrying the man who shot down the Italian plane."

And that had been it. That night they reached Almería, where El Lobo was deposited at an aid station to lie beside a hundred other wounded men. He was given coffee and brandy. An officer came by to congratulate him on his marksmanship, and to tell him that such as he were the hope of the Republic. He seemed full of confidence, and announced to El Lobo that at this moment the International Brigades were on their way to retake Málaga.

After one day in Almería, El Lobo was put on a hospital train and taken to Valencia to recuperate. The International Brigades did not retake Málaga, though one heard that they had fought very bravely until driven back somewhere around Motril, where the front had stabilized.

———————

The lights of the *alpujarreño pueblos* were turning on by the time Rosales reached the snowline, and he had little difficulty in descending along the muleteers' trail, which had been widened and graded at some point in his thirty-seven-year absence. He passed a large electrical power station that was another recent addition. Large clusters of wires ran from it down the mountainside. So now there's electricity in Poqueira, he thought with some surprise. It had not really entered his mind before this moment that anything might have changed in the years he had been away. He had assumed that all would be as it had been, and he found this evidence of progress a little disquieting. But, he reassured himself, Poqueira would still be Poqueira: This or that detail might be different, but it would still be his *pueblo*, the place where his name and date of birth were inscribed in the registry in the village's tiny *ayuntamiento*, the town hall, where all the records had been kept for centuries. There might be few who remembered him, but the people of Poqueira, once they knew who he was, would accept him as one of them. Of this he was quite sure. He continued his descent with confidence, forgetting his fatigue and hunger and laughing quietly at the difficulties of his journey home. Since 1939, when he stood in the sand of the French concentration camp near Perpignan, he had known he would return, and now he had.

# Chapter 6

Rosales rounded the last turn of the road down from the Sierra and entered Poqueira. Electricity, it appeared, was not the only change the years had brought. Directly ahead of him was a new hotel—so new that lime had not yet been painted over the raw, factory-made blocks that had been used in the construction of the building. Above the entrance were flying the flags of several European nations, and beneath them was a sign that read: PENSIÓN SIERRA NEVADA. The building was three storeys high, taller by far than any he remembered in the Alpujarreño *pueblos*. Outside the *pensión* a very modern bus was parked, with a painted inscription on its side announcing that it was the property of something called MAUPINTOURS. What in the name of God, he wondered, would bring European tourists to Poqueira?

He passed quickly by this ugly new building, shaking his head in tired incredulity. Ahead of him was a corner he well remembered: the one where there was the café of old Luís, at the top of Poqueira's single main street. He did not expect to find Luís there, of course—thirty-seven years were thirty-seven years—but he did hope that there would be someone he might remember in the café, someone who could tell him what was what in Poqueira.

Luís's place was more brightly lit than in the old days (electricity, Rosales reminded himself: progress), but there was the same bar, with many bottles behind it, and the pedestal with the stuffed owl on it that he used to stare at when a child. Over the bar, as always, hung several *serrano* hams; and in the back of the room were the familiar flimsy tables, at which the old men of the *pueblo* sat smoking and playing their card games. But there were differences that disturbed him. For one thing, against one wall was one of the abominable jukeboxes, playing at top volume the new music he despised so; for another, there was a large television set, showing great festivities in—he supposed—Madrid; and, strangest of all, there were foreigners standing at the bar. *And some of them, by God, were women.* He consoled himself with the thought that these were, after all, only foreign women, not to be taken too seriously; and approached the bar, slightly bewildered and irritated at the noise these *extranjeros* were making.

The bartender, a shy young man with reddish hair and pale blue eyes, nodded to him and smiled. "*Muy buenas,*" he said, waiting for Rosales's order. If he felt any curiosity about where such a weathered and haggard stranger could have come from, his sense of politeness kept him from showing it.

"*Muy buenas*," Rosales responded. "You have good business tonight, especially from these *extranjeros*."

The young man shrugged. "These live here with us, here and in Bubión. We see a good deal of them, especially in the evenings. And now, of course, they are celebrating *Navidad*."

"Ah," said Rosales. "I thought perhaps they had come in that bus in front of the new *pensión*. What do they do in the Alpujarras? Are they rich?"

"Some are," answered the young man. "Some, I believe, are quite poor. They are painters and writers, mostly, I think." He continued to wait patiently for Rosales's order.

Realizing that he was expected to ask for something, Rosales said, "Look, *hombre*, I'm sorry I can't buy anything. I have no money. But I would like to ask a couple of questions, if I might."

The young man smiled shyly, turned away from Rosales for a moment, then returned with a glass of wine and a small plate on which were several olives and a slice of ham. "*Feliz Navidad*," he said, putting the glass and the plate in front of Rosales.

"I thank you." This was the kind of courtesy Rosales had expected in Poqueira. As he took a sip of the wine, he glanced in the mirror behind the bar and caught some of the men on either side of him looking at him out of the corners of their eyes. Even one or two of the foreigners had noticed him, and seemed to be talking to one another about him. Well, he thought, to everyone here

I'm a *forestero*, and I suppose I look old and strange enough to make people curious. It was nothing to worry about, he felt sure.

When he could catch the attention of the young bartender again, he beckoned him over, and said, "When I was a boy here, this café was run by a man named Luís. Are you of his family?"

The young man looked surprised, and the men along the bar now turned to stare frankly at Rosales, abandoning their own conversations. Most were young, he noticed; but some were of his age, and might remember him. "You are from here, *señor?*" the bartender asked. Rosales nodded, smiling. "Luís was my father," said the young man, "but he died many years ago, when I was a boy."

"I am sorry to hear that," said Rosales. "He was always a man of good reputation, and generous, too." He paused, wondering how cautious he still needed to be, then continued: "I am called Rosales, and have been gone from Poqueira since the war. Now I have come back, and would like to know if there are any of my family here, and where I might find them."

Before the young man could answer, one of the *extranjeros*, a slight, florid man with large ears and a broken nose, stepped to a space at the bar, flipped a five-hundred-peseta note in the direction of the young man, and hollered, "*¡Bebidas para todo el mundo!*" Drinks for everyone. This kept the bartender busy for many minutes, as he raced about opening beers, reaching for bottles of *coñac* and sherry, and pouring glasses of wine. Everyone mumbled their thanks to the little man, then returned to what they had been doing.

"Don't look surprised, Rosales," murmured an old man who stood next to him. "They always behave this way, and we have grown accustomed to them. Sometimes they even brawl. Generally they do little harm here, though, and some even give us work to do. They are only a minor annoyance in Poqueira." He took out a pack of Bisontes, and offered one to Rosales, who took it gratefully: his first cigarette in days.

"Perhaps I know you," the man said, keeping his voice low. "Which of the Rosales' might you be?"

"Sebastián." Rosales had to think for a moment: *What were the names of the others?* "I had two older brothers, Ángel and Jaime, and a younger sister, Josefina. My brothers were in Sevilla, serving as pharmacist's apprentices, when the war began. I was thinking they might have returned here." The man shook his head.

"I knew them. They never came back. Few did, after the war. Most died, I suppose. Or found work elsewhere." He paused, thinking. "Sebastián. I knew you, too, though you were only a boy when I was already in the fields. You left with the CNT, right?"

Rosales nodded. Why was this man speaking so quietly, almost furtively? Was there something to fear?

"And what brings you back? The amnesty?"

"If there *is* an amnesty, I suppose so," said Rosales. "I wanted to return to Poqueira, to find my family, to work a little. No special reason. May I ask if you know anything of my sister?"

"She is here, married to a man named Mario Rodríguez. Do you want me to take you to her?"

"No, *hombre*, but thanks," answered Rosales. "I

would not want to take you from the café, and if you'll just tell me the way . . ."

The man smiled. "It's no trouble, *compadre*. I was ready to go, anyway. The noise in here bothers me, and my wife will be expecting me back. Besides, after so many years Poqueira's streets might seem a little complicated to you, and it would be easier to take you to Rodríguez's house than to tell you where it is."

As they were leaving, the little *extranjero* who had bought them all drinks ran to the door, shook both their hands, and hollered "*¡Feliz Navidad!*" into their faces. The older man nodded gravely at the foreigner, as did Rosales.

Once they were out in the cold night air, walking down Poqueira's main street, past other noisy cafés and the darkened doorways of shops and offices, the older man leaned toward Rosales and said, "One has to be a little careful with these *extranjeros*, Rosales. The *policía* allow them to stay here because they bring in money and provide work for us. That one just now hires many of us to rebuild old houses that have been abandoned. Which he sells at great profit to other *extranjeros* who wish to spend their vacations here. But the *policía* do not really like these people, because of their strange ways, and are suspicious of those of us who are too friendly with them."

"What strange ways, *amigo?*" Rosales asked, a little worried at the old man's obvious anxiety about the *policía*. In the old days, the *policía* had consisted of two middle-aged *Guardias Civiles*, who had been so benign that the people of Poqueira had not even bothered to kill them at the beginning of the war, and had only disarmed them and sent them walking down to Órgiva in the valley.

"Oh, the way they behave with their women, and the way they drink, and now and then there's some trouble with a little marijuana. Nothing extreme, you know: just —different." The older man steered Rosales onto a side street that led downhill into a little *placeta* in the middle of which was a fountain he did not remember. The buildings around the *placeta*, too, were quite elegant by *alpujarreño* standards, and obviously of recent construction. Clearly, some kind of prosperity had come to Poqueira. When Rosales remarked on this to his guide, the man shrugged.

"It seems we are a town that is interesting culturally, a sort of showplace *pueblo* for the *Ministerio de Información y Turismo*. Some very big men from Madrid came here a few years back, looked around, and told us to clean ourselves up: to put fresh *cal* on the walls of our houses, and to pour concrete down along our paths so tourists would not have to walk in dirt, and to decorate our houses with more geranium plants so as to seem as authentic as possible. They gave us a lot of money to do this. Now they come up every few months to see that we are keeping ourselves clean. They still complain about the smell; but they have not been able to convince our dogs and burros not to shit in the streets. Nor have the flies deserted us. Nonetheless, as you see, we have electricity in our homes, and there is a bank in case someone might have something to put in it, and there is a real *correos*, too, with a little clerk who sends out the postcards the tourists write. There are telephones in the village. We have a school building with six rooms and two *maestras* educated in Granada. Many of us have bathrooms inside our houses, and running water. So, Rosales," the man concluded, "prosperity has indeed come to your old *pueblo*." He smiled cynically, and shrugged again.

Rosales was not pleased to hear any of this, especially when it occurred to him that so grand a town as Poqueira had become would no longer be governed by a single pair of complacent *Guardias*. "And the *policía?*" he asked the man, as they continued on down the narrowing lane toward the *barrio de abajo*, the lower section of the town where the Rosales family had always lived.

"*Hombre*, we have a complete *garrison*," said the man, puffing out his chest in mock pride. "Twelve men, at least: six to watch *us*, and six to watch the *extranjeros*. And they know *everything, hombre*: They know who comes, who goes, who's looked at whose wife, who got a letter from his cousin in Ugíjar—*everything*. Tomorrow they will know that that little *inglés* back there laid down five hundred pesetas for drinks."

"And tomorrow they will know I have arrived," said Rosales.

"*Claro, hombre*," the older man laughed. "If they don't know already. Maybe you were seen coming up through Pampaneira and Bubión. Maybe someone saw you on the road."

"No," said Rosales. "I didn't come that way. I came from above, from Granada across the Sierra."

The man stopped, looked at Rosales, and whistled softly. "Is this true?" he asked. Rosales answered his gaze, and said nothing. "By all the saints," the man laughed, "I believe you. Don't tell me why you did that, instead of coming down from Granada the normal way, and then climbing up from the valley. Don't tell me: I don't want to know." They resumed their walk, the older man still shaking his head in wonderment.

In a few more minutes they turned down another lane, this one like all the others lit up brightly by lamps strung along the walls. "There it is," said the older man, indicating a small house, white like all the others, with a small door of wood that had been stained dark. This was certainly not his old house, though he could not have said where his old house was. The man was right: Either Poqueira's streets had changed a great deal, or his memory of the village was not as clear as he thought it would be.

"Do you want me to come with you, Rosales, or shall I leave you here?"

"Thank you for everything, but I would not keep you. You have your own home to go to, and it's late."

"As you wish," said the old man. "*Buena suerte*, then; good luck, and may they welcome you there. You'll be a curious *Navidad* present for them, I'm sure." He laughed, shook Rosales's hand, and began his way back uphill. Before he rounded the corner, though, he stopped and called back, softly, "Sebastián: are you the one they called El Lobo in the war?" Rosales nodded, a little surprised that his name should have been carried back to Poqueira. The old man whistled faintly again, and resumed his climb.

Rosales stood outside the door. Josefina, he said to himself. My God, I haven't thought of her for years. He remembered her now as a baby, still being suckled when he had left for the war. What would she be now?

Thirty-nine? Forty? Well, Josefina, he thought, little sister, here is your Sebastián, beard, scars, dirt, and all the rest. He knocked sharply on the door.

In a few seconds it opened. A man of about forty-five stood in the doorway, his shoulders bunched a little against the cold wind that poured down the lane. "*Muy buenas noches,*" he said politely to Rosales, his face full of curiosity and perhaps a little anxiety.

"*Muy buenas,*" Rosales said. "Are you Mario Rodríguez, husband of Josefina Rosales?" The man nodded, opening the door no further.

"Then I am your brother-in-law. I am Sebastián Rosales, the brother of Josefina. Is she here with you?" Rosales felt to his surprise that he was almost as nervous as this Rodríguez.

"Josefina," Rodríguez called, not taking his eyes from Rosales.

"*Sí,* Mario. *¿Quién es?*" a woman's voice answered from somewhere within.

"Come here, woman. Now. Here is someone for you to see." In a second, a tall, stout woman with hair already gray and brown face already heavily lined appeared behind Mario. She nodded to Rosales, wiping her hands on the apron she wore over her plain black dress.

"*Buenas noches, señor,*" she said to Rosales. "*¿Mario, qué hay?*": What's going on? she said in the same breath to her husband.

"This man says he is your brother, Sebastián. What do we do?" Mario had not moved from the doorway. Rosales, standing before them, felt rather foolish, and began to suspect that this Mario was not too quick.

The woman pushed Mario aside and came close to

Rosales, peering up intently into his face. "Who were your parents?" she demanded.

Rosales recited, as if at catechism lessons: "José María Rosales and Concepción Martín, from this *pueblo*. I assume they are long dead."

"You are right," said the woman, her eyes widening. "Do you have brothers?"

"Ángel and Jaime, apprenticed in Sevilla in 1934. I do not know what became of them. Am I your brother?" Rosales smiled faintly.

"I don't know," said Josefina, looking agitated and unhappy. "Are you Sebastián, truly? Where have you been? Why have you come back?"

"This is my *pueblo*, Josefina. Here is where I belong. I was away in the war, and then in France for many years. Now I have returned. Why would I lie? I realize that this must be a trial to you, and I know I look like the *mantequero*. But I am Sebastián, no more nor less than your brother. May I come in, or must I go away?" Rosales held his hands out at his sides, a gesture as close to supplication as he could bring himself to make.

Josefina was tall for an *alpujarreña*. She came forward now and embraced Rosales, and her head reached almost to his shoulders. "I believe you," she sobbed into his vinyl jacket. "You are like our father, *duro y terquísimo*": hard and stubborn. She drew him into the little *salón* that lay beyond the doorway, crying out to her husband as she did so: "Mario! Bring the wedding photograph from our room!" Mario scuttled off out of sight, then returned with a small framed picture in his hands, as Josefina, still crying, pushed her brother into a small cane chair beside the corner fireplace, where a small limb from an olive tree was burning, along with a clump of rosemary for kindling and, Rosales supposed, for fragrance. Mario presented the photograph to his wife, who held it up next to Rosales's face. "Look at this, Mario," exclaimed Josefina, pointing to a figure in the photograph: "Here is my father, twenty-one years ago, on the day of our wedding—and here in this chair is his exact image. Is this not Sebastián?"

Mario looked dubiously from the wedding photograph to the scarred and bearded man seated in his living room. "Well," he said cautiously, "they're both tall and thin. But it's hard to say, with . . . with this one's beard, and—"

"This is Sebastián," Josefina announced with certainty. "Look, *hermano mío*, at the face in this photograph. Might it not be yourself?"

Rosales looked, and saw a much younger Josefina and Mario, standing with great formality for their wedding picture, taken no doubt by the old man who came up on muleback from Órgiva for such occasions, his wooden camera stuck in the *alforja*, the cotton saddlebag, across the animal's rump. Behind the bride, stiff and austere in his best, his only, suit, was his father, glaring out at the cameraman and looking as if no smile had ever crossed his face. Except for the beard and the scars from the German barbed wire, Sebastián Rosales could indeed have been this ferocious old man. "Be glad that I, and not you, resemble our father," he said. "Mario would not have married you, otherwise."

Mario, apparently convinced, or at least persuaded to make the best of a complex situation, shook Rosales's hand and sat down opposite him, taking from his pocket a couple of Bisontes, one of which he gave to his brother-in-law. Josefina ran from the room to her kitchen, returning moments later with a tray of little cakes and a bottle of *montilla*, lightly chilled. She pulled another chair up, close to Rosales, served him a glass, and said, giggling like a schoolgirl, but pretending great severity: "All right, *hermano mío*, account for yourself. Where have you been? And eat these *pasteles* before they are stale."

It took Rosales perhaps five minutes to say all he wished to say about his life since 1936. He mentioned a little about the war, and spoke briefly of his life in France. For reasons that he could not have explained to himself, he said nothing of Inés, nor of his daughters and grandchildren. Perhaps he did not wish to complicate things. The dead gypsy in the Albaicín did not cross his mind. He had only one question to ask Josefina. "Do you remember Ana María Delgado? The *chica* who was to have been my *novia?*"

Josefina put her hand on her brother's knee, and smiled softly at him. "It's more than twenty years that she's been dead, Sebastián. She died in the hospital in Lanjarón, of typhus."

Rosales only nodded, saying good-bye in an instant to the fantasy he had carried with him for so many years.

After a pause, Mario said, very diffidently, "And what will you do now, *señor?* Will you stay in Poqueira?"

Understanding Mario's concern, Rosales threw his cigarette butt into the fireplace and answered, "I shall of course stay here, in my *pueblo*. But in my own house, as soon as I have found work to pay for one. I am sure there is no room here, and I would not wish to impose myself on another man's family—"

"*Ya basta*," said Josefina firmly. "We have a small room that was our son's until he went away last year, and it is now your room as long as you want it. Why would you live elsewhere? Look: Here we have a television"—she pointed to a small box in the corner of the room—"and a real bathroom, and a *bomba* that gives hot water. Here is your house. Enough, now."

Mario nodded in affirmation, trying to seem as enthusiastic as his wife.

"I accept for the moment, with gratitude," said Rosales, very tired now from the intensity of the occasion, and from the warmth of the fire. It came to him suddenly that he must still smell strongly of the mountain-goat scent from the cave of last night, and that Josefina and Mario must have noticed this in the small, hot room. To distract himself and them, he said, "You live very well, clearly. Mario must have a good job."

The husband lifted his shoulders in self-deprecation. "I work for the *inglés* here in Poqueria who rebuilds our old houses. He pays us well enough. It's work, anyway: I can't complain."

And Josefina, her voice full of pride, added: "The television and the refrigerator are from our son, who sends us money often. He works in Germany, in a *fábrica* making automobiles, and comes to visit us every year. You would be proud of him, Sebastián."

"Ah," said Rosales, remembering his first ride many days ago, away from the Pyrenees, and feeling some doubt about the possibilities of his being proud of this generous nephew. Josefina talked on, at some length, about the family, life in Poqueira, the new prosperity, and many other things. He held his eyes open with difficulty, and found himself wishing that this conversation would end, so that he could go to bed.

Josefina, seeing her brother's struggle to stay awake, stopped her chatter and leapt to her feet. "For the love of God, Mario, what's wrong with you? Can't you see the man is tired? Let's leave him alone now, and show him his bed." Mario, who had said almost nothing, nodded obediently, rose, and pointed down a narrow hallway that led past the kitchen. "The room is there. The bathroom is across the hall. Do you wish to bathe before going to sleep?"

Rosales, tired as he was, understood that Mario was hoping he *would* wash himself before getting into the bed of the generous son, but either fatigue or perversity made him say, "Tomorrow I'll bathe, if I may. Now I'd like to sleep, with your permission."

Josefina took him by the arm and led him to her son's bedroom. She turned on a table lamp beside the bed, drew back the covers, and patted the mattress. "Real wool," she said with pride. "You'll sleep like a prince, and tomorrow we'll get to know one another. Good night, my brother." She stood on tiptoe and kissed Rosales's grizzled cheek, then left the room and closed the door behind her, giving a last wave to Rosales as she did so.

Once she was gone, Rosales took off his clothes, hung the bayonet on the bedpost, and lay down on the soft mattress, pulling up to his chin the thick quilt that Josefina used as a bedspread. His head sank into the downy pillow, and his body began to relax in a series of involuntary jerks. That he was in Poqueira finally, after all these years, and in the house of a member of his family, had not yet sunk into his consciousness very deeply. He began to sleep, and woke only briefly after a few minutes to hear Josefina and Mario in muted but obviously agitated conversation in the *salón*. Tomorrow, he said to himself, tomorrow I'll worry. And fell asleep. It was a deep sleep, but full of dreams—of rushing water, of thin girls with large liquid eyes, of whiteness.

At dawn he was lying awake in the quiet house, staring at the ceiling. It was, like all Alpujarreño ceilings, very low—low enough so that Rosales would have to stoop most of the time when indoors. Its beams were thick, necessarily: Laid across them were laths made of stout poplar or oak branches; and atop these were the large flat rocks, put together in several layers, that constituted the roof proper. From the dirt that had been packed between the rocks for insulation came a constant sifting of fine gray dust. It was all completely familiar to him, even though he had not seen a ceiling constructed in this old *moro* fashion since leaving Poqueira. He softly touched the surface of the table by his bed. It, like every other thing in an Alpujarreño house, was covered with a light film of the gray dust. The room was cold and damp, and smelled complexly of lime, old wood, dust: exactly like every room he had ever been in until 1936. He climbed quietly out of bed and walked over to the one small window in the room. Its shutter was closed against the wind by a wooden slat. Rosales lifted the slat, pulled back the shutter, and looked out into the lane down which he had come last night. It was as the old man had said: Every house was freshly coated with a coating of white lime, and the lane itself had been smoothed over with concrete, so that there were only lumps now to indicate that cobblestones lay beneath, as they had always done since put there by the *moros*.

As Rosales stood looking out, a very old man came down the lane leading a large burro weighted down with *bombas*, large red canisters containing butane gas for heating the running water that was another innovation since his time. In the old days the women of the *pueblo* had gone each morning with large jars carried on their heads to one of the three fountains in Poqueira, where they drew their day's supply of water. The *urbanización* of Poqueira: Rosales felt a little uneasy about all this, without knowing why, until he remembered what the old man had told him about the large numbers of *policía* who had come as part of the town's progress. He would have to talk to Josefina about what he was to do and say when the *Guardias* learned of his arrival, as they surely would before many days had passed. There had been not more than three hundred inhabitants of Poqueira in his time; and, even with the *urbanización*, it did not seem probable that the *pueblo* had grown much over the past three decades. A new face would not go unnoticed for very long, he realized.

What would these *Guardias* do about a man who had no papers to prove who he was? Arrest and detain him in the *cuartel*, certainly, until they had established his identity. What more they would do, he could not guess. Whatever, he would have to behave like a real *perro viejo*, a cautious old dog, and stay out of the town's streets until Josefina could help him decide what to do. He knew only that there could be no imprisonment for him: The mere idea was impossible to contemplate. He closed the shutter and returned to his bed.

At eight o'clock there was a gentle knock on his door. He called a greeting, and Josefina entered, smiling brightly, and wearing what must have been her best dress. About her head and over her shoulders was a heavy woolen shawl. Mario, looking as worried as he had last night, hung in the gloom of the hallway behind her, bobbing his head in greeting.

"Well, our brother," said Josefina, "today, as you may have heard, is *Navidad*. No Rosales I ever heard of went to Mass; I don't suppose you're any exception. You certainly don't *look* very pious. But that's where *we're* going, Mario and I, and perhaps you'd like to get up and bathe while we're gone. Then we'll have a real fiesta of a breakfast, and begin talking in earnest."

Rosales smiled: that bath again. Well, it would be as much a pleasure to his hosts as to him, so he'd really go the whole way: take a long, hot bath, and perhaps even borrow Mario's razor to shave off his beard.

He saw a look of consternation suddenly come over his sister's face, and realized that she was staring at the bayonet, hanging by its wire necklace around the bedpost, next to his head. Mario had apparently seen it, too, and was gazing at it as he would at a serpent. My sister has married a rabbit, Rosales thought; perhaps he doesn't even *have* a razor for me to borrow.

"Holy Mother of God," Josefina breathed, "what are you doing with *that* thing?"

Rosales smiled. "Don't worry," he told them, "I won't

226

stab you. But a man traveling alone has to be able to defend himself."

"Against what?" Josefina asked. "Have you been fighting with tigers on your way here? No one needs such a weapon in Spain today."

Suddenly he thought of the gypsy. "*I* needed such a weapon," he said matter-of-factly. "I used it on a gypsy in Granada only a couple of nights ago."

Josefina and Mario crossed themselves simultaneously, and Mario retreated farther into the hallway. A little surprised at their reaction, Rosales related, in his expressionless way, what had happened: "I was attacked and humiliated by this gypsy. He took my money, and tried to steal my *bota*. It was only normal and proper to take my revenge." This explanation seemed quite sufficient to him, but it did not appear to have any calming effect on Josefina and Mario. Josefina now appeared not only frightened, but angry as well. "This is 1973, Sebastián. No one kills in Spain now, not even for honor. You have done a terrible thing." Mario had disappeared entirely, now.

"Are you going to turn me out, then, my sister?" Rosales asked, still not understanding Josefina's reaction. "It was, as I said, only a gypsy." He felt a little embarrassed, as if he had committed a minor social error.

"You fool," said Josefina. "Do you think the *policía* will care whether it was a gypsy you killed? You killed *some*one, that's enough for them. Were you seen?"

Rosales pondered this a second, then answered, still not really concerned, "Perhaps. Anyway, his friends know who killed him. But no one would look for me here, in Poqueira, surely."

Josefina leaned against the door frame, gathering her

thoughts and calming herself. This is a strong woman, Rosales thought; she and I will be able to handle whatever happens. The bell in the church tower tolled briefly. After several minutes, Josefina straightened her shoulders, pulled her shawl more tightly around her, and looked with great severity down at her brother, her black eyes bright in her dark, lined face.

"Of course I am not going to turn you out, Sebastián. But we must think. Were you seen entering the *pueblo* last night?"

"*Claro*, woman," Rosales answered. "I was at Luís's café for a time; and I was led here by a man."

"What man?"

"I did not ask his name."

"Did he ask yours?"

"Of course I told him who I was. How else would I have found my family?" Rosales was admiring his sister's quickness: She reminded him of the lawyer in Casas Ibáñez.

"Then, whoever this man was, the whole *pueblo* will know who you are and where you are in a matter of hours. You ought to know how things are in Poqueira." Josefina might have been his mother, lecturing him for some childish stupidity. "Now we're going to Mass. Have your bath, and keep out of sight. We'll discuss this later. *¿De acuerdo?*"

"*De acuerdo*," said Rosales: agreed. Feeling rather chastened, he waited until he heard the front door close, then climbed from the bed again and padded across the hall to the bathroom. It was small, but more opulent by far than anything he could have imagined in Poqueira. There was a large tub, a sink, and a toilet. Beside the sink was a small wooden table. On it he saw Mario's razor. He looked at himself in the small mirror that was hung on a nail over the sink. To hell with it, he said to himself: Why bother with shaving? I'm no beauty either way. And he felt in any case a certain distaste about using the razor of this Mario.

A half hour later, clean at last, his stiff gray hair plastered down with water, Rosales put on his clothes (these could do with cleaning, too, he thought, noticing the faint goat smell that still clung to them) and began an inspection of the house. There was not really much to see: the tiny *salón*, the bedroom of Josefina and Mario, with a painting of San Sebastián (at the moment of his martyrdom, bristling with arrows) hanging over a small cabinet, and a statuette of the Virgin on the bedside table. It surprised him that his sister was so pious, but perhaps it was Mario who was the real believer. He looks the type, Rosales thought sourly. After a glance into the kitchen, where a ham hung from a peg on a ceiling beam, next to strings of blood sausages and dried peppers, and where a *bomba* stood on the floor, attached by tubing to a gas stove, Rosales returned to the *salón*. He was bored and restless, and knew he could not remain inside the house. I'll just take a walk in the forest below the *pueblo*, he thought, and be back in time for lunch. He returned for a moment to the kitchen, cut a large slice from the ham hanging there, returned to the son's bedroom for his *bota*, and went to the front door.

He peered out cautiously, up and down the lane: no one. He stepped out, closed the door behind him, and set off for the end of the lane, where a path led downhill, past the tin-roofed shed where the women had always done their washing, and into the forest of live oak, chestnut, and poplar where he had played as a boy. The day was chilly, but below the town the wind was muted, and he felt quite comfortable in his old clothes. In a few minutes the *pueblo* was out of sight above him, and the path dropped sharply downward into the ravine made by the Río Poqueira. The water was moving sluggishly when he reached it, and when he bent to drink from it his lips were numbed by its coldness. It tasted as fresh as it always had, pouring as it did straight down from the Sierra Nevada. In the summers he had come here with his friends to catch trout; and not far upstream was a waterfall, with a pond below it in which they had splashed about noisily. To the west, far above him, was the high ridge where many *alpujarreños* had owned small parcels of land, living for weeks at a time in communally owned *cortijos*, large farmhouses that could each accommodate several families. Snow covered most of the ridge, now, but Rosales could see traces, just below the snowline, of groves of fig trees and apple orchards. He counted three *cortijos*, abandoned now for the winter, along the crest of the ridge. Squinting into the sunlight on the slopes of the Sierra Nevada above Poqueira, he looked for flocks of sheep there, but saw nothing. Then he remembered that when winter came the shepherds would march their flocks all the way down through the valley below, across the Sierra de Gador, and into their winter grazing land in the lush fields along the coast. He would not have minded the life of a shepherd, Rosales thought: One needed to see humans very little, there was the mute companionship of the animals, and a shepherd could live in the clean openness of the land, moving along through the seasons as the weather dictated. Perhaps this was something he could do now. He had no money to buy a flock of sheep, but he could certainly tend someone else's, and earn enough to keep himself furnished with what little he required in the way of clothes, food, wine, and cigarettes. He would have to ask Josefina about this.

With some surprise, he noticed that the sun was now directly overhead. It would be a long climb back to Poqueira, and Josefina and Mario must already have returned from Mass, and be worried at his absence. Coming down to the river had been easy; climbing back was hard enough to make him realize how near exhaustion he still was. By the time he reached the shed of the washerwomen and turned into the lane where his sister lived, he was panting as if he were an old man, and he told himself that he would need a little time to accustom himself once again to the steep and rugged terrain of the Alpujarras. Villagers were out in the streets and paths of Poqueira now, gossiping and exchanging greetings on this day of *Navidad*. Several nodded to him as he climbed up the lane, and looked with curiosity at him as he passed. A couple of children, young boys, followed him with great solemnity, stopping when he turned to smile at them, and resuming their walk when he resumed his. Well, to all of these I'm a stranger, he thought. That would pass.

Before he could knock, Josefina opened the door and drew him in quickly. She and Mario had been waiting for him for some time, evidently, and he sensed trouble. "I'm sorry if I worried you," he said, "but I just went for a little walk down to the river. No one saw me until just now. Is anything wrong?"

"Sebastián," Josefina began, her voice sounding

frightened and urgent. "The *Guardias* have been here. They asked who you were, and I told them. They want you to come to the *cuartel* immediately, and will come back for you if you do not do so. Mario did not go to Mass. He was stopped by the *Guardias*, and brought back here by them." Mario confirmed this with a nod, his face pale and his lower lip trembling.

"Well, Josefina," said Rosales, "they were bound to know about me soon. What are we to do?"

"*Do*, my brother? Why, you must go to the *cuartel*, of course. Do you think we want the neighbors to see the *policía* dragging you from our house and taking you through the *pueblo* as if you were some criminal?"

Rosales thought with some alarm that he *was* a criminal, depending on how much this Mario had told the *Guardias*. He might now be to them not just a man with no papers, but a man who had stabbed a gypsy to death. He glanced at Mario, and thought of asking how much he had talked; but Mario would not look at him, and Rosales realized that Mario had probably said enough to ruin him. It did not occur to him that the television or radio might have brought word of his crime to Poqueira, and that Mario might have done no more than confirm to the *policía* what they had already learned. For a moment he was almost overcome by a great sense of hopelessness, and slumped against the wall of the *salón*. *Well, that's it; that's the end of my life in Poqueira.* The whole thing, from the sudden and certain urge to leave Cambó to this dead moment now, had been for nothing. He had done all that, come all that way, to reach his land, his *pueblo*, and Poqueira would not have him. The homecoming had lasted less than a day. Where could he go, now? Back to France? The idea was unthinkable. To a city, maybe Sevilla or Córdoba? No: The *policía* could track him down in a city almost as easily as they could in Poqueira. He felt hopeless, knew himself to be absolutely trapped. The only answer was flight, with no destination ahead of him. All right, he thought, if that's all there is, that's it. An old *refrán* that had been current during the war came suddenly to his mind: *Hay que tomar la muerte como si fuera aspirina:* One has to take death as if it were an aspirin. Of course— that was all there was to it. As in war, the important things were simple. His moment of despair lifted from him. A man does what he must. One can choose to survive, and do so if he is strong enough. Or a man can choose *not* to survive, and die—if he is strong enough. The simplicity of his solution almost pleased him. He stood straight again, and looked at his sister, smiling faintly.

"No, Josefina, no *cuartel* for me, no *nothing* with the *policía*. I must go, now, before they return. I am sorry to have brought this sorrow on you." He turned to go to the son's bedroom for his blanket, and Josefina threw her arms about his neck.

"Where can you go, Sebastián?" she cried. "What can you do? Don't go: Just speak to the *policía*, and explain that you have lost your papers. These things can be repaired. We can hire a lawyer in Órgiva or Lanjarón to represent you, and in a few days things will be settled. Stay, Sebastián."

Rosales looked over his shoulder at Mario. "No, Josefina, I think it would be harder than you imagine," he said. "I will go into the hills, and hide there until I can

233

think of something. Don't worry: I'll be back soon," he lied. "Just give me a little food to take with me now, and hurry." The *Guardias* won't wait for me long, he thought, if Mario has told them of the gypsy. Which he has, surely.

Josefina gave him a long look, and then ran to the kitchen. As if afraid to be alone in the room with Rosales, Mario leapt to his feet and ran to fetch the blanket roll, which he brought out and silently handed to his brother-in-law, as Josefina emerged from the kitchen with a yellow plastic shopping basket bulging with whatever she had been able to lay her hands on.

Rosales took the blanket roll and the bag of food, shook hands briefly with the still-silent Mario, and gave a quick embrace to Josefina. "I thank you for your kindness," he said to her. "I'll go off now on the Busquístar road, and look for a safe place to stay, until I can return. I'll send word when I find a way." Looking at Mario, he thought, Did you hear that, *maricón?* I said the Busquístar road. Make sure the *policía* get it right. Then he turned, and went out the door.

He walked as swiftly as he could without attracting attention, even though, at dinner time, there were few in Poqueira to notice his departure. Down he went again on the path below the village; but this time he turned left along a narrow way that led to Bubión, two kilometers away. Fifteen minutes later he had reached the lane that wandered upward through Bubión. He followed it, heedless of the *bubioneros* who watched him pass by. At the top of the town, on the edge of the road that wound downhill, he saw a café. He entered, approached a group of men who stood nearest the door, and said, without any preliminaries, "I am looking for an old *castillo* between here and Busquístar. Can you tell me how to find it?" A trail as wide as a herd of cattle, he thought; even the stupidest of *Guardias Civiles* should be able to follow it.

Startled at this intrusion, the men he had accosted looked first at him, then at each other. Finally, one of them answered, "If you mean the old ruins on Miguelito's land, it's off to the right of the road, just past the *Fuente Agria*. There's a path—"

"*Muchas gracias,*" Rosales interrupted. "I know the place you mean." He turned abruptly, and pushed his way out of the crowded room and onto the road that would take him toward Busquístar. It was already mid-afternoon, and he had a long walk ahead of him: If he remembered rightly, the place he had in mind was at least six kilometers along the road, with a difficult track to follow once he turned into the countryside.

The road out of Bubión was filled with young people sauntering along on their afternoon *paseo*, enduring the rigors of peasant courtship. Bands of young girls, dressed in their fiesta finery, walked past bands of young men in jackets and collarless shirts, each band pointedly ignoring the other. Here and there were individual couples: those who had advanced far enough in the ritual to be seen together, and who would, within a year or two, marry and begin their families. Once or twice he passed a couple already married. Predictably, the young wife, already growing plump, would be proudly pushing a baby carriage before her. Behind her would come the husband, walking with hands behind his back and head down, clearly wishing that he were at the café instead of being part of this ancient and necessary parade. Few of these young people gave Rosales more than a passing glance—but they would remember him easily enough when the *Guardia* asked them, he knew.

In another half hour he came to the *Fuente Agria*, where a shrine had been built above the springs that gave out the bitter, iron-flavored water that was supposed to remedy everything from goiter to impotence. A few pilgrims were there, filling bottles they had brought with them to collect the water. He waved to them. Remember me, he said to them under his breath; they will ask you if you have seen a tall man with a gray beard. Say YES. He felt exhilarated, happy to be part of a chase with such an inevitable conclusion. He thought of himself as being in control of things, determining the direction of the hunt, choosing his own terrain. *El lobo viejo*, the old wolf.

The trail he knew from his childhood appeared on his right. He took it, trotting now in his haste to reach the place before dark. It ran along an irrigation ditch at the edge of a wheat field, heading toward tall rock formations and thickets full of squat ilex trees and clumps of *rasea*, the prickly-leaved shrub used by the *alpujarreños* for the weaving of baskets. Before he left the open trail, he stopped and peered into the shopping bag Josefina had given him. The ham was there, and the blood sausages he had seen hanging in her kitchen, and several of the *Navidad pasteles* she had offered him last night. He took the ham, and left the rest on the trail, in the yellow plastic shopping bag. They'll be able to see this, he thought, even if they come for me at night.

He needed all his agility now to follow the intricate trail as it wound around the large, rounded boulders and through the thickets. He fell once, tripped by a tree root exposed above the trail, and lay still for a moment where he had fallen, catching his breath. Then he pulled himself to his feet and went on, his *bota* under one arm, Josefina's ham under the other. He caught a brief glimpse of white in the dusk ahead, and knew he was almost there. In another moment he was out of the woods, and standing on a grassy terrace, looking at the ruins of what had once been a small *moro* fortress. It was exactly as he remembered from his boyhood: a series of rooms hacked from the single enormous limestone boulder that rose at the end of the steep ridge along which he had been traveling. The outer walls of these cave rooms were, like the houses in the Alpujarreño villages, constructed of many small rocks held together by *cal*, white lime. Into the front wall of each room was built a doorway, and several still had doors attached to them, their vertical slats half-rotted by hundreds of years of harsh weather. Beneath the lawn on which he was standing was a *moro* cemetery (or so the village lore had claimed), and beyond the great boulder, at the edge of a precipice, which fell hundreds of meters down to the valley below, was a rounded threshing floor made of cobblestones worn almost flat.

Rosales walked to the edge of the cliff and sat down on a stone to look out over the valley. A perfect place for such a fortress, he thought: It commanded the entire valley of the central Alpujarras. No one could move down there, even if he were forty kilometers away, without being seen by a sentry up here. From where he sat he could see at least five *pueblos*, and the almost vanished ruins of three more. Directly below him, looking from here like a twisted length of white thread, was the Río Guadalfeo, which ran westward, past Órgiva and down to the sea near Motril—probably not very far, he thought, from the place on the coast road where he had been wounded during the retreat from Málaga. To the southeast were the steep slopes of the Sierra de la Contraviesa, on which he could see many goat trails, white against the brown of the hills, zigzagging up to the crest of the Sierra. He knew that if he climbed to the top of the boulder, onto the monolithic roof of the fortress, he would be able to look back at the *pueblo* of Busquístar, and perhaps even the tips of the Sierra Nevada, far to the north. The evening wind was sharp now, especially on this exposed promontory, and Rosales discovered that he was shivering. He rose slowly and stiffly from the stone on which he had been sitting, and walked back to the fortress. He had to pick his place of best defense, some place where he could not be seen until he chose to be.

The front rooms, those facing west, would not do. Their doorways were on a level with the small lawn, and he needed some elevation above the ground, as at the much grander *castillo* in Puente de Génave five days earlier. He walked around to the rear of the fortress, that which looked out to the east, and found two small rooms, both more than a meter above the uneven path that ran around the boulder. One of these was large and light, and contained sacks of grain stored there, evidently, by the farmer who owned this land. But there was no door to this room, so he looked in the other. Here there *was* a door, at least one that could be leaned against the entrance, but the room itself was not much. It was not more than a small cave, with a mound of packed earth for a floor, and a ceiling so low that he could barely stand once inside. In the rear of the cave, in total darkness, he heard a few faint rustling noises. Bats, probably, or rats that fed on the farmer's grain. All right, he thought; this would be the place. He climbed out of the cave room and stepped over to the edge of the precipice to look back at the fortress. Just to the north of the two rear rooms was a tall stone wall, over which his pursuers would have to climb. They would almost certainly approach the fortress as he had, from the western side. This was good, since it would give him more time to hear them coming.

It was almost dark now, and bitterly cold. Rosales unrolled his blanket and wrapped it around his shoulders. He climbed back into the larger, more comfortable room and sat down, leaning his back against one of the sacks of grain. He took the bayonet from around his neck and began carving away at Josefina's ham. It was coarse and hard, and the bayonet's edges were barely sharp enough for the job; but he managed to scrape a few pieces loose, and ate them slowly, washing them down with wine from the *bota*. When he had finished his meal, he stood, grasped one of the sacks of grain, and hauled it over to the other, smaller cave where he would spend the night. At least he would have some sort of pillow to rest his head on, he thought. He sat for a moment in the doorway, looking up at the night sky, clear and full of stars. "I should have been a shepherd," he said aloud. Then he climbed into the cave, covered himself with his blanket, lay the bayonet by his right side, close to his hand, and composed himself for the night. They won't come tonight, he told himself: It's *Navidad*, after all, and they know where I am. They'll wait until morning, when they can make their way more easily, and when I won't be as hard to find.

Still, he could not sleep. The small animals, behind him in the depths of the cave, never ceased their scurrying about; and tired as he was, he could not help thinking of how things might have been, ought to have been. He imagined himself living in Poqueira, in a small *casita* perhaps not far from Josefina, spending most of his days and nights in these mountains, watching over the flock of sheep that he might have had. He would have trained a young dog to help him guide the flock across the hills, to protect them from foxes, and to keep them from falling over such cliffs as the one not far from where he lay. Well, he thought, in the end I ran out of luck; or perhaps I wasn't shrewd enough. At least he had done what he had set out to do: He had come home. This was his land, after all; and if he could not live in it, he could at least die in it. And die well.

In this manner, thinking a little and—finally—dozing a little, Rosales passed the night. Some time shortly after dawn he heard them coming for him. They were thrashing their way through the woods along the ridge, making no attempt at a silent approach. Or maybe, he thought, these *Guardia* were city men, clumsy at country walking. He half rose, and leaned his face against the slats of the door, tense and listening carefully. It seemed to him that there were at least four of them, possibly several more than that. They probably planned on surrounding the fortress, to make sure he could not escape.

He crouched peasant fashion behind the door, bayonet in hand, and waited. His mouth was dry, and his hands were trembling a little with anticipation, but he was glad to realize that he felt no fear. The old Lobo of the war years would not have been ashamed of him.

As he had expected, they came around the west side of the fortress, moving cautiously past the rooms there, and continuing on until they had reached the narrow strip of land outside his room. He heard whispering, and the sound of weapons being readied.

Then one of them spoke: "Sebastián Rosales! We know you are there. You are accused of the murder of a Cayetano Heredia, called 'Barrillos,' in Granada, on the night of December 22." Mario did it, all right, smiled Rosales to himself; Josefina could have done better, surely, than to marry an informer. "Will you submit to our arrest, or must we take you by force?" The man's voice sounded hard, Rosales thought: One should not underestimate the men of the *Guardias Civiles*. But he said nothing.

"Rosales!" The voice called again. "We want no violence, but you must understand that we will not hesitate to kill if we must. Now come out, and surrender."

Slowly Rosales rose to his feet, and pushed open the door, his bayonet held lightly in his right hand. Before him, five meters away, stood a row of six *Guardias Civiles*. They wore crash helmets, heavy leather jackets, and black field boots. The officer in charge held a semi-automatic pistol; two of the others were pointing submachine guns at him; and the rest carried carbines, ready also to fire. These were truly tough men; Rosales was satisfied that they should be the ones.

"*Qué grupo de chulos*," laughed Rosales, standing

241

now in front of the doorway: What a bunch of pimps.

"Do you surrender?" demanded the officer.

Rosales looked for a second over the heads of the men in front of him. The sun had risen now all the way over the ragged escarpment on the far side of the valley. It would be a good day: bright and clear and maybe even warm. The silence was almost complete, except for the faint murmuring that came from the Río Guadalfeo as it ran along its twisting course to the sea. Rosales felt something close to joy rising in his heart. He was home: He was where he belonged, with his own earth beneath his feet and his own sky above his head. This was all a man required. He put his hands on his hips, leaned his head back, and laughed.

Then he looked at the officer and, still grinning, said to him, "*Me cago en tus muertos.*" As the officer continued to stare, stony-faced and unmoved by the insult, Rosales drew back his arm and flung his bayonet at him. The man leapt aside, and the bayonet glanced off the ground at the edge of the cliff, then flew over it, down into the valley far below. Rosales could hear it clanging against the rocks as it fell.

"*¡Fuego!*" cried the officer, and his men obeyed the order. The volley tore into Rosales, hitting him with such force that he was hurled back into his cave. He felt for an instant how cold the cave floor was against his cheek, knew himself to be content, and died.

*Son buenas gentes que viven,*
*laboran, pasan y sueñan,*
*y en un día como tantos*
*descansan bajo la tierra.*

They are the good ones who live,
work, walk, and dream,
and on one day just like all the others
they lie down under the earth.

ANTONIO MACHADO,
*He Andado Muchos Caminos*

# *Afterword*

There is no *pueblo* in the Alpujarras called Poqueira, though historians of the region tell us there used to be, in the days of the Moorish glory. And of course there is no Sebastián Rosales, though I have known dozens of Spaniards very much like him, and admired them all.

For those who might be interested in the fact behind my fiction, I should indicate that, in addition to using knowledge acquired directly from people and places in Spain, I have employed material from such works as: Gerald Brenan, *South from Granada;* J. A. Pitt-Rivers, *The People of the Sierra;* V. S. Pritchett, *The Spanish Temper;* various essays in the *New Yorker* and elsewhere by those most acute of Hispanophiles, Alastair Reid and Allen Josephs; Franz Borkenau, *The Spanish Cockpit;*

Eduardo Pons Prades, *Republicanos españoles en la segunda guerra mundial;* Juan Llarch, *Batallones de trabajadores;* Robert Goldston, *The Civil War in Spain;* José María Bueno, *Uniformes militares de la guerra civil en España;* Gustav Regler, *The Owl of Minerva;* T. C. Worsley, "Málaga Has Fallen," *New Writing* (Spring 1939); John Sommerfield, *Volunteer in Spain;* Gabriel Jackson, *The Spanish Republic and the Civil War, 1931–1939* and *The Spanish Civil War;* Herbert L. Matthews, *The Yoke and the Arrows;* Robert Payne, ed., *The Civil War in Spain;* F. Pérez López, *Dark and Bloody Ground;* Estanislau Torres, *La batalla del Ebro;* José Manuel Martínez Bande, *La gran ofensiva sobre Zaragoza;* Tomás Salvador, *La guerra de España en sus fotografías;* Amaro Izquierdo, *Belchite a sangre y fuego;* Rafael Casas de la Vega, *Teruel;* and, of course, the definitive history, Hugh Thomas, *The Spanish Civil War.*

But if there is any authority to this book, it comes chiefly from my friendships with the men and women, native and foreign, of the villages of Capileira and Bubión, in the region known as the Alpujarras, in the province of Granada. They are people who are noble in the sense that a great wine is noble.

## FOR THE BEST IN PAPERBACKS, LOOK FOR THE

In every corner of the world, on every subject under the sun, Penguin represents quality and variety – the very best in publishing today.

For complete information about books available from Penguin – including Pelicans, Puffins, Peregrines and Penguin Classics – and how to order them, write to us at the appropriate address below. Please note that for copyright reasons the selection of books varies from country to country.

**In the United Kingdom:** For a complete list of books available from Penguin in the U.K., please write to *Dept E.P., Penguin Books Ltd, Harmondsworth, Middlesex, UB7 0DA*

**In the United States:** For a complete list of books available from Penguin in the U.S., please write to *Dept BA, Penguin, 299 Murray Hill Parkway, East Rutherford, New Jersey 07073*

**In Canada:** For a complete list of books available from Penguin in Canada, please write to *Penguin Books Canada Ltd, 2801 John Street, Markham, Ontario L3R 1B4*

**In Australia:** For a complete list of books available from Penguin in Australia, please write to the *Marketing Department, Penguin Books Australia Ltd, P.O. Box 257, Ringwood, Victoria 3134*

**In New Zealand:** For a complete list of books available from Penguin in New Zealand, please write to the *Marketing Department, Penguin Books (NZ) Ltd, Private Bag, Takapuna, Auckland 9*

**In India:** For a complete list of books available from Penguin, please write to *Penguin Overseas Ltd, 706 Eros Apartments, 56 Nehru Place, New Delhi, 110019*

**In Holland:** For a complete list of books available from Penguin in Holland, please write to *Penguin Books Nederland B.V., Postbus 195, NL–1380AD Weesp, Netherlands*

**In Germany:** For a complete list of books available from Penguin, please write to *Penguin Books Ltd, Friedrichstrasse 10 – 12, D–6000 Frankfurt Main 1, Federal Republic of Germany*

**In Spain:** For a complete list of books available from Penguin in Spain, please write to *Longman Penguin España, Calle San Nicolas 15, E–28013 Madrid, Spain*

### The Rebel Angels   Robertson Davies

A glittering extravaganza of wit, scatology, saturnalia, mysticism and erudite vaudeville. 'He's the kind of writer who makes you want to nag your friends until they read him so that they can share the pleasure' – *Observer*. 'His novels will be recognized with the very best works of this century' – J. K. Galbraith in *The New York Times Book Review*

### Still Life   A. S. Byatt

In this sequel to her much praised *The Virgin in the Garden*, A. S. Byatt illuminates the inevitable conflicts between ambition and domesticity, confinement and self-fulfilment while providing an incisive observation of cultural life in England during the 1950s. 'Affords enormous and continuous pleasure' – Anita Brookner in the *Standard*

### Heartbreak Hotel   Gabrielle Burton

'If *Heartbreak Hotel* doesn't make you laugh, perhaps you are no longer breathing. Check all vital signs of life, and read this book!' – Rita Mae Brown. 'A novel to take us into the next century, heads high and flags flying' – Fay Weldon

### August in July   Carlo Gébler

On the eve of the Royal Wedding, as the nation prepares for celebration, August Slemic's world prepares to fall apart. 'There is no question but that he must now be considered a novelist of major importance' – *Daily Telegraph*. 'A meticulous study, done with great sympathy . . . a thoroughly honest and loving book' – *Financial Times*

### The News from Ireland   William Trevor

'An ability to enchant as much as chill has made Trevor unquestionably one of our greatest short-story writers' – *The Times*. 'A masterly collection' – *Daily Telegraph*. 'Extremely impressive . . . of his stature as a writer there can be no question' – *New Statesman*